F TROOP

and Other Citadel Stories

This book is dedicated to the Citadel's long gray line.
Especially to the Class of 1968 and to the F Troopers.
And to the boys who did not make it.

F TROOP

and Other Citadel Stories

Tom Worley

The University of South Carolina Press

© 2014 University of South Carolina

Published by the University of South Carolina Press
Columbia, South Carolina 29208

www.sc.edu/uscpress

Manufactured in the United States of America

23 22 21 20 19 18 17 16 15 14   10 9 8 7 6 5 4 3 2 1

Library of Congress Cataloging-in-Publication Data

Worley, Tom.
    [Short stories. Selections]
    F Troop and other Citadel stories / Tom Worley.
        pages cm
    ISBN 978-1-61117-333-8 (hardbound : alk. paper) — ISBN 978-1-61117-334-5
(pbk. : alk. paper) — ISBN 978-1-61117-335-2 (e-book)
    1. Title.
    PS3623.O37F38 2014
    813'.6—dc23

                                                        2013036698

This book was printed on a recycled paper with 30 percent postconsumer
waste content.

CONTENTS

AUTHOR'S NOTE

F Troop and Other Citadel Stories is a work of fiction. The Citadel and all the settings are real places. Some of the dates are real, but others are fictionalized. Some of the events are inspired by actual experiences, but the details are fictionalized. All the major characters, with the exception of the Boo, are fictional. A few characters are inspired by persons I've known, but as portrayed in these stories, are entirely fictional.

KNOB YEAR BEGINS

The Guidon is a small booklet, published annually by the Citadel, designed to provide information about the school to incoming freshmen. The goal of the fourth class system, also known as the plebe system, is to turn Citadel freshmen into Citadel men. The term plebe is from the Latin word *plebis,* meaning common people. There is nothing common about a Citadel freshman, for he is the lowest form of life on the campus. *The Guidon* defines plebe as a first year cadet, a fourthclassman, a freshman. Also a doowillie, knob, smack, or squat. The term by which freshmen at the Citadel are most often known is knob. It is thought that the term originated from the fact that the freshman haircut, a shaved head maintained throughout the first year, closely resembles a doorknob.

Tuesday, September 8, 1964, the day after Labor Day. Midmorning. Pete Creger stood outside the front sallyport of Number Two barracks, Padgett-Thomas barracks, on the Citadel campus, located on the banks of the Ashley River in downtown Charleston, with his parents. On the sidewalks nearby other plebes and their families milled about, saying their final goodbyes before entering the barracks to begin the knob year. Mothers kissed and hugged their sons, dabbing the moisture from their eyes with fingers or handkerchiefs. Fathers were more restrained, making do with a pat on the shoulder, a firm handshake, or a look in the eyes that said *I know you're man enough for the Citadel. Make me proud. Don't come crying to me that it's too rough and you want to come home.*

It was the same with Pete's family. Pete felt weird shaking his dad's hand. He felt far more comfortable embracing his mom. He stole a furtive

1

glance past the sallyport's wrought iron gate and fought back a momentary doubt. Outside the barracks was calm and peace, family and friends; inside was a cacophony of sound, a noisy din, organized, efficient chaos. Pete took a deep breath, waved a final goodbye, picked up his large brown canvas bag stuffed full with articles he was required or allowed to bring with him, and walked past the gate into the sallyport. Pete's knob year, the first day of his Citadel career, was underway.

In the sallyport Pete was immediately accosted by a cadet, a member of the training cadre, carrying a clipboard. "Name?" the cadet asked.

"Pete Creger."

The cadet hit Pete hard in the middle of his chest with the side of his right fist. Pete dropped his bag and staggered backwards a few steps. "Pop to when you address an upperclassman, nutbrain," the cadet hollered at Pete. Consulting his clipboard, he checked off Pete's name, and said, "Mr. Creger, the correct way to answer that question is to say sir, my name is cadet recruit Creger, P.R., sir. Now, pop off." Pete was slow to respond. "I can't hear you, knob," the cadet said with a raised voice.

Pete got it. "My name is cadet recruit Creger, P.R., sir," he mumbled.

"Put a sir in front of that, mister."

"Sir, my name is cadet recruit Creger, P.R., sir."

"Louder. I can't hear you," the cadet shouted.

Pete shouted back, as loud as he could, "Sir, my name is cadet recruit Creger, P.R., sir."

Looking at his clipboard again the cadet said, "Mister Creger, you've been assigned to F Company. May God have mercy on you. Follow me." Pete followed his cadet guide through the sallyport on to the red and gray checkered concrete quadrangle. Spaced at intervals throughout the quadrangle were card tables. Several cadets sat behind each table on metal folding chairs. Beside each table was a thin white pole, and atop each pole was a white placard with black lettering designating the various companies. The cadet Pete was following pointed in the direction of the F Company sign and told Pete to go there. "The F Company cadre will eat you alive," he told Pete.

About half a dozen cadet recruits were already in line at the F Company table. Pete joined them at the back of the line. They stood in silence. While waiting, Pete glanced about the barracks. The place was general mayhem, a madhouse. Cadet recruits, would-be knobs, dressed in civilian clothes, far outnumbered the cadre, distinguished by their uniforms of gray trousers, short sleeved gray shirts, and black garrison hats with shiny bills. Some of the recruits were being marched around, some were doing pushups, others were formed up in lines, many were being hollered at and cursed. All of them, like Pete, appeared harassed and anxious. Pete began seriously doubting the wisdom of his choice of a college. What had he gotten himself into?

When Pete made it to the front of the line, one of the cadets at the table asked, "name?"

Pete was ready. "Sir, my name is cadet recruit Creger, P.R., sir."

"What the hell kind of a name is that?" Pete wasn't prepared for the question. He had no idea what to answer. "Well? Pop off, squatbrain."

Pete said the first thing that came to mind. "Sir, it's a good name, sir." Derisive laughter.

"You think Creger's a better name than any of your classmates' names?"

"Sir, no, sir."

"Damn right it's not. It's a dumbass name and you're a dumbass. Isn't that right?"

"Sir, no, sir."

"Bullshit! Only a dumbass knob ever disagrees with an upperclassman. Give me fifteen pushups for being a dumbass." Pete dropped prone to the quadrangle floor and began pumping out pushups.

"Count'em out," he was told. When he was done and back on his feet, he was asked, "now, are you a dumbass?"

Pete was a fast learner. "Sir, yes, sir," he responded. More laughter.

"Damn right you are. I want to hear you say it. Say sir, I'm a dumbass, sir."

"Sir, I'm a dumbass, sir."

"Louder, with feeling."

Pete shouted as loud as he could, "Sir, I'm a dumbass, sir." He hoped it was with feeling. A paper with writing on it was shoved at Pete across the table and he was told to sign his name. He had no idea what he was signing, but he wasn't about to question or disobey. He signed.

"Congratulations, dumbass. You're now officially enrolled in the Citadel." Pete felt like a dumbass, sure enough. He was told to go stand in yet another line off to the side. This line was longer than the line at the table. No one in the line said anything. No one moved. The line kept growing. The heat and the humidity were bone crushing. Sweat popped out all over Pete and began trickling down his legs into his socks. After what seemed an eternity, but was probably only twenty minutes, more or less, several cadre members approached, and began calling out names and handing out yellow index cards with numbers written on them.

After the cards were all passed out, one of the cadre members, standing at the front of the line, said, "listen up. These cards contain your room assignments. We are now going to march over to the F Company area and up the F Company stairwell. Other F Company cadre members will meet you there and direct you to your rooms. Laid out on the bunks in your rooms are PT uniforms consisting of dark blue Citadel shorts and white Citadel T shirts. You are to remove your civilian clothes and put on the PT's. You should have brought with you white socks and white tennis shoes, which complete the PT uniform. Once in the PT uniform you are to remain in your rooms awaiting further orders. Are there any questions?"

There were no questions. The march began. Pete looked forward to getting out of the sun. They had only gone a few steps when there was a commotion to his rear. The march stopped. The boy immediately behind Pete was struggling trying to carry several bags and other items and had dropped one. Noticing Pete only had one bag, the annoyed cadre member unceremoniously thrust the offending item, a white pillow case filled with miscellaneous personal articles, into Pete's free hand, and the march resumed. Soon there was a logjam in the F Company stairwell. There was a stairwell in each of the four corners of the barracks. They rose four stories high like circular towers. Within each was a spiral staircase. The staircase could accommodate two climbing abreast, but only one at a time when burdened with baggage. As each boy reached the second floor, he was momentarily set upon by the cadre, and harassed and harangued before receiving directions to his room.

When Pete reached the second floor, he was surrounded by a bevy of cadremen who pressed in close to him shouting obscenities. One of them then stood back, pointed to silver insignia on his collar, and asked in a malevolent voice, "what's my rank, screwhead?"

Pete had taken the time to study *The Guidon* before reporting to the Citadel and he recognized the rank. "Sir, you hold the rank of F Company Guidon Corporal, sir," he answered properly and correctly.

The Guidon Corporal was not pleased with the correct answer. An unpleasant smile crossed his face. A smirk. He thumped the nametag fastened above the right pocket of his uniform shirt and asked, "what's my name, knob?" Pete silently read the nametag. *Osterhout.* A name capable of any number of pronunciations, only one correct one. A trick question. The Guidon Corporal would be unhappy if he mispronounced the name, equally unhappy if he didn't. Pete hesitated. "Come on, knob, you're so smart. What's my name? You'd better get it right."

Pete took a wild stab in the dark. He pronounced it "usterout," making the first letter a u instead of an o and keeping the h silent. Again the evil smirk. Wild, raucous laughter among the other cadremen.

Pete could sense Osterhout wanted to laugh too, but fought to restrain himself. "Holy shit, knob, you're the first one in your class to get my name right. You deserve a prize. Hit it for fifteen." Pete hit the floor of the gallery, only to be pulled to his feet by Osterhout. "Not here, knoblet. You're holding up the line. Shitting all over your classmates who want to get to their rooms." Osterhout pulled Pete around the corner and to the other side of the gallery. When Pete finished the pushups and was on his feet again, Osterhout got up close to him again, right in his face, and said, "I hate all knobs. I hate smart knobs especially. I hate you. I'm going to make you my special project. I'm personally going to run you out of here within the week. Hell, you may be gone before the sun rises tomorrow. Think about it. There's a place for you at Clemson." Osterhout walked away, leaving Pete standing alone on the gallery.

Pete stood there not knowing what to do or where to go. He was without directions to his room. Clueless. He noticed there were numbers above all the doorways to the rooms on the gallery where he was standing. The room number directly across from him was 2211. He looked at his yellow card: 2219. What luck! Something had finally gone right. He had to be close. He turned to his left and walked briskly along the gallery, trying to act like he knew what he was doing and keeping an eye on the numbers above the doors. The numbers were getting higher.

All the rooms had screened doors as well as thick, heavy wooden doors. The wooden door to 2219 was open, the screened door closed. Pete could see through the screened door into the room. He could see someone in the room. He hoped it was a fellow recruit and not a cadreman. He burst into the room with his heavy brown bag and the bulky, troublesome, white pillowcase, dropping both of them on the wooden floor.

Pete looked at the room's other occupant and breathed a sigh of relief. Before him stood a boy his own age, with shaggy brown hair, already dressed in the PT uniform. Obviously a fellow recruit, not a cadreman. "You took a while getting here," the fellow recruit said.

"Little trouble out on the gallery," Pete replied.

"Ya ask me, this whole place is trouble."

The two of them talked while Pete changed into his PT's. Bo Warner was from Savannah. After learning Bo had gone to a military high school, Pete couldn't hide his astonishment Bo had come to the Citadel. "Wasn't high school enough military for you?" Pete asked.

"Actually," Bo answered, "I liked the military in high school. I've got an uneasy feeling, though, that the military there was nothing like here."

"I don't know what it was like there, but I'm pretty sure this place is going to get worse before it gets better."

Before Bo could answer, they heard someone outside hollering and shouting in a loud voice: "F Company knobs, F Company knobs. Attention,

6

F Company knobs. All F Company knobs, down to the quadrangle. In your PT's. On the double."

They both went to the open screen door and looked out. Neither one was about to poke his head out the door or step out onto the gallery. A cadreman on the quad in the F Company area was doing the shouting. They couldn't tell if any knobs had made it to the quad yet, but they were hearing the slamming of screen doors. "I think the worse is beginning," said Bo as he sprinted out the door, Pete close on his heels.

Everything from that point on was mostly a blur. A blur of frenzied activity, running and marching, pushups and sit-ups, running in place and bracing. More running. More marching. Running and marching in squads, in platoons, in companies. Learning left face, right face, and about face. Ceaseless movement. Never stopping. Running and marching all over campus.

Thin, lumpy mattresses were on the single bunk beds in the rooms, each with a mattress cover. Stripped from the beds, the mattress covers served as giant duffel bags. Before the end of the first day the cadet recruits were marched from location to location around the campus filling the mattress cover duffel bags with Citadel issued items: gray cotton trousers, both short and long sleeved gray cotton shirts, blue bedspreads and blankets emblazoned with the Citadel emblem, laundry bags, blue corduroy Citadel bathrobes, raincoats, garrison hats, field caps, webbing, cartridge boxes, blue Citadel cloth belts, brass belt buckles, breastplates, waistplates, shakos, and desk blotters. It took a minor miracle to stuff it all in the mattress cover; a major one to lug it all around the campus and back to the barracks in the stifling, exhausting, sub-tropical heat of a late summer Charleston day without passing out, suffering stroke, or worse. Some made it, some didn't. Back in their room, Pete and his roommate Bo glanced at each other without speaking and took turns gulping water from the faucet of the room's single sink. Too tired to speak, they collapsed on their bunks for only a moment before the call came to return to the quad and the heat.

That first day included a visit to the Citadel barber shop in Mark Clark Hall, the student activities building across the parade ground from the barracks, for the Citadel knob haircut. Mark Clark Hall, like the mess hall, was air conditioned. The barracks were not. The lines were long. They went in with hair and came out without any. The haircut itself took about thirty seconds. Including the wait, though, it offered about twenty minutes of air conditioning, a welcomed, if too brief, respite from the heat and the terror of the cadre. The haircut was a pivotal moment for Pete. Until then he had been seriously considering Mr. Osterhout's suggestion he should try Clemson. Once he was shorn of his locks, he couldn't bear the embarrassment of appearing at Clemson or anywhere else with a bald head. The haircut made it official. There was no turning back.

He was now a knob.

The next few days were much like the first: filled with running, marching, exercising, and verbal and physical abuse at the hands of the cadre. They were interspersed with trips into the cool, refreshing air conditioning of Mark Clark Hall, where the freshmen were lectured on various subjects important to the Citadel. Among others, there was a talk on discipline by the school president, General Mark Clark, an impressive figure, a genuine World War II hero, and a talk by a member of the cadet honor committee on the honor code: a cadet does not lie, cheat, or steal, nor tolerate those who do. A simple concept, complicated by reality.

About three days went by. The days were so busy that Pete and Bo scarcely had time to put their room into ship shape military order. Some things had been arranged in proper fashion, but others had not. A number of things were still piled in the middle of the floor, among them the white pillowcase. Pete had forgotten its existence. He still did not know the names or faces of most of his classmates. He was trying hard to be able to identify the members of the F Company cadre. A rumor began circulating within F Company that there had been a theft within the company. The victim was a knob. Pete had heard the name, but couldn't put a face with it. Among the items missing were a small clock radio, a Bible, a calendar, and several framed pictures of family members. David Weston, the victim of this despicable deed, was distraught over his losses, particularly the Bible and the pictures of his family. He had looked everywhere for his missing possessions and they couldn't be found. He couldn't imagine anyone stealing his Bible and pictures of his family, but they were nowhere to be found and theft was the only plausible explanation.

The F Company commander called a special meeting of the F Company knobs to discuss the theft. The meeting took place within a day or so of the honor code lecture at Mark Clark Hall. The company commander said, "I'm not accusing anyone, but if anyone knows anything, under the honor code that person by withholding information, like the thief, is guilty of an honor violation." He paused to let his words sink in. Then he added, "the guilty party knows who he is. If he's in this room, perhaps the best thing would be for him to quietly return the items to Mr. Weston's room. Neither Mr. Weston nor anyone else need know his identity. If the thief is discovered, the mandatory punishment is dismissal from the Citadel. The school administrators in that situation normally help the dismissed cadet gain admission to another school. Mr. Weston, anything you'd like to say?"

"I don't want to see anyone get hurt by this. I don't even want to know who took my things. I just want them back."

"That's it," said the company commander. "You're all dismissed."

Back in their room, Pete and Bo discussed the meeting. Bo said, "this really, really sucks. I hope we don't have a thief among us, but if there is, I hope he gets caught, and soon."

"The sooner the better," Pete agreed.

Looking around their room, Bo said, "this place is still a mess. If Weston and his roommate are anything like us, the missing stuff is probably right there in their room and they just haven't come across it yet."

"Yeah," said Pete, agreeing again. "Chances are there hasn't been a theft at all."

"We have a few minutes before lights are out," Bo said. "Let's spend them picking up some more."

Like Bo, that first day when he returned to the room with his full mattress cover, Pete had dumped its contents in the middle of the floor and had slowly been picking up since. The empty mattress cover was back in the bunk housing the lumpy mattress. The bed was made, the blue Citadel bedspread on top; the Citadel bathrobe hung on a hook on the wall, as did two laundry bags; the desk blotter was in its place on Pete's desk, some of the gray trousers and most of the short sleeved shirts were in Pete's press; the rest of the trousers, some of the short sleeved shirts and all of the long sleeved ones remained on the floor, along with the blue Citadel blanket. Pete tackled the pile on the floor. He put the rest of the trousers and shirts in his press. Then he noticed it. The corner of something white protruding from beneath the blanket. He moved the blanket and revealed a white pillowcase. Pete remembered.

At first he didn't associate it with David Weston, but immediately there was an odd feeling in the pit of his stomach. He picked up the pillowcase and put it on his bunk. He turned back one corner of the open end and discovered a name label: David Weston. An involuntary groan escaped from Pete and he sat down on the bunk beside the pillowcase, looking dejected.

Bo noticed. "What?" he asked.

Pete was busily pulling items from the pillowcase: the missing Bible, the missing clock radio, the missing calendar, the missing framed pictures of David Weston's family. Pete looked at Bo and said, "they're going to think I'm a thief, but I'm not." Pete told Bo what had happened.

Bo said, "I don't know if you're a thief or not, but I'm turning you in. I'm taking no chances of being involved in an honor violation. Right now, I wish I was at any school in America other than this one, but being kicked out on an HV is not the way to extricate yourself from this hellhole. My family would never get over it."

"Mine either," said Pete. He felt like he was going to throw up.

Bo burst out laughing. "Just kidding, just kidding," he exclaimed.

"What if they don't believe me?" Pete asked.

"They'll have to believe you. Weston will remember what happened."

"But what if he doesn't? He obviously hasn't remembered yet."

"You didn't remember either, not until you saw the pillowcase."

"Maybe the cadreman who handed me the pillowcase in the first place will remember."

"Do you remember him?"

Pete thought about it. "No. No, I don't remember him at all. There's been so much going on. It's a wonder I can remember anything. I guess that's why Weston doesn't remember. Do you know Weston?"

"I do now. But not before."

"You were in the room first. Do you remember seeing me come into the room with the pillowcase that first day?"

Bo thought about it. "Can't say that I do."

"But you do believe me, don't you?"

"I told you I was just kidding when I said all that other."

At that moment taps began sounding. That meant lights out. From outside on the gallery Pete and Bo could hear the sounds of *all in* being taken.

"We need to let the cadre know about this," Bo said. "Now's the time."

They left the lights on. Pete opened the wooden door to their room and stood in front of the screen door. His heart seemed to thump louder and harder as the sounds of *all in* grew louder and nearer, approaching their room. He was somewhat heartened by the sight of a familiar face in the doorway, that of Mr. Bruton, his squad sergeant. "All in, Mr. Creger?" Bruton asked when he saw Pete.

"Why aren't your lights out?"

Mouth dry, heart pumping fast, fearing the worst, but knowing it had to be done and hoping for the best, Pete said, "sir, Mr. Bruton, sir, request permission to make a statement, sir."

"First tell me if your room's all in."

"Sir, all in, sir."

"Now, Mr. Creger, you may make your statement. Pop off."

Pete took a deep breath. "Sir, I have information about Mr. Weston's missing property." Pete intentionally did not use the word "stolen."

"Oh?" Bruton had been standing outside the room on the gallery, talking through the screen. Now he came into the room. "Let's hear it."

The missing items, including the pillowcase, were still on Pete's bunk. Pete showed them to Mr. Bruton and said, "here they are." He folded back the corner of the pillowcase, revealing the name *David Weston,* and told Mr. Bruton what had happened, the how and the why. He ended by saying, "so, you see, they were never stolen at all, just forgotten."

Bruton returned the items to the pillowcase. He took the pillowcase with him as he left the room, saying, "keep your lights on. I'll be right back."

Pete had been amazingly calm while telling the story, but now he panicked. Was he going to be accused of an honor violation? Bruton wasn't right back. He was gone a full half hour. Bo tried to reassure Pete. "Don't worry," he said, "Bruton believed you."

"Why didn't he say so?"

"He's coming back and he'll say so then."

When Bruton returned, he had with him two other cadremen: the company commander Mr. Freeman, and another whose face was familiar to Pete and Bo, but whose name neither could remember. Pete noticed the pillowcase wasn't with them. "This is Mr. Lakeland," Freeman said. "He's F Company's representative on the honor court." Pete's face fell. He was sure his goose was cooked and he was going to be facing an honor violation. Seeing the stricken look on Pete's face, Freeman said to Pete, "don't worry, Mr. Creger. We believe you. Mr. Bruton and I just brought in Mr. Lakeland to help us mull this over. He is the honor representative and we felt he should be consulted. We don't want this to get messy. We've handled it and came here to tell you what we think and what we've done.

"As you know, we're past lights out. The three of us have quietly placed the pillowcase in Mr. Weston's room. He'll find it there tomorrow morning at reveille. He'll never know how it came to be there. Only the five of us in this room will ever know. That's an order! This is the best way to handle the situation. We understand that knobs have lots of distractions, particularly as knob year begins. The three of us, one junior and two seniors, were once knobs too. We understand how both you and Mr. Weston, with everything else going on, easily and completely forgot about the pillowcase being handed off to you. Even though you remembered once you saw the pillowcase, Mr. Weston may not. Despite what he said in the meeting, his reaction may be different if he hears the story. He may be sore about his things going missing. He might even accuse you of an honor violation. No need to chance that. Things sometimes have a way of getting out of hand. I suppose we could go looking for the cadreman who gave you the pillowcase. My guess is he may not remember either. We believe you. No need to seek corroboration. If we didn't find him, the whole thing could get really messy. The important thing is Weston has his stuff back, and that's an end to it. A good end. Good night, gentlemen. Get these lights out."

Relief flooded over Pete. Relief and gratitude. He said, "thank you, Mr. Freeman. Thank you."

"No need to thank me, son. I'm not your friend. I'm your company commander. Don't ever forget that."

Lying awake in his bunk with the lights out, Pete said, "I don't know about any of the other upperclassmen, but at least Mr. Freeman is human."

"Only part of him. The other part is company commander," Bo replied.

"A damn good one, too."

"You may have dodged a bullet."

"Maybe." Pete drifted off to sleep, dreaming dreams of being at Clemson, wondering what his freshman year there would have been like, praying he would make it through knob year, and that in the end it would all be worth it.

TO THE SHOWERS

The showers were the scene of many knob hazings. Knobs came to hate the showers. The hated term *sweat party* originated from the frequent hazings that took place there. All knobs in the company would be required to put on their Citadel sweat suits, hoods pulled over their heads. Over this would be added Citadel raincoats, thick, heavy materialed contraptions complete with capes. Lastly, garrison hats, protected with rain covers made of the same heavy material as the raincoats, would be donned.

For footwear the knobs would wear tennis shoes with thick, white socks. It was a hot get up. The knobs would be sweating like hogs. Then they would be marched off to the showers. Before entering, some kind, obliging upperclassman had turned on all the hot water shower heads, all seven of them, full blast, so when the knobs went through the door of the shower room, the place was steamed up. Sauna-like temperatures, only wet, very wet, not dry. Knobs were lined up around the perimeter walls of the showers, an area designed to accommodate seven at a time, thirty plus of them, three or more deep against the walls. Then the fun began. Running in place, hitting the tiled floor, and doing pushups and sit-ups, scalding water flowing between finger tips and running off stomachs and backs. Knobs sickened and vomited. Pushups and sit-ups continued amidst vile, putrid puke. Lucky ones passed out, were picked up and thrown out onto the cool gallery, to the welcomed fresh air, where they were revived and returned to the showers.

This was the picture knob Sammy Graham envisioned when he was first asked by upperclassman Homer Powers, "ya wanna go to the showers with me?" He thought he was being invited to his own personal, one on one, sweat party. Not an invitation to be readily accepted. But Pete Creger found this out later, talking to Sammy after the fight. Pete was the only knob who witnessed the fight, except for Sammy, who fought it.

Pete happened to be tooling along the gallery near the latrine, which is next door to the showers, when he was grabbed by a couple of upperclassmen and forced into the shower area with them. He had no idea what was up. In the showers was his classmate Sammy Graham, surrounded by about twenty upperclassmen, among them Homer Powers. Powers snarled at Pete. "Mr. Creger, your wasted classmate Graham challenged me to a fight. He wants one of his classmates to witness the fight, to make sure it's a fair fight. You willing to do that for your classmate, waste product that he is?"

Sammy and Pete were standing in the middle of the showers surrounded by twenty plus upperclassmen, both bracing as hard as they could. "Sir, yes, sir," shouted Pete.

"Mr. Graham," Powers asked, "is Mr. Creger a satisfactory witness for you? Are you satisfied he'll render an accurate report of our fight?"

Sammy, like Pete still in a full brace, yelled out, "sir, yes, sir."

"Do you want any more of your classmates present?" Powers asked Sammy.

"Sir, no, sir."

"At ease, then, both of you."

Powers, followed by Sammy, took off his shirt and undershirt and handed them to one of his classmates. Sammy handed Pete his shirt and undershirt. Sammy wore glasses and he took them off and handed them to Pete. Looking at the two of them, Pete thought Sammy had little chance of beating Powers. He was taller than Powers, but Powers was more muscular. Sammy was thin and the plebe system had made him thinner still. Hardly any knobs had not lost weight. Powers, though, failed to take into account Graham's dogged determination, fueled and made stronger by the abuses of the fourth class system.

As the fight began Powers and Sammy stalked each other in a narrowing circle, fists clinched, their guards up, feinting blows, each waiting for an opening. The noise from the spectators grew louder and louder, all shouting encouragement to Powers. Pete alone rooted for Sammy, and he was too afraid to offer verbal support. The first blow landed was a left handed punch by Sammy to Powers' stomach, which drew a grimace. There was a lot of clinching and pounding on the shoulders and backs, none of it significant.

All of a sudden Powers landed a right off Sammy's nose, which started to bleed. After that it was as though Sammy literally saw red. He became the clear aggressor. At one point he had Powers against the tiled wall, hitting him again and again in the stomach and ribs. When Powers dropped his guard, trying to cover his midsection, Sammy let loose a roundhouse right that caught Powers solidly on the left side of his head. Powers staggered against the wall. The blow boxed his left ear. Powers shook his head, reached up, and felt his ear. Pete thought *that must have hurt; I hope the bastard's ear drum is busted.* Powers was evidently stunned. Sammy moved in for what Pete hoped would be the kill. He managed another hard left to the stomach and a right to the jaw, a glancing blow that barely landed, when there was an excited commotion, the crowd parted, and upperclassmen scampered for the exit.

Neither Sammy nor Pete ever knew how Mr. Freeman, the company commander, a senior with the rank of cadet captain, learned a fight was in progress in the showers, but the commotion was him, a furious, frantic, whirling dervish, shouting, hollering, pushing, and shoving his way into the melee. The fight was over. "What the hell is going on here?" Freeman screamed, his face set in anger. "Get to your rooms, all of you. Not you, Powers! What the hell are you thinking?"

"He wanted to fight me. I obliged."

All the other upperclassmen had left. Pete started to leave, but Mr. Freeman said, "stay put, Mr. Creger. What are you doing in here?"

Addressed by the company commander, Pete popped to in the brace position, an instinctive reaction, and replied, "sir, they brought me in here to witness the fight, so Sammy, I mean Mr. Graham, wouldn't be in here by himself, sir."

Mr. Freeman looked quizzically at Pete and said, "you get to your room, too. I'll talk to you about this later."

Pete never knew precisely what went on in the showers between Mr. Freeman, Powers, and Sammy. After Pete left, the three of them were alone together. He imagined Mr. Freeman probably gave them a pretty good dressing down, probably checked them over for injuries, though he was likely more concerned about Sammy than Powers, him being a knob. Pete knew Mr. Freeman was worried.

Freeman was concerned about word of the fight getting over to the commandant's department. He wanted to handle it within the company. He told Pete as much when he came to Pete's room to talk to him about it afterwards.

Pete guessed Mr. Freeman wanted to hear about the fight from both sides. Pete tried to be objective, but he knew his telling of it was slanted toward Sammy. He told Mr. Freeman it was too bad he'd come in when he did, because a few more minutes and Mr. Powers would have been laid out on the floor. Mr. Freeman smiled but didn't say anything to that. Pete couldn't shed any light on what caused the fight. Sammy only told him about it later.

Sammy had been assigned to a mess with Powers. Powers was a junior private who'd been giving Sammy a pretty rough time. The two of them were seated next to each other at the table in the dining hall. To serve the table, Sammy sometimes had to reach in front of Powers. Powers had taken to jabbing Sammy with a fork. Sammy had fork puncture marks on his hands, wrists, and forearms. You'd have thought the mess carver would have put a stop to it, but he and the other upperclassmen at the table thought it funny. On the morning of the fight, Sammy had already been jabbed once. The jab drew blood. Sammy finally had enough. The next time Powers picked up his fork to jab him, Sammy picked up a knife and glared at Powers. Powers smiled at Sammy, a twisted, sardonic smile that all the knobs knew well, more an evil grin than a smile. "What do you think you're going to do with that knife?" Powers asked Sammy.

"Unless you put down that fork, you're damn well about to find out," Sammy answered.

Powers went ballistic. He did put the fork down. "Do you hate me, knob?" he shouted. "Ya wanna go to the showers with me?" he screamed.

At first Sammy thought Powers meant he intended to give him a personal sweat party in the showers. He didn't answer. But then it became clear Powers was challenging him to a fight. "Come on, Graham," Powers taunted. "We'll settle this right now. A fair fight. In the showers. You and me. If you have the balls."

"Oh, I've got the balls," Sammy screamed back. The entire mess hall was always a din of sound, near bedlam, so the goings on at this particular mess drew no particular attention. As soon as mess was over, Sammy and Powers, accompanied by the entire mess, double timed to the barracks and into the showers on F Company's first division.

Freeman was irate with Powers. He was also concerned for himself. He feared if the commandant's department learned of this episode, he might be broken, reduced in rank for failing to maintain company discipline. He had to be careful. He talked to Powers and told him he was meting out a month's company restriction to him for fighting in the barracks. He handed out the same punishment to Graham. He made it clear to both Powers and Graham there could be serious repercussions to F Company if word leaked out. Both Powers and Graham agreed to accept the punishment. Freeman breathed a sigh of relief.

The punishment meant that both Powers and Sammy would be confined to the barracks for four consecutive weekends. Sammy stayed in the first weekend. Powers did not. Shrewd mind that he was, he figured Freeman couldn't do anything about it. Freeman certainly wasn't going to report him to school authorities. Freeman was powerless to enforce the punishment. All his classmates, including Pete, urged Sammy to break the restrictions as Powers had done. Sammy considered all that during the next week.

He was a knob. Freeman might not be able to enforce the punishment, but he and all the other F Company upperclassmen could sure as hell make life even harder. They could take it out on all the knobs. Talk about shitting on your classmates!

As the weekend neared, Sammy's dilemma was reaching a climax. A class meeting was called by Squeaker Dorfner, who had become the acknowledged leader of the knobs. The meeting was held that Thursday night during evening study period in the room of Squeaker and his room-mate Bob Williams.

All the knobs quietly sneaked into the room one or two at a time. It was essential the meeting be kept secret from the upperclassmen. No one knew, nor wanted to find out, what would happen if the knobs were discovered having an unauthorized assembly. Squeaker presided over the meeting. He and everyone else spoke in whispers. The meeting was brief. Squeaker said the purpose of the meeting was to assure Sammy everyone was behind him, regardless of the consequences, if he chose to ignore Mr. Freeman's restrictions. It wasn't fair for Sammy to stay in if Powers wasn't going to. To a man, every knob assented and urged Sammy to go on general leave beginning that Friday after parade. Sammy was moved. He said "thanks," but didn't say what he was going to do. Everyone left the meeting not knowing what Sammy decided.

Every Friday afternoon at three forty-five the Citadel holds a retreat parade, an impressive display. The parades are graded by a panel of tactical officers. Competition between the companies is fierce. At the end of the year the company accumulating the highest total points in all areas, including parade, wins the designation of Honor Company, a dubious distinction, since it entails the additional duty of serving as an honor guard, welcoming visiting dignitaries to campus. F Company had won Honor Company the previous year and a big push was under way to repeat, something seldom achieved in the history of the school. Up until this particular Friday afternoon, F Company had failed to win, or even place, in a parade that year. The knobs were blamed for the poor performance. Things were about to change in a big way. Following each parade, the results were announced in the barracks over the PA system, beginning with third place, then second place, then the winner. The afternoon it was announced that F Company had won the parade, it was as though a major sports championship had been won. Ecstatic cheering. Wild celebration. Jubilation. Tremendous relief among the knobs. A burden lifted.

Perhaps it was the euphoria of winning a parade. Whatever it was, all the knobs gravitated to Sammy's room. Together, as a class, the knobs insisted Sammy take general leave. Real celebration was to take place, and

Sammy was needed to help. Freshmen were required to sign out for general leave in a book kept for that purpose in the guard room just off the front sallyport. The guard room was small. Only a half dozen or so cadets could fit in the room at one time. Sammy and Pete signed out at the same time. Pete signed the book first. While waiting for Sammy to sign, Pete looked around and there was Mr. Freeman, watching Sammy sign. Pete punched Sammy. Pen in hand, Sammy looked over and saw Mr. Freeman. Their eyes met. Sammy didn't hesitate. He finished signing. Pete didn't know whether it was an act of great courage or terrible stupidity. Mr. Freeman, acting as if all was well, said, "You knobs did a good job at parade today. I'm proud of all of you. Enjoy yourselves."

Sammy and Pete together said, "thank you, sir." They looked at each other and left. They got out of that guard room and off campus as fast as they could. The F Company knobs gathered at Gene's Haufbrau, a favorite watering hole in West Ashley. The beer flowed freely. Pitcher after pitcher was consumed. A wild and wooly celebration. Toasts all around. To each other. To the Citadel. To Mr. Freeman. To winning parades. One, of sorts, to Homer Powers. *May he flunk out of school, never wear the ring, and rot in hell.* They were happy for a little while. They left Gene's that evening plastered, but content, at least as content as Citadel knobs were capable of being. A new hero was among them, Sammy Graham. They'd won a parade. But they had to return to the barracks. The rest of knob year still loomed.

There were no repercussions from Sammy's boldness in breaking restrictions. Nothing more was ever said of the incident with Powers in the showers. The brutal first year at the Citadel continued on, hard as ever, but somehow now a bit easier. It was the beginning of the coming together as a class for the F Company Class of 1968. All for one and one for all. Word of worthy exploits has a way of getting around. Word came back to Sammy that the story of his fight in the showers with an upperclassman had made the rounds at his old high school, and that he'd become a hero of legendary proportions. Sammy knew the accolades were undeserved. It was the bonds being formed between classmates that was worthy of praise.

After that first win at parade, F Company either placed or won every parade the rest of the year. The company was good in other areas too, and repeated as Honor Company. Sadly for Homer Powers, the ill meant toast became a prophesy. He wasn't back at the Citadel for his senior year. No one knew for certain, but rumor had it that he'd flunked out. What was known was that he never graduated from the Citadel, never wore the ring. No one in the Class of 1968 ever lost any sleep over it, especially not Sammy Graham. He wears the ring.

COLONEL SYDNEY AND THE
SWEET POTATO SERMON

When he entered the Citadel, though he was from Charleston, Pete Creger, like most of his classmates, had not heard of Colonel Sydney. He had heard of Summerall Chapel, but until his time at the Citadel began, he paid the structure little attention, although on several occasions he had walked past it on The Avenue of Remembrance and had read the inscription carved in stone above its front portals: "Remember Now Thy Creator in the Days of Thy Youth." He hadn't taken the time to reflect on what that meant, nor did he have any idea that Colonel Sydney was the Citadel's chaplain. Pete had never been inside the chapel and did not know the colonel's office was located at the rear of the finely proportioned Gothic edifice that bore the name of General Charles P. Summerall, heroic World War I soldier and former president of the college. The colonel's famous sweet potato sermon, perhaps better known as the "tater discourse," by tacit agreement between the colonel and the corps' upperclassmen, was kept secret from the freshmen until its annual delivery, a tradition which enhanced the sermon's shocking surprise, if not its message. The corps never knew from year to year exactly when the sermon would be given, but generally it was sometime in the first semester. As Sunday after Sunday rolled past with no mention of taters, anticipation grew among the captive cadet congregants, except among the freshmen, who had no clue it was coming.

The sermon played upon words ending in "tator." On the morning the colonel at last launched into the sermon, there was a collective murmur of amused approval among the upperclassmen, whispers of "don't forget to duck," and looks of bemused bewilderment on the faces of the freshmen. Had Pete Creger known to duck, he would have done so, but he would not have formed a special bond with Colonel Sydney nor would he ever have found his way to the colonel's office at the rear of the chapel.

Pete came from a family of church goers. He had formed a substantial relationship with God in early childhood, but he kept it to himself. In fact, he graduated from high school never having joined the church, his only sign of teenage rebellion. His parents, however, kept hammering at him, insisting he join the church before going off to college. The summer before he entered the Citadel, to please his parents, Pete broke down and officially became a church member. The transition contributed nothing to Pete's outward display of faith; inwardly, though, he had to admit he felt more in touch with spiritual matters.

Perhaps it was Pete's increasing inner sense of spirituality that gave him his disdain for the way worship services were conducted at the Citadel. That, and guilt over his own behavior and the behavior of the entire corps of cadets. Almost to a man, Citadel cadets were an irreligious bunch. Their language was atrocious. So much for the third commandment. The rest of them pretty much went by the board too. The focus of a cadet's weekend was carnal. Getting laid, or at least talking about it and trying, was foremost in the minds of the corps. When that failed, as it often did, the next best thing was getting drunk. Most of Charleston's young maidens during Pete's days as a cadet were chaste, but the liquor stores and bars were wide open and welcomed cadets.

On Sunday mornings the regimental band marched back and forth on one end of the parade ground playing "Onward Christian Soldiers." The corps, hung over from the debaucheries of Saturday, but clad in their dress grays, dutifully marched company by company across the parade field to the soulful strains of the band, and followed the Sunday color guard into Summerall Chapel for what passed for worship services. Mandatory worship services. Attendance not an option. Considering the condition and attitude of the corps, arguably a sacrilege.

On a cold Sunday morning in early December of his knob year, Pete Creger, hung over like the rest, his head pounding with each step, the blaring of the band adding to the sense of nuisance, made his way along with his company into the chapel. Like the others, his vision was too blurry, his mind too numbed, by the activities of the previous evening to appreciate the beauty of the setting, the performance of the choir, or the exhortations of the sermon. Heavy, ornate, black wrought iron chandeliers hung from the vaulted ceilings, along with flags from the fifty states. The cadet choir, accompanied by the cadet congregation, sang "A Mighty Fortress is Our God." The service seemed more one of patriotism and remembrance than worship.

Colonel Sydney ascended the pulpit. He began the sermon. Like the other freshmen, Pete had no understanding of the light chatter, the laughter, which increased as the sermon progressed. Colonel Sydney said he was going to tell the young men of ways not to be and one way they ought to be. The ways were "taters." Most of them were bad.

"There's the dictator. *Dick Tater.* Some people," he said, "like to tell everyone what to do. They're bossy, but they never soil themselves by actually doing anything themselves. No one likes them. Never be a *Dick Tater.*" There was scattered laughter.

"Then there're the spectators. *Speck Taters.* They're people who never seem motivated to participate in anything. They're content," the Colonel said, "to watch while others do. They let the world pass them by. Never be a *Speck Tater.*" More laughter.

"Next are the commentators. *Common Taters.* They're people who never do anything to distinguish themselves, unless you mean those TV reporters, or the modern day political analysts, who call themselves commentators. They think they're smarter than those who do, and they try to tell everyone how to interpret others' actions. Trouble with them is they never do anything themselves and they're not as smart as they think they are. Make sure you never turn into a *Common Tater.*" By this time some of the freshmen were joining in the laughter, but they didn't know where this was going.

"Some of the worst are agitators. *Aggie Taters.* They look for ways to cause problems. They try to get others to agree with them. They like to stir things up, never in a good way. Generally, they're never for anything. They just look for ways to be against something. Beware of the *Aggie Tater*."

The upperclassmen knew the "sweet tater" was coming soon, and they began speaking low to each other. Things like, "how many more *taters* before the big wrap up?"

Colonel Sydney was just warming up. "I know all of you have met hesi-tators," he went on. "*Hezza Taters*. Those who say they will, but never seem to get around to doing it. Please, please, don't let me catch any of you turning into Hezza Taters.

"A really bad thing is the imitator. *Emma Tater*. They're false. Put ons. They put on a front, try to act like someone they're not. They really don't know who they are. Don't be an *Emma Tater*. And lastly, thank the Lord, there is one good kind of *tater*." This was the moment all the upperclassmen had been waiting for. They got ready to duck. They knew what was coming. "There are those who live what they talk. They talk the talk and walk the walk. They're always prepared to stop what they're doing and lend a helping hand. They bring real sunshine into others' lives. They're called *sweet taters!*"

Shouted out. All the upperclassmen ducked. The freshmen sat there looking dumbfounded. Colonel Sydney reached behind the pulpit and pulled out a large, raw sweet potato, hand-picked for the occasion. It was thin and pointy on one end, long, fat, and wide everywhere else. He held it up a split second, reared back like a quarterback heaving a hail Mary, and chucked it out into the corps with all his might. Every year the sweet potato hits an unsuspecting freshman. It's as though the colonel picks one out and aims at him. They're easy targets. The upperclassmen ducked, their heads down and protected. Usually there's no damage done.

Pete Creger was sitting up straight, looking straight ahead. Afterwards, those sitting closest to him said they thought he had plenty of time to duck. Pete didn't duck. The sweet potato smashed broadside into his face. Pete happened to be sitting in an aisle seat in the center of the chapel. He went down like a felled ox. He crumpled sideways out of his pew into the aisle. Blood everywhere. The impact knocked his glasses from his face, and they fell by his side, the lenses unharmed, but the plastic frames broken in half.

Silence. No one laughed. Colonel Sydney, alarmed by the sight of the fallen cadet and the blood, rushed from the pulpit to Pete's side. Pete was out cold. The colonel whipped out a white pocket handkerchief and futilely attempted to staunch the flow of blood. He kept repeating, "I'm sorry, son. I'm so sorry," but Pete couldn't hear him. He was still out. Ludicrously, the colonel rose from his kneeling position at Pete's side, stood, and announced, "this concludes our service."

Some enterprising soul produced a stretcher and poor Pete was carted unceremoniously off to the infirmary, accompanied by a near frantic Colonel Sydney, fearing he may have committed murder with a sweet potato. Pete awoke in the infirmary. He had no idea where he was or how he came to be there.

He remembered marching into the chapel that morning. Everything from that point on until he awoke was a blank, missing from his memory. He could not recall the sermon. When told he was struck in the face by a sweet potato thrown by Colonel Sydney, he didn't believe it. Pete's injuries exceeded the limits of the Citadel's tiny infirmary. There was a concussion. There was the amnesia. His nose was broken. Surgery was required. He was transported to St. Francis, one of the downtown hospitals.

Pete's parents were notified of the accident. "Accident!" Pete's father exploded. "That sweet potato was deliberately, willfully, and intentionally thrown from the pulpit by that looney chaplain with a reckless disregard for the safety of others." Pete's father was a personal injury lawyer. He threatened to sue Colonel Sydney and the Citadel. He didn't have to. The Citadel paid all Pete's expenses, plus some. The some turned out to be payment in full of Pete's tuition and college fees for the remainder of his Citadel career. The sweet potato scholarship.

Pete was hospitalized a week. Colonel Sydney visited every day. He brought flowers, magazines, and snacks. At first Pete was uncomfortable with all the attention, but by the end of the week the colonel had won him over. Sydney was sincerely contrite.

Upon Pete's release from the hospital, the colonel and Mrs. Sydney invited Pete to their house, located on campus, for dinner. Soon this became a regular event, and from time to time included Pete's friends. Mrs. Sydney was a terrific cook. No before, during, or after dinner drinks, though. Pete and the colonel became fast friends. The colonel treated Pete like one of his old army buddies. He even set Pete up on a date with his niece, a pretty young thing who was a freshman at Columbia College. The relationship lasted longer than Pete expected and when the colonel's niece finally ended it by writing Pete a "Dear John" letter, the colonel wasn't at all sore at Pete, even though the bad things written about Pete in the letter were all true. Pete's relationship with Mrs. Sydney was strained a bit by it all, though, particularly when Pete got the letter published in the "Dear John" column in the *Brigadier*, the school newspaper. Pete missed a few of Mrs. Sydney's home cooked meals before she forgave him.

Colonel Sydney sometimes served as a counselor to troubled cadets and his office door was always open to anyone. Pete never needed counseling, but he often dropped by the colonel's office at the rear of Summerall Chapel to talk and visit. On one of these visits about half way through the first semester of Pete's sophomore year, Pete inquired as to when the colonel intended to deliver his annual sweet potato sermon. With great regret, the colonel informed Pete the sweet potato sermon had been delivered for the last time. "Because of your injury," the Colonel said, "the administration has banned it."

"Colonel," Pete exclaimed, "that can't be! Not because of me! I should have ducked! It's all my fault."

"I'm afraid the administration doesn't see it that way, Pete."

"But Colonel," Pete continued to protest, "I don't even remember it. It's like I never even heard it." The colonel offered to tell it to Pete again, right there on the spot in his office. "No, Colonel," Pete said. "It wouldn't be the same. It must be from the pulpit in the Chapel."

"Well," said the colonel, "I suppose I could give the whole thing again, without throwing the sweet potato. I could just hold it up, so it could be seen. The administration couldn't complain about that."

"It wouldn't be the same, colonel. The corps deserves to see you throwing that sweet potato. It's a Citadel tradition."

"I don't think there's anything that can be done."

"We'll see about that," Pete said. He left the colonel's office and hurried across the parade ground to the barracks, determined to have the sweet potato sermon reinstated, he just didn't know how. He conferred with his roommate and most of his classmates. Someone suggested a petition. With the help of most of the sophomore class, a petition was circulated throughout all four barracks. Freshmen weren't asked to sign, the freshmen surprise being part of the tradition. Every upperclassman signed.

To no avail. The petition was rejected.

Someone suggested taking the petition to the alumni association, known then as the Association of Citadel Men. The petition was presented at one of the regular board meetings. It was approved by unanimous vote. When presented to the entire membership, it passed without a dissenting vote. The alumni were behind them. The petition was then put before the Board of Visitors, the college's ruling authority. There was some rough sledding, but the petition was granted in a close vote. The sweet potato sermon lived on. A compromise was that instead of being thrown, the sweet potato must be *gently tossed.* That year the sermon was delivered much later than usual, but it was delivered. Citadel traditions were hard to kill off.

As the sermon was delivered, Pete kept thinking that his memory of having heard it before would return, but it didn't. It was exactly like hearing it for the first time. It was thrilling. Pete was proud of the success of the petition drive. The colonel was happy, too.

Another action of the colonel's was a Citadel tradition. The colonel drove around the Citadel campus in a Christmas green Volkswagen beetle. Every year the week before the cadets were furloughed home for the Christmas holidays the colonel parked his beetle beside the mess hall early in the morning as the cadets marched to breakfast. Perched atop the little car was a large, square music box. Standing beside the car and the music box, usually dressed in overcoat and gloves, for Charleston in mid-December could be a cold, damp place, was the colonel, waving to the corps as they marched by, spreading Christmas cheer while the music box filled the air with carols, the sounds of Christmas. Sometimes the colonel rang a brass bell as he waved, other times he jingled a string of sleigh bells. Often he sang along with the music.

Pete held the rank of platoon sergeant in his junior year. Platoon sergeants march in front of the platoon. That Christmas as Pete's company marched into the mess hall for breakfast the colonel pulled him from the ranks and insisted Pete stand beside him to help lead the corps in singing the carols. The following year, Pete's senior year, Pete held the rank of cadet captain and was a company commander. He marched in front of his company. That Christmas, once again, the colonel insisted Pete stand with him and help lead the singing.

At Christmastime that year the colonel had not yet delivered his sweet potato sermon. He gave it the first Sunday back from the Christmas holidays. It was the next to last sweet potato sermon Pete would hear. That year, as required by the Board of Visitors, the Colonel gently tossed the sweet potato, but before throwing it he called Pete's name and tossed it to him. This time Pete caught the sweet potato with his hands, not his face. Pete carried it back to the barracks. It was the largest sweet potato he'd ever seen.

During his senior year, Pete began dating a young woman from Charleston. It took a while to convince her, but two years after Pete's graduation from the Citadel, they were married in Summerall Chapel by Colonel Sydney. Her name was Emma. As part of the wedding service the colonel gave a shortened version of the famous sweet potato sermon. When he pronounced them husband and wife the colonel said Pete was Emma's tater now and the two of them were sweet taters for life.

DOUGHNUTS AND
CHOCOLATE ICE CREAM

K nob year. A little past the half way mark, first semester finished, the
second just begun. Most of the knobs, at least those taken with El
Cid, were well settled in, accustomed to the routine of upper class harassment, drill, PT (physical training), sweat parties, classes, studying,
marching, more upper class harassment, parades, inspections, meeting
formations, and more upper class harassment, the constants of their lives.

Pete Creger and Bo Warner had become good friends with Don Palassis and Ed Leverette, the two knobs who lived in the room next door. The
four of them felt they had El Cid well in hand. The year was better than
half over and they had handled everything the system had thrown at them.
They were on the verge of becoming brash.

Evening study period was from seven thirty to ten thirty P.M. Sunday
through Thursday, and all cadets, without exception, were required to be
in their rooms studying. Lights out was at eleven. Pete and Bo discovered
there were vending machines in the back sallyport with soft drinks, crackers, chips, and candy bars. Unknown to them, only upperclassmen were
allowed to visit the machines. They began considering how great it would
be to have a snack once in a while before going to bed. They contemplated
this for a time before putting a plan into action.

F Company area was nowhere near the back sallyport. The danger was
that to get there F Company area plus the areas of two other companies
had to be traversed. Knobs never ventured into other company areas. The
galleries were a veritable mine field of upperclassmen, all prone to explode

into handing out pushups and worse, much worse, to innocent, harmless freshmen.

At first Pete and Bo decided against it. Then they thought, what the hell, they could handle it. They were brash. They pooled all their loose change. Only one would make a run at a time, vending for all four. They drew straws to see who would go first. Pete Creger lost.

Pete sneaked over to the room next door to take orders from the Golden Greek and the Brute before the bugle blew, ending evening study period. Most of the knobs had acquired nicknames, bestowed upon them by the upperclassmen, worn proudly as symbols of their near acceptance, signs that they were on their way to becoming full-fledged members of the corps. Don Palissis was called the Golden Greek because his last name was Greek, and he was into weight lifting and body building, with a golden physique. Ed Leverette was strong, muscular, and tough, and was known as Brute. Bo Warner's nickname was Blitz because he was the most shined up knob in the company. Pete Creger was called Pink Panther after Inspector Clausseau, the bumbling detective played by Peter Sellers in the *Pink Panther* movies, because he was tall, skinny, too clever thinking for his own good, and a bit of a klutz.

Pink Panther probably wasn't the best choice for making the maiden run to the vending machines, but it was the luck of the draw. He bolted out of his room at the sounding of the first note of the bugle. By the last note he had already descended F Company stairwell and was fleeing along the ground floor gallery, deep in forbidden territory. He turned the corner by G Company stairwell before he was accosted. "Halt, dimwad," rang out from a band company upperclassman. "What the hell are you doing out here on my gallery?"

"Sir, running an errand, sir." Technically the truth, and the answer agreed upon as the response to any such query.

"Stop and give me fifteen, nut." Pete hit it for a quick fifteen pushups, pumping them out like they were nothing. Pete was wearing his Citadel light blue corduroy bathrobe with two deep pockets in front. As he hit it the loose change in one of the pockets rattled, but, thankfully, none of it rolled away onto the gallery. He counted out the pushups and jumped to his feet at fifteen. The upperclassman wasn't around and Pete didn't wait for him. He flew toward the back sallyport without further mishap.

Once there, it felt strangely like sanctuary. He couldn't believe his luck. He was alone in the sallyport. He acted nonchalant, like he belonged there. He quickly vended two cokes to be split, a candy bar, and a pack of nabs, also to be split. Two upperclassmen entered the sallyport as he exited, but paid him no attention. Back on the gallery Pete sprinted toward F Company stairwell, the vended goods in his bathrobe pockets. Upperclassmen were everywhere, but he treaded past them as if they weren't there. He was within two doors of his room before being stopped again.

"Where you been, Creger?"

"Sir, to the latrine, sir." The response agreed on if stopped on their own gallery near the latrine.

"Carry on." Planning helped. The Golden Greek and Brute were in the room with Blitz waiting for the Pink Panther. A successful run. The entire adventure had consumed only ten minutes. Twenty minutes to enjoy bedtime snacks. They laughed and celebrated. They were cool. They agreed to make only one run a week. No need to press their luck.

The two weekly runs after that, carried out by Brute and Blitz, were equally successful. Like Pink Panther, they both were stopped and harassed, light pushups, running in place, nothing too bad; like Pink Panther, they both returned with the loot relatively unscathed. They thoroughly enjoyed their before bedtime snacks, and thought they had hit on something really good, something which, to a small degree, held off the drudgery of life in the barracks. The Golden Greek was the last to make a run. Lo and behold! He was back as quick as that; no encounters with upperclassmen, no mini sweat parties. A totally free ride. No punishment inflicted. As the four of them sat together that night, eating and drinking their refreshments, they discussed the Greek's incredible luck.

Pete's next turn loomed on the horizon. Not that he minded badly, but there was a certain risk. Not really intending it as a new course of action, just mulling out loud, Pete said, "since the Greek hasn't enjoyed the same fun as the rest of us, I think it only fair he keep making runs until he has a little sweat party of his own." Brute and Blitz were quick to agree.

The Golden Greek, a cooperative soul, said, "I feel lucky." The Golden Greek indeed was fortunate. He made three more consecutive, successful runs. Unscathed. They discussed going back to taking turns. After all, the Greek was sitting on four lucky runs. How long could his luck hold? Something bad, really bad, was bound to happen. It wasn't fair that he continue to run all the risks. Somewhere in all of this a run had been made on a Wednesday night. They had been wondering about an ice cream chest at the back of the sallyport that was always padlocked shut. They discovered that on Wednesday nights, and only on Wednesday nights, an upperclassman attended the ice cream chest and sold ice cream from it. Not only that, he also sold doughnuts. They had begun fantasizing about doughnuts and ice cream. Not just any ice cream, chocolate ice cream. Dare they attempt a purchase? The Golden Greek put himself in jeopardy. He declared he would make one more run. The run of all runs. The run for doughnuts and chocolate ice cream. After that, he would retire for a while.

It was an exciting time. The prospect of consuming clandestine, contraband doughnuts and chocolate ice cream thrilled them, for by this time they had learned knobs weren't allowed to visit the back sallyport, unless they were there to make purchases for an upperclassman. They realized the reason none of them had ever been bothered while in the act of vending probably was because it was assumed they were on a hunger mission for upperclassmen. That was good news. It improved the chances of successfully purchasing doughnuts and chocolate ice cream.

Even so, there was tension connected with the new enterprise. They worried they were tempting the fates. As the slated Wednesday evening approached, they revisited the issue of who should be the runner for the run of all runs. Pete's turn was next. The consensus was that their doughnuts and chocolate ice cream were better off in the hands of the Golden Greek than the Pink Panther. Pete volunteered that he was ready and willing to go, but secretly he was relieved when the Golden Greek said, "I still feel lucky." That sealed it.

On the evening of the big run Blitz and the Pink Panther quietly left their room for the room next door. The Greek was in good spirits. He was like a prize fighter entering the ring in a match he expected to win. They all wished him luck. There was a grin on his face as he hurled himself from the room at the stroke of ten thirty, with the first note of the bugle heralding the end of evening study period. If all went well he should be back in a matter of minutes. They could already taste the doughnuts and chocolate ice cream.

Ten minutes went by. Fifteen. Twenty. The Greek hadn't come back. There was a problem. At five till eleven Bo and Pete went back to their room, planning to return after all in. Surely, the Greek would be back by then. Bo and Pete waited until after all in, kept their lights out, and went back to the room next door. Brute was still up, he had blankets over the windows and the lights were on, but the Golden Greek wasn't there. It was ten past eleven and they were worried.

The first thing Blitz and the Pink Panther asked Brute was, "did you report him all in?"

"I had to. What else could I do?"

Blitz and the Pink Panther agreed with that, but silently wondered if Brute might be courting an honor violation. Where could the Greek be? Surely he would be back any minute. They all knew where he was. In some upperclassman's room, hanging from the pipes. Sweating. His luck had run out. They determined to wait up for him, no matter how long it took. Midnight passed. Still no Greek. This must really be some badass. Doesn't he need sleep? One A.M. came and went. Two A.M. crept along and still no Greek. The unknown upperclassman, whoever he was, must be a sadist. This was unbelievable.

They took turns venturing onto the dark, vacant, silent galleries, searching for the Greek, listening for sounds. Wherever he was, they didn't think he was in F Company area. By three A.M. they were beside themselves with anxiety. When the vigil had begun there was a sense of urgency, compounded by their need for sleep. Now they were wide awake, past the need for sleep, waiting and hoping for the safety and return of one of their own.

As the hour approached three thirty Brute once again slipped noiselessly onto the ominous, unlit gallery. Blitz and the Pink Panther remained in the room. All speculation had ceased and they sat in shocked silence.

Suddenly, there was a faint sound from outside, and the door swung slowly, eerily, open, followed by the sight of Brute all but bodily carrying into the room a limping, wounded Greek, no longer golden.

In later years, the four friends, reminiscing about the spectacle of the Greek that night, would laugh uproariously, but that night no one was laughing. It wasn't a laughing matter. The ice cream came in small single serving cardboard containers. One of the containers, melted, had been poured onto the Greek's head, where it had run down his face, mingled with great beads of sweat on his forehead, nose, and chin. He couldn't stand on his own. Brute had spotted him on the gallery, crawling toward F Company area and his room, and had run to his rescue. His bathrobe was wet with absorbed sweat. The smushed remains of doughnuts, along with smashed cups of chocolate ice cream, were still in the pockets of his bathrobe, but the melted ice cream was everywhere, a sticky mess down his front, his legs, even onto his feet and between his toes.

The Greek breathed heavily. Panting. Like a long distance runner just finished running a race. He was sore and unimaginably tired. Talking slowly, at times gasping for air, he told them what had happened. He had no trouble buying the doughnuts and ice cream, but they were waiting for him as he turned the corner by G Company stairwell. He wasn't sure how many. He didn't know any of them, but he would recognize them. He thought they were all from G Company, but he wasn't sure. They took him to a room on the top gallery in G Company area. They worked on him in pairs, taking turns. He asked the time. When told it was past three thirty, he couldn't do the math and asked how long he had been gone. When told five hours, he said it seemed longer. When finally released, they had to help him from the room. He described the pushups, the sit-ups, running in place, holding a rifle up across his held out arms, standing bracing against the wall, hanging from pipes, constant, without let up.

The other three marveled that he was conscious and alive. Five hours without let up. They took his bathrobe off, sponged him off with wet towels, and put him to bed, though none of them slept. Sleep wasn't possible. While the Greek lay in his rack, eyes closed, the other three talked quietly, trying not to disturb him, about what was to be done. They talked seriously about reporting the incident to the commandant's department, though even as they said it, they knew it wouldn't be done. All of them had gone through some tough rackings, but this was unheard of. In the end, the only decision made was that there would be no more runs to the back sallyport for snacks. So much for doughnuts and chocolate ice cream.

Reveille was at six fifteen. A few minutes before six Bo and Pete returned to their room to prepare themselves for morning formation. They dressed quickly and glided back next door to help Brute with the Greek. He needed assistance dressing. They prayed he could make it down to formation on his own and wouldn't have to do more than march to the mess hall for breakfast. He made it fine. After all, he was the Golden Greek.

None of them ever mentioned the activities of that night to an upperclassman. They did tell the tale to their classmates in F Company. The legend of the Golden Greek and his night of torture was born. One or more of their classmates, they never knew who, must have repeated the story to a F Company upperclassman. Two weeks later the F Company commander visited Don and Ed's room.

He said he'd heard a rumor about Mr. Palassis having some trouble over in G Company. He said he didn't need or want to know names, he just wanted to know if it was true. Both Don and Ed said they'd rather not say.

"That's all I wanted to know," was the reply. "Don't worry, nothing official's going to happen, but I promise you this. No one from G Company will ever again touch an F Company knob."

They never knew what their company commander did after that. Rumor had it there was a serious heart to heart talk with G Company commander, which included the threat of reprisals. What is known is no F Company knob after that ever had any trouble with anyone from G Company. Of course, they all made a point of staying away from G Company area.

The legend of the Golden Greek's night of terror grew. Part of the legend was that the Greek never again ate doughnuts or chocolate ice cream, but the truth is they became his favorite dessert.

Neither the Pink Panther, Blitz, the Brute, nor the Golden Greek so much as cast a sideways glance toward the back sallyport the rest of knob year. After that, though, once they were upperclassmen, they sent many a knob on runs to the back sallyport with instructions to say, if stopped on the gallery, "the Golden Greek sent me. Mess with me at your peril." The Greek meant it, too.

The Golden Greek's unforgettable ordeal, coupled with the all-night vigil of the other three, bound the four friends together in a way that nothing else would have. Brute, Blitz, and the Pink Panther felt as though the Golden Greek had sacrificed himself for them. They felt his exertions, his sweat, his aching joints, his pain, his suffering along with him. It was as if all four had personally experienced the ultimate, out of control extremity of the plebe system. The Greek was sore physically and exhausted mentally for weeks afterward. The other three covered for him when they could, supported him, and nursed him back to health emotionally. The Greek never forgot the terror of that night nor the fact that his recovery from it was spearheaded by his three friends.

After graduation, the four stayed in close touch with each other, though separated by miles and state lines. They were ushers, groomsmen and best men in each other's' weddings and, with their wives, godparents for each other's' children. They supported and encouraged each other through good times and bad. Though separated by distances, they saw each other as much as possible. Whenever their families shared meals together, they always had doughnuts and chocolate ice cream for dessert.

COMPANY BARBER

S ammy Graham's dad was a barber. Owned his own shop. At age thirteen Sammy was taken into the shop to learn the trade, first under a learner's permit, then as an apprentice, and finally as a licensed registered barber, or as his dad referred to it, a master barber.

By the time Sammy entered the Citadel he was an excellent barber. Barbering was his weekend and summer job all through high school and at the Citadel it became his saving grace. As Sammy often said in later years, "if it wasn't for barbering, I wouldn't have survived the freshman year."

Sammy had as hard a time that first semester as anyone. Not an outstanding physical specimen. Not an athlete. Painfully skinny. Thick glasses. Bookish. Inept militarily, the last one in the company to learn to march. At five feet eleven inches and 155 pounds, Sammy didn't have any weight to lose, but lose it he did. By Christmas the daily regimen of constant rigorous exercise and little food reduced him to a paltry hundred and nineteen pounds and a twenty-six inch waistline. He looked like a concentration camp refugee, but his spirit wasn't broken. He did have a few things going for him: he was smart, determined, well liked, and respected by his classmates. Over Christmas break he seriously considered not returning for the second semester, but hey, he was half way through the grueling first year, and the thought of what others would say about him if he quit gnawed at his soul.

Hard as it was, and it was extremely hard, for Sammy dreaded going back, he returned to the Citadel in early January, having regained a few of his lost pounds. Fortune smiled on Sammy that first week back in a chance remark to an upperclassman during a sweat party on the gallery. Sammy was being racked by his platoon leader, a senior first lieutenant with the unlikely name of Grant Bloodworth.

Bloodworth claimed he was amazed Sammy had the balls to return from Christmas furlough. "Why'd you come back, knob?" Bloodworth shouted at Sammy. "You're the most worthless waste product I've ever seen. You can't do anything right. Not one god damned thing. Tell me one thing, just one thing, you can do. What are you good at, dumbhead?"

With his chin tucked in, bracing hard, Sammy blurted out, "sir, I'm a licensed barber, sir, and a good one, too." Until that moment none of the upperclassmen had been aware of Sammy's tonsorial skills.

Bloodworth wasn't impressed. Worse, he expressed disbelief. "Bull shit, knob!" he exclaimed. "I can't believe the State of South Carolina would issue a license allowing an uncoordinated turd like you to perform barber services on the heads of the state's unsuspecting male populace." Grinning and turning to Jimmy Williams, the knob standing next to Sammy, sweating and suffering alongside him, he asked, "Mr. Williams, you ever heard of this? You know anything about Mr. Graham being a barber?"

"Sir, no, sir." Sammy had told a number of his classmates, but Jimmy wasn't among them.

"Mr. Graham, if you're a barber, how come you never told your classmate Mr. Williams?"

"Sir, no excuse, sir."

"Damn right there isn't." Bloodworth made a fist and struck Sammy in the middle of his chest. "I don't even believe you, douchebag, but I'm going to give you a chance to prove it." Bloodworth knew Sammy was from Charleston. "This weekend I want you to go home, get your license, and bring it to me. I want to see it."

"Sir, yes, sir." The next weekend, returning from general leave, Sammy dutifully brought his license as a South Carolina registered barber from home. Bloodworth's roommate, a senior private named Bob Andrews, was in the room when Sammy came by to show his license. Andrews never racked knobs. He was friendly to them and always tried to help them, so much so that the knobs called him "Uncle Bob."

Looking at the license, Andrews said to Bloodworth, "looks authentic to me."

"So it does," said Bloodworth. "Got the state seal and everything. Still," he added pensively, "this doesn't prove you're any good at it. Tell you what, Mr. Graham, next weekend I want you to bring your barber tools into the barracks and give Mr. Andrews a haircut. He'll be the guinea pig. I'll watch. Do a good enough job on him and I'll even let you cut my hair. That okay with you, Bob?"

"Sure," Andrews said. "He's licensed. He couldn't possibly do any worse than those butchers in that so-called barber shop over in Mark Clark Hall." The campus barber shop and its barbers had a notorious reputation. Cadets were required to have their hair cut weekly and at the beginning of the school year were issued haircut tickets to last the year. The barbers didn't bother themselves with quality work. They had a captive clientele.

Sammy was concerned about bringing the tools of his trade into the barracks. What if an enterprising tactical officer found them in one of the frequent random room searches carried out by the commandant's department? They might be confiscated and lost forever. They'd be expensive to replace. He'd receive demerits, maybe even a punishment order. He could wind up walking tours. What if he was accosted by an upperclassman while bringing them into the barracks? No telling what might happen.

Sammy's fears proved unfounded. He had no trouble getting the barber tools inside the barracks and up to his room. He placed them inside a small, gray, metal box with a lock and key and placed the box inside a laundry bag while carrying it into the barracks. He made it safely to his room without being stopped on the gallery. In his room, he decided putting the box out in the open in plain view was the best bet for keeping it from being confiscated as contraband. He locked the box and put it on his book shelf. The key he put in his wallet, which he kept locked away in his lock box, with a combination lock, in his press. He hoped for the best.

The first barbering session in his platoon leader's room was swimmingly successful. Sammy even brought a haircloth and paper neck strips, signs of his professionalism. Uncle Bob Andrews went first.

40

One of the wooden desk chairs, placed in the center of the room, served as a barber chair. Bloodworth looked on with rapt attention. It was evident Sammy knew his business. Sammy brought two small hand mirrors so his customers could view the results. "That's perfect," exclaimed Uncle Bob, looking in the mirrors at his finished haircut when Sammy was done.

"I'm next," said Bloodworth, smiling at Sammy and plopping himself in the chair as soon as Uncle Bob vacated it. Bloodworth was as pleased with his haircut as Uncle Bob was with his. After Sammy swept up the hair from the floor, Bloodworth asked, "Mr. Graham, how'd you like to become the *official* company barber?"

Sammy didn't exactly know what that meant, but he wasn't about to say no. "Sir, that'd be great, sir," he said.

"Bob has an idea. He's going to work on it. He'll let you know. In the meantime, don't take your tools home. Leave'em in the barracks." Sammy didn't have a clue what could be in the works, but he had a good feeling. Bloodworth was actually being nice to him.

Within the week Uncle Bob came to see Sammy in his room. Since it was Uncle Bob, Sammy didn't bother to pop to in the brace position when Uncle Bob entered the room. Uncle Bob took no notice.

"I have such a deal for you," he said. He was holding one of the red haircut tickets in his hand. "The barbers at Mark Clark Hall are paid a dollar for every haircut ticket they turn in," he said. "One of the barbers has agreed to pay me fifty cents for every one of these I give him. Grant and I will set you up as the company barber. You'll cut hair in our room once a week. You'll be paid in haircut tickets. The barber will make fifty cents, and you and I will split the fifty cents the barber pays me, thirty cents to you and twenty cents to me. Handling fee. How 'bout it? Do we have a deal?"

The year was 1965. The going rate for a haircut in Sammy's dad's barber shop was a dollar fifty. Sammy received seventy percent of that, but he didn't even think about it. He didn't even do the math. He stuck out his hand. "Deal," he said. For Sammy it was a great deal. For him, the plebe system was effectively over.

That semester Sammy had no Friday afternoon classes. After the noon formation and completion of the noon meal, around twelve-thirty, Sammy made a bee line back to the barracks. He grabbed the metal box containing his barber tools and hustled to his platoon leader's room. First, he cut Uncle Bob's hair, then Bloodworth's, just as he'd done that first day, the tryout day. After that, it was first come, first served. The clientele was exclusively seniors, from the company commander, through the company officers, down to the senior privates. The customer base even included members of the battalion and regimental staffs. On average, Sammy cut a dozen or so heads every Friday afternoon between twelve thirty and three thirty.

At thirty cents a haircut it wasn't much money, but Sammy would have done it for free. He had been adopted by the senior class, and was under their protection. He still received an occasional racking, but never by a senior, and as the year wound down they were lighter and lighter and fewer and fewer. Most of the seniors even began calling him by his first name, sort of an early recognition. He still called each of them "mister," but during barber shop hours on Friday afternoons he was treated as an equal.

The weekly retreat parade was held every Friday afternoon at three forty-five, so the barber shop closed at three thirty. This meant Sammy had only fifteen minutes to dress for parade, not much time to don his full dress uniform, webbing with brass waist plate and breastplate, including cartridge box, and shako, grab his rifle, and meet formation. Personal appearance inspections, including rifle, were made before marching out to parade. Sammy's personal appearance, never the best, suffered. He looked more like a senior private than a knob. The good news was that the platoon leaders conducted the inspections, each inspecting his own platoon. Bloodworth never stopped in front of Sammy, never took his rifle, and scarcely glanced at him as he walked by. Sammy never received demerits at these inspections, while some fault frequently was found with even his most shined up classmates.

One Friday afternoon, while in the middle of cutting Bloodworth's hair, another platoon leader, George Todd, one of the few officers whose hair Sammy didn't cut, stopped by the room. "Say, Grant," Todd asked with a sly grin "how about you and me swapping platoons this afternoon? You inspect my platoon and I'll inspect yours. I want to jack it up Graham's ass."

This could be trouble, thought Sammy. Bloodworth considered. Then, to Sammy's relief, Bloodworth said, "naah, I couldn't let you do that to my barber. I have to look out for him. You wanna be an asshole, go burn your own knobs, the ones in your platoon. Leave mine alone."

After Todd left, there was a general grumbling about him, mostly from the senior privates waiting in line for haircuts. One of them said, "that guy's a real dickhead. Can't believe he came in here saying that shit."

Uncle Bob said to Sammy, "don't worry about him. You have any trouble from him, let me know, I'll take care of it."

All of this made Sammy feel much better. He had always hated Todd. No doubt the feeling was mutual. By the time the company was assembled on the quadrangle for the pre-parade inspection, Sammy had mostly forgotten about it. As usual, he barely had time to make it to the formation, and he was looking his normal bedraggled self. In appearance, he was no model cadet. He was aghast when Bloodworth and Todd switched platoons and Todd came over to conduct the inspection.

Sammy had not cleaned his rifle in several months. There was no need. Bloodworth never inspected it. Sammy came to inspection arms snappily enough, and opened the breech of his rifle as Todd stood in front of him. Todd leaned forward and peered inside the rifle through the open breech. For a moment Sammy thought Todd might not take his rifle and all might be well. Then Todd said quietly, "lint in rifle," and snatched the rifle forcefully, so hard and fast had Sammy somehow not been able to check himself, he would have lost his balance and stumbled backwards. Sammy knew it was all over.

Todd looked down the rifle's bore. "Dirty bore," he said firmly without looking at Sammy. He handed the gun back to Sammy, who returned to order arms. Todd continued standing in front of Sammy. He looked at him up and down. The list was long. It started at the top of Sammy's head and ended at his feet: "Dust on shako, dirty webbing, tarnished breast plate, tarnished waist plate, no crease in trousers, improper shoe shine.

No, make that no polish on shoes." All of this was dutifully recorded by the accompanying platoon sergeant on a notepad attached to a clipboard. Then, "scratch all that. Just put him down for filthy rifle and gross personal appearance." Unsmiling, Todd said, "Graham, you're going to be sitting in for a long time." Then he moved on. No other member of the platoon was written up for anything. Only Sammy.

The delinquency list came out once a month. It was a computer generated sheet put out by the commandment's department. Reading across from left to right it gave the date, the offending cadet's name, the infraction, and the assigned punishment. The dreaded list was posted on the company bulletin board for all to see. Excessive demerits meant confinements. Sammy's name, though he was a knob, had not appeared on the delinquency list since he had become the company barber, a distinction Sammy knew he did not deserve. Sammy couldn't believe this had happened to him. He wanted to talk about it, if not to Bloodworth, to Uncle Bob, but he didn't have the nerve to bring it up, and neither had mentioned it to him. All he could do was accept his fate and wait for the next DL to come out. The jig was up. It wasn't a question of whether he would have excessive demerits, but how many. How many confinements would he face?

The next DL came out about two weeks after the fatal inspection. As soon as Sammy heard the DL was out, he sucked it up and headed to the bulletin board. With pounding heart he searched for his name. It wasn't there! How could that be? Must be some cruel mistake. He sensed someone standing close to him. He looked to his right. Grant Bloodworth. "You didn't really think I'd let Todd jack it up your ass, did you?" Bloodworth smiled. Relief flooded over Sammy. He was so happy he couldn't speak.

Not a mistake. A practical joke. A pretty mean one, but who was Sammy to complain? The whole plebe system was a joke. Laughing about it was the only way to get through it. The seniors laughed their asses off. They had all been in on it. At the next haircutting session Bloodworth said to Sammy, "it was your Uncle Bob's idea."

"Oh, no," Uncle Bob protested. "Sammy knows I'd never do him that way. It was all Todd. The rest of us just went along."

44

"Mr. Todd sure was convincing," Sammy ventured.

"His part was easy," someone said. "He just had to be himself."

"It's easy to act like a dick when you are one, "Uncle Bob said.

"Who's a dick?" asked Todd, coming into the room.

"You are!" all the seniors shouted at him. "What are you doing here?"

"I came to get a haircut," he replied, holding up a red haircut ticket. Todd was last in line, but everyone stayed to watch him get his haircut. Sammy was egged on to take his revenge by giving Todd a botched haircut. "He doesn't have the balls," Todd said. "I'm not worried."

"He's too nice a guy to mess up even your hair, George," Uncle Bob told him.

The truth was, Sammy didn't have the balls. He was, after all, a knob. As the semester wore on some of the seniors, including Grant Bloodworth, became bolder and bolder in the directions they gave Sammy for cutting their hair, instructing him to leave it a little longer, a little longer. The haircuts were still on the short, military side, but they were becoming noticeably less so. Occasionally the company tactical officer, a regular U.S. Army officer stationed at the Citadel, would conduct the Friday afternoon before parade inspections. During one of these inspections the company tac looked closely at Bloodworth's haircut and questioned him: "I've been noticing, Mr. Bloodworth," the tac said, "you seem to be wearing your hair a little longer. You haven't graduated yet, you know. You need to set an example."

"Yes, sir," was Bloodworth's short reply.

"That haircut doesn't look to me like it came from the Citadel barber shop. Did you get your hair cut there this week?"

"No, sir." Listening to this exchange from his place in the platoon's first squad, Sammy cringed. His heart beat faster. Please, please, he thought to himself, don't tell him where you got that haircut.

"I didn't make it over to the barber shop this week, sir. Too busy."

"So you didn't get your haircut this week?" Sammy held his breath. Bloodworth didn't reply. "I was going to write you up for improper haircut. I'll have to make it no haircut." The conversation ended and the tac went on with the inspection, accompanied by Bloodworth, who scowled at Sammy as he and the tac stood in front of him.

Sammy was immensely relieved when the inspection was over. The commandant's department was still clueless about the barracks barber shop. He worried about repercussions from Bloodworth, but there were none. Bloodworth took it well. "It's not your fault, Sammy," he said. "You cut it the way I told you." After that, Bloodworth and all the seniors returned to shorter haircuts.

The school year ended. Sammy and his classmates were no longer knobs. Sammy was amazed he had made it through the year without the commandant's department discovering he was running a barber shop in the barracks. Sometimes he wondered if maybe they knew and turned a blind eye. No matter what, his barbering skills had seen him through knob year. Some of his classmates urged him to keep the barber shop open but he declined. He was no longer a knob and there was no reason to go on giving cheap haircuts. There also was no reason to press his luck with the commandant's department.

He retired permanently as company barber. Sammy continued working summers at his dad's barber shop while attending the Citadel. No other summer job would have paid more, or been easier. The barber tools made one appearance on campus sophomore year. The Citadel's big instate rival in all sports was Furman University in Greenville. Their teams were called the Paladins and at football games a knight in armor rode the sidelines on a horse, a beautiful white stallion. Before the big game that year a group of cadets paid a nocturnal visit to the Furman campus and kidnapped the horse. It was rumored Furman students were planning a raid on the Citadel campus in retaliation. The commandant's department approved a special task force of cadets to patrol the campus at night to thwart any raid by the Furman students. Sammy volunteered for the night patrol. Enter his barber tools and barbering skills. Three Furman students were captured coming onto campus in the dead of night. They were held while Sammy shaved their heads, giving them knob haircuts. Next morning they were paraded through the mess hall to the applause of the corps. So ended the Furman threat.

After that the company barber made only two other brief appearances. At the beginning of junior year Sammy shaved the heads of the company's two top ranking members of his class as they competed for spots on the prestigious Junior Sword Drill. Toward the end of that year he performed the same ritual for all his classmates who became Bond Volunteers, seeking to become members of the elite Summerall Guards silent drill team.

Being company barber ruined Sammy as far as ever having anything remotely resembling a proper military bearing. Uncle Bob, that quintessential senior private, was Sammy's hero, first and last. Emulating him came natural to Sammy. The irony is that late in his senior year Sammy was promoted to the rank of cadet second lieutenant, assistant platoon leader. How that ever came about, God only knew. Sammy didn't. His commission was dated March 21, 1968, arguably making him the lowest ranking officer in the Class of 1968. He was a singularly undistinguished officer. He is and always will be best remembered as company barber.

KNOB REBELLION

T.S. Eliot wrote, "April is the cruelest month." F Company knobs at the Citadel, Class of 1968, in the spring of 1965 knew he was wrong. March is the cruelest month. As hard as the knob year was, March was the month that was the hardest, cruelest month of all.

As the month of February of that year neared its close, rumor spread throughout the F Company knob world that the sophomores had something special planned beginning in March. The knobs weren't worried about the rumors. By then, those knobs left, about twenty-five of the forty plus who had begun the year, were hard core veterans of the plebe system. They had weathered the appalling worst. They had come together as a class. They were fit and ready. The end of the year was in sight, drawing nearer each day. Those not going to make it through to the end of the year had already quit and left. Barring unpredictable family crises or poor grades, those remaining, so they thought, were destined to wear the ring. There would be no more dropouts due to the physical or mental rigors of the system. The sophomores had other ideas. They were poised for one more run, one more effort to drive out the weak, to see that only the best remained.

At the beginning of the school year only members of the training cadre were allowed any contact with the knobs. Only two members of the sophomore class were cadre members, the guidon corporal, who was also the company clerk, and one other corporal. Cadre lasted but two weeks. After that period, the other eight sophomore corporals were allowed to join in the fun of racking knobs. The remaining sophomores, all cadet privates, had to wait until the start of the second semester in January.

The thinking of the sophomore class was that once the whole class was loosed upon the knobs, the knob class unity would break and droves of them would leave the Citadel in despairing surrender. That didn't happen and the sophomores were indignant about their failure. They met and came up with a scheme designed to be the final undoing of the knobs. They sought and received permission from F Company's commanding officer to carry out their plan. All of this was unknown to the knobs.

The first Monday morning in March as the knobs returned from breakfast in the mess hall to the F Company area in the barracks, they were met on the first division gallery by the sophomores en masse. One by one as the knobs ascended the F Company stairwell, they were accosted, told to hit it, and dragged and placed along the gallery in lengthening line, where they were made to brace, run in place, and do pushups and sit-ups. A full blown sweat party. The entire knob class racked as one by the entire sophomore class. Something new.

Not really. Just more of the same. The knobs had long since adjusted to it. The timing was new. Once classes had begun back in the fall, except for isolated incidences when one or more knobs might be subjected to rackings lasting only a few minutes, this time of morning had been devoted to cleaning and straightening rooms, or a last minute look into the books before leaving the barracks for the first round of classes that began at eight A.M. The Citadel day revolved around a tight schedule. Following breakfast, normally there was about forty-five minutes, the only unscheduled time of the day, a blessed time, a time to attend to personal needs, and to relax a moment before jumping into the cares of the day. On this particular day, the sweat party lasted a half hour, leaving scant time for the knobs to recover, remove the sweat from their bodies, and to attend to anything else. Those with an eight o'clock class barely had time to do anything before heading out. At the Citadel being late to class wasn't an option.

The next day it was more of the same. And the day after that. And the day after that. The entire week. The knobs expected the weekend to be different. Surely it wouldn't continue on Saturday and Sunday. But it did. No let up. The following week the same. The din grew louder and louder. A major aspect of collective racking was the noise. The sophomores screamed obscenities, an unending barrage of foul language hollered at close range into faces and ears, loud enough to set ears to ringing, ear drums near to bursting. Upperclassmen from the other companies took to wandering over to F Company, attracted by the noise, to see what was going on. They walked around smiling, laughing, and shaking their heads, amused at the F Company zealots. The sophomore voices were growing hoarse, and still it went on.

All the knobs were in top flight shape. But the daily thirty minute workouts, coupled with the ordinary rackings of the day, were beginning to wear. A toll was being taken. Shoulders and other body parts ached. One morning, near the end of the third week, as Pete Creger came up the stairs to the F Company area, he was told to hit it for a hundred push-ups. He popped those out pretty quickly and was told to keep going. He quickly pumped out another hundred and decided to keep count of the rest. The total count for the morning came to 475, a personal record for Pete. The first fifty perfect, after that passable, the last one hundred or so nothing to brag about.

A knob meeting was called to discuss the situation. It was held in the room of Squeaker Dorfner, who had become the acknowledged knob leader. The general consensus was that little could be done other than to ride it out. Surely, the sophomores would tire and wear out soon, before the knobs did. A few of the more rough and tumble suggested a revolt of some kind, but the suggestion had little support. It wasn't taken seriously. Something like that was unheard of, and had never been known to occur in the annals of the Citadel. Squeaker proclaimed something of that nature would probably bring the other two classes, the juniors and seniors, into it too. Perhaps the worst of it, the most disheartening factor, was that in the other companies the plebe system was winding down, easing up. But not in F Company. Rumor throughout the rest of the corps was that the F Company knobs had been too arrogant, even disrespectful of the system. Thus the crackdown. F Company knobs were being punished. In the end, the meeting came to nothing.

The next morning brought business as usual. Another week went by. The sophomores had heard of the meeting and racked the knobs even harder. The whole situation was intolerable. Was this going to go on the rest of the school year? Something had to be done. This had been going on for nearly a month, the month of March, the cruelest month. Another meeting was agreed to, this one to be held off campus over the weekend at the home of Pete Creger, one of only two F Company knobs from Charleston. Absolute secrecy had to be maintained. Without anyone openly saying so, all had come to the same conclusion: the rough and tumble crowd had been right. The only way to put an end to this was to rebel. The purpose of this meeting was to plan a knob rebellion.

At one time or another Pete Creger and Sammy Graham, who also was from Charleston, had brought all of their classmates home with them, but this was the first time all the classmates had been in one of the homes at the same time. Pete's mom was great. She cooked up a big meal, a Charleston meal. Fried shrimp, hush puppies, French fries, and cole slaw, washed down with sweetened iced tea. Any other time would have been festive, but the mood was somber. A revolt was being planned. Everyone was frayed physically and mentally, which did not bode well for a successful revolution. There was unanimity when a revolt was called for; the difficulty was in going about it. The discussion was heated. As usual, Squeaker's plan was adopted. It was as good a plan as any. There was considerable skepticism as to whether or not it would work. The plan was for all the knobs to meet outside the barracks, line up, run into the barracks together, go straight to their rooms, and lock themselves in until time to go to class. If confronted by the sophomores, which was expected, the plan was to fight through them and continue to the rooms. The key was to not stop, to keep going, and not to submit. This would be done every morning. The hope was that this would bring the morning sweat parties to an end and things would return to normal.

The meeting was held on a Saturday afternoon during general leave. It was decided not to implement the plan until the following Tuesday. This was to throw the sophomores off in case they had gotten wind of the plan. It meant there would be two more sweat parties, one on Sunday and one on Monday. Coincidentally, d-day happened to be April 1, April Fool's Day. The significance of that day was not lost on anyone. It was ominous, but was laughed off. They might be fools, but they were determined. If there were two more sweat parties, they would have endured them every day of March. Thirty-one consecutive days. That had to be a record, a record that had to end.

To Pete's dismay, he was scheduled for guard duty along with two of his classmates, to begin the afternoon of the thirty-first and to end the afternoon of the first. If the rebellion went forward as planned, it would be shorthanded by three. The sophomores already outnumbered the knobs. The knobs thought it was because the sophomores had suffered through an easier system. The sophomores thought it was because they were tougher than the knobs. There was a faint, lingering hope that the sophomores planned to end the sweat parties at the end of March. Most, though, thought the plan was to drive more knobs out of the Citadel, and that had not happened; therefore, the sweat parties would continue until the knobs somehow put an end to it.

On the morning of the rebellion, as an orderly of the guard, Pete was stationed in the center of the quadrangle, a front row seat. Pete would have preferred to be in on the action. As the hour approached he was nervous, expectant, and apprehensive. He continuously checked his watch. Cadets began arriving back in the barracks after breakfast, but no F Company knobs were among them. That could only mean one thing: they were forming up outside the barracks. Pete could see everything inside the barracks, but nothing on the outside. He assumed that his classmates were forming up outside the sallyport nearest the F Company area. He kept his eyes in that direction.

Then he noticed something very disturbing. The sophomores were forming up inside the sallyport. News of the planned rebellion must have leaked. The element of surprise was lost. The sophomores appeared to know something was up and were waiting, ready to meet it. This isn't good, Pete thought.

Suddenly the knobs, Pete's classmates, burst through the sallyport. They came in silence. Determined faces. Running single file. Hard and fast. Toward the F Company stairwell. The sophomores, faces set, equally determined, ran to meet them. Pete expected Squeaker to be out front leading the way. Instead, it was Ed Leverette. Called the Brute by the up-perclassmen because of his muscular build and tough, no nonsense ways, he lived up to his nickname that morning. Rich McCarthy, a sophomore corporal who had been on cadre and had been a knob nemesis all year, led the sophomores running up to meet the charging knobs. As the Brute and McCarthy met, both running at full speed, Brute, head down, deftly side-stepped and stiff armed McCarthy squarely in the chest. The blow knocked McCarthy backward and upward. Both feet, spread eagled, left the ground. Unbelievably, he somersaulted in the air before returning to the ground. Luckily for him, Tuesday was laundry day. A huge pile of laundry bags, stuffed with dirty laundry, was lying on the gallery waiting to be picked up. McCarthy landed on the soft laundry bags, which probably saved him from the death or serious injury Pete felt he deserved as he watched in joy-ful awe, wishing McCarthy had landed on the hard concrete of the gallery.

The Brute's perfectly delivered stiff arm was a glorious sight to behold. Pete's admiration of Brute, his athleticism, his strength, and his grace un-der pressure grew. But it was far from over. Fist fights broke out all along the gallery. McCarthy jumped back to his feet and joined the fray. He took off after Brute, cursing and calling his name, vehemence flowing from his every breath. By this time, Brute, running and fighting like most of the knobs, had made it up the first flight of F Company stairs. Fights con-tinued all along the upper galleries. Pete feared someone was going to be shoved, pushed, or thrown over the guard rails to the quadrangle below, the fighting was that fierce. There was the slamming of doors as knobs, fighting through the melee, reached their rooms and locked themselves in.

As suddenly as it had begun, the fighting was over. All the knobs had made it to their rooms. There followed the pounding on doors, as the sophomores, indignant, screamed obscenities and demanded the knobs unlock the doors and come out. Fat chance! Pete was exultant. It appeared the knobs had won. At least this round. The company commander ap-peared and ordered the sophomores to their rooms. The quiet was eerie. F Company was engulfed in silence. No activity. None whatsoever.

The calm continued until a few minutes before eight, when knobs and upperclassmen alike emerged from their rooms, laden with books, and headed off to class. Definitely not a normal morning. For the F Company knobs it was a wonderful, beautiful morning. Welcome April. Goodbye cruel, cruel, March.

The following morning after breakfast, as the morning before, all the F Company knobs, this time bolstered by the three who had pulled guard duty the day before, formed up outside the barracks. As the morning before, they entered the barracks in single file, running, Brute leading the way. Nothing happened. No resistance. They went to their rooms and locked themselves in. They continued the routine the rest of the week with the same results.

That Friday, after parade when F Company marched back into the barracks and before being dismissed, the company commander announced that all knobs were to report to his room immediately. Reporting to the company commander's room probably meant bad news. The knobs were apprehensive. Crowded into their captain's room, they waited, hushed and silent, filled with dread. He made them wait. Every eye was glued upon him. Finally, his face broke into a smile. Then, he looked serious again. He said, "gentlemen, the war is over. I've told the sophomore class there will be no more morning, post-breakfast sweat parties. Congratulations to all of you. You've won a victory." Wild, unrestrained cheering and back slapping broke out. Heretofore unknown knob jubilation. The captain held up a hand to command quiet. In the silence before he spoke again, the PA system crackled, announcing F Company had won that afternoon's parade. Again loud cheering, ending with the chant *F's the best, to hell with the rest,* repeated over and over again. Again their leader held up his hand for quiet. This time he said, "let me remind you, there's still two months left in the school year. I haven't graduated yet and all of you are still knobs. The plebe system isn't over." Then he raised his voice and shouted, "now get the hell out of my room! When you hit the gallery, find a spot and give me fifteen."

Those fifteen pushups were the only ones performed gladly that year.

All the knobs who performed those fifteen pushups that glorious April afternoon finished out the year. Most of them graduated from the Citadel three years later. They wear the ring and they are bound together by that first year, the three that followed, and all the ensuing ones. They reflect and realize their genuine love for one another. The Citadel taught them discipline, teamwork, duty, honor, and perseverance. They remember that March and the knob rebellion that April morning. With due respect to Mr. Eliot, a great poet who may or may not ever have visited Charleston, April in Charleston is the finest of all months, not the cruelest.

THE LONG GRAY LINE

The United States Military Academy at West Point is the school most closely associated with the phrase "long gray line." In the 1950s there was a book and a movie, set at West Point, with that title. The term connotes the continuum between cadets and the graduates of a military institution, and is appropriately applied to all of them.

Pete Creger was a good student in high school and it was a given in his family that he would attend college. Arriving at his senior year, he knew he wanted to go to college; he just didn't know where. He sent off for information about a number of schools, and made more than a few visits to campuses during his junior year. None of them stood out. They all seemed about the same to him. He was looking for a college that was uniquely different in some way; he just didn't know precisely what he was searching for. That's where things were for him on a certain fateful day in early December of his senior year in high school.

Pete lived with his family in Charleston. That particular day in Charleston County was designated College Day. All the public high school students in the county who planned on going to college were bused over to the Citadel campus in downtown Charleston. The buses were unloaded near the front entrance to McAlister Field House, the Citadel's basketball arena, and the students were herded inside.

Representatives from various colleges, most of the instate ones and many out of state ones, were there to speak to the students about their schools. The idea was to help the students choose the right college. Each representative was assigned a relatively small area within the building and was to give talks and answer questions about their school during a designated time. Each session would last about half an hour and there would be three sessions. Signs were placed and each representative stood by his sign. The students were told to attend the three sessions of their choice, and to carefully compare what they learned about each school.

Pete had attended the first two sessions and had about been bored out of his mind. Nondescript. Average. He was becoming resigned to attending some average college, it didn't matter which one, they were all the same, and becoming an average college joe. The third session had just begun. Clemson. No different than the others. If such a thing were possible, Clemson's rep was more boring than the other two. He reminded Pete of an unsuccessful insurance salesman.

The areas where the sessions were held were relatively small and were crowded in upon one another. Pete was seated on the edge of the Clemson area. The area next to it was for the Citadel. Pete had no interest in the Citadel. Pete knew very little about the Citadel. Being from Charleston, Pete knew of the Citadel, but everything he had heard about the place was bad. The military and all that. You'd have to be crazy to go there. Why subject yourself to all that. College certainly wasn't supposed to be anything like the stuff he'd heard about the Citadel. The Clemson guy was so bad that Pete, not meaning to at first, found himself listening to the Citadel guy. Pete was seated as close to him as he was to the guy from Clemson, and could hear every word he was saying.

The guy was dressed in an air force uniform, and he was a terrific speaker. He was animated. He said he was a Citadel graduate. He was convincing. Pete was certain the guy believed everything he was saying about the Citadel, and he was saying some amazing things. He did not mince words. He said the first year was hard, as hard and challenging as anything you'd ever do, harder than you could ever imagine. The Citadel wasn't for everybody, but if you came there, and survived the first year, he guaranteed that afterwards you'd fall in love with the place. You'd be a member of the "long gray line." Pete had never heard the phrase. The guy in the air force uniform explained that the long gray line included Citadel cadets and Citadel graduates everywhere. All over the world. He took off his Citadel ring and held it up. "This ring," he said, "is a symbol. A symbol of the school and its graduates. Recognized and respected throughout the world. You can go to some other college, and maybe join a fraternity, and have some friendships that may last a while, but the bonds formed at the Citadel are enduring. Those bonds extend not just to your own classmates, but to all Citadel graduates. The advantages of being a Citadel graduate are second to none. The Citadel alumni network will open doors to you that otherwise would remain closed. Graduating from the Citadel means something, it carries with it a distinction unavailable at any other college. If you come here, and if you measure up, you'll be a Citadel man, a member of the brotherhood, a member of the long gray line. The world will be your oyster."

Pete was mesmerized. He was close to being hooked. This was definitely different. He had never before considered the Citadel. The most appealing aspect to him was the talk of the Citadel alumni network, membership in the long gray line. Was it true? As he boarded the bus to return to his high school, he was oblivious to the noise around him, sitting contemplative and silent. The bus circled the parade ground on its route to exit the campus. Pete had managed to grab a window seat, and he surveyed the campus. All the buildings were of Spanish-Moorish architecture. Cadets in gray uniforms strolled about. Pete tried to picture himself as one of them. His thoughts excited him. No college had excited him in the least, before now. Was it just the oratory? Was he being sold a bill of goods? As the bus rolled through Lesesne Gate, the Citadel's main entrance/exit, Pete came to a sudden, but conditional, decision. Subject to confirming that business about the Citadel network, the truth about the long gray line, he was going to the Citadel.

He told Bobby Grimes, one of his good friends, who was in the seat next to him on the bus. Bobby laughed. "You're not Citadel material," he said. "You won't last the first day. You're nuts." That was the reaction he got from just about everyone he told.

Jennifer, his girlfriend, didn't laugh, but she sensed he was serious and expressed concern. "Oh, Pete," she said. "I don't know. You need to think this through. I'm going to Carolina. You could come there with me. It'd be great."

His parents didn't laugh. His mom was laid back about everything. She smiled, shrugged it off, and said, "it's your choice. In the end, I'm sure you'll choose the right one for you."

His dad, on the other hand, was very opinionated. Like Pete he had heard things about the Citadel and, like Pete until his College Day experience, everything he'd heard was bad. He made a face and said, "I hear it's a great place to be from, but an awful place to be at."

"Well," said Pete, "that's pretty much what this air force guy said. Only he was very convincing that the challenges are worth it." Pete was pretty sure his dad would come around if all the stuff about the Citadel alumni network turned out to be true. If the long gray line was real.

Pete sent off for an application. When it came, as college applications went, it was pretty straightforward. Pete had already requested and received about a dozen applications, but had yet to complete any of them. Several even required the writing of an essay, and Pete decided against those schools out of hand. Pete figured the purpose of the essay requirement was to intimidate and eliminate students, such as himself, who weren't all that interested in the school in the first place. The Citadel did not require an essay. It used another form of elimination by intimidation: the applicant was required to obtain recommendations from two Citadel graduates. What a pain! Pete, however, was definitely interested in the Citadel. Plus, he figured it was a chance to maybe find out about the alumni network.

Pete asked his dad if he knew any Citadel graduates and told him why he needed to know. It turned out his dad knew quite a few. His dad made phone calls to two of them, and set up appointments for Pete to meet with them. One was a lawyer and the other a doctor. Pete was impressed. Pete was sure his dad had come around. It was like his dad to help by seeking recommendations from professionals.

The lawyer's office was in the People's Building on Broad Street. Pete made the trip alone. He was glad his dad didn't suggest accompanying him. Pete had been to Broad Street before but this was his first time in the People's Building. He was impressed with the lawyer's office, but not so much with the lawyer. His mother probably would have described the office furnishings as old Charleston antique. Running to heavy. Somewhat ornate. Pete wasn't into interiors; even so, he found the décor imposing.

Prominently displayed on one wall were Mr. Burrough's framed degrees. The law degree from the University of South Carolina was signed by the entire law school faculty, but it was the Citadel degree which held Pete's attention. It displayed the American war eagle at its center top, with the American flag flowing from its talons and scrolling down the sides. Pete had never seen a degree from the Citadel. As he looked at this one, he felt a yearning to earn his own, to become a member of the long gray line. The degree was signed by a number of men, among them General Charles P. Summerall, president of the Citadel, which marked Mr.Burroughs, in Pete's eyes, as ancient. It had been a long time, Pete knew, since Summerall's retirement as president of the Citadel.

In appearance Mr. Burroughs was not what Pete had expected. Short of stature. Thin. Gray hair on the sides of his head, bald on top. Furrowed face. Wire-rimmed spectacles. Pete supposed even Citadel men grew old. It was only when Mr. Burroughs began talking that Pete's impression of him improved. He spoke with confidence and authority, kindly, but firmly. As they conversed, Pete imagined he could detect in Mr. Burrough's voice the resolve and determination of a stalwart member of the long gray line.

"So, you're Harry's boy?" Mr. Burroughs asked. More a statement than a question.

"Yes, sir."

"Known your father for many years. Good man. Good businessman."

"Thank you, sir." Pete couldn't recall his dad ever speaking of Mr. Burroughs, but his dad knew a lot of people.

"Tell me why you want to go to the Citadel."

Pete recounted his encounter with the air force officer on College Day, and asked, "is the network of Citadel graduates as amazing as he said it was? If so, that's the main reason I want to go to the Citadel."

"And what if it isn't?"

Pete was momentarily taken aback by the question. He had to think about his answer. He replied truthfully, "I guess I've been assuming it is, but I'm just seeking confirmation."

Mr. Burroughs smiled. He said, "as a lawyer I've learned it's usually best not to assume anything. Check it out, which is what you're doing. Add some determination in there and you've got a winning formula. Your reason for wanting to attend the Citadel is a good one, and yes, the Citadel alumni network is very strong. Citadel graduates do have a knack for sticking together and staying in touch with each other. They're very loyal to each other and to their school. The Citadel has a reputation for turning out graduates of the highest caliber. By way of example I'd say that within this state if two young men fresh out of college, one a Citadel graduate, applied for the same job, both being equally qualified and their resumes otherwise being equal, the Citadel grad is more likely to get the job."

"You're just as convincing as that air force officer," said Pete.

"Neither of us is trying to sell you a bill of goods. The Citadel isn't for everybody. Don't go there unless you're absolutely sure you want what the Citadel offers."

"Yes, sir," said Pete. "I'm sure."

"Do you have a form for me to sign?"

Pete handed Mr. Burroughs the form. As he signed the recommendation, he said, "your reason for wanting a Citadel education is one of the better ones I've heard. One young man came in here and told me he liked the uniforms. Good for attracting girls, he said. He didn't last. I don't want to hear of you even thinking of dropping out."

"Oh, you won't, sir," Pete said.

"Welcome to the long gray line," Mr. Burroughs said as he handed Pete the form.

"Thank you, sir," said Pete, standing to go, the interview concluded.

The two of them shook hands. "Give your dad my best regards and remember what I said."

"Yes, sir. I will sir. You don't have to worry about me, sir."

A week later Pete arrived at the office of Dr. John Purcell for his second interview. The office was a sharp contrast to the lawyer's. It was located in a newly constructed building in downtown Charleston near the medical university. Rows of tinted glass. Modern art and a fountain in the lobby, alongside a building directory and a bank of elevators. Dr. Purcell's office was on the sixth floor. There was a large waiting room filled with empty chairs. It was late afternoon and Pete assumed the appointment had been scheduled after the doctor had seen his last patient of the day. Nonetheless, Pete was kept waiting a full half hour. Typical of all doctors, Pete thought. Only seventeen, Pete had yet to meet anyone connected with the medical profession he really liked. Maybe a Citadel graduate will be different, he mused.

Finally ushered into the doctor's presence, the meeting was brief. Dr. Purcell didn't seem particularly interested in Pete or the purpose which had brought him to his office. "I've never been asked to do this before," he said as Pete entered the office. "Do I need to write a letter or what?"

"No, sir, just a form to sign," said Pete, handing him the form.

Dr. Purcell took the form, hurriedly scribbled his name on the bottom, scarcely glancing at what he was signing, and handed it back to Pete. "Good luck to you," he said. "the Citadel's a great school. I'm sure you'll do fine."

"Thank you, sir," said Pete.

"Glad to be of help." The meeting was over. Pete left. He had stood the whole time. The whole thirty seconds. Pete barely had time to notice the medical school degree and the Citadel degree hanging on the wall. The Citadel diploma was signed by Mark W. Clark, the current school president. Pete guessed Dr. Purcell maybe was in his early thirties. He would have liked to ask him about the long gray line. He decided to content himself with what he'd learned from Mr. Burroughs. He still hadn't met a doctor he cared for, but all was well because he had his two recommendations in hand.

The Citadel also required each prospective cadet to spend a weekend at the Citadel living in the barracks with an assigned freshman. During that weekend the future members of the long gray line were referred to as weekend visitors. Pete's weekend visit was scheduled for the last weekend of February, 1964. By then, he had already been accepted by the Citadel as a member of the Class of 1968, and was eager to find out what went on in the barracks. He didn't believe the plebe system could possibly be as difficult as everyone claimed.

Weekend visitors were instructed to report to the guardroom of the main barracks, Padgett-Thomas Barracks, after the Friday afternoon parade between four and six P.M. Pete's dad had to work, but Pete and his mom arrived on campus around three thirty, in time to watch the parade, which began at three forty-five. Though they were from Charleston, it was the first time either Pete or his mom had viewed a Citadel parade. Pete thought it was glorious. He also thought his mom was impressed. "Can you believe this time next year you may be out there marching around on that field?" she asked Pete.

"I will be," he replied. "I'm going to join the long gray line. I love it already."

"Are you sure?" his mom inquired. She looked a little worried.

"I'm absolutely certain," Pete said. His mom still looked anxious. "Don't fret, Mom," Pete reassured her. "I'll be fine."

The parade ended a little after four. Pete and his mom left the parade field and walked over to Padgett-Thomas Barracks. They waited a few minutes longer. Pete quickly told his mom good-bye.

"Dad and I will pick you up here around eleven Sunday morning. Have a good time," she told him. She looked like she was about to cry.

"It's just for the weekend," Pete said.

"It's just that all this military stuff is new to me," she said. "It's a little scary."

Pete didn't reply. He ducked into the front sallyport. Inside the guardroom one of the cadets on guard duty looked up Pete's name on a list of weekend visitors. "Your host cadet is cadet Ed Swanson," the cadet said. He's in Tango Company. That's in fourth battalion. Number Four Barracks. This is Number Two Barracks." He gave Pete simple directions and told him to report to the guard room in Number Four Barracks. "Mr. Swanson is there, eagerly awaiting your arrival," Pete was told, with a hint of sarcasm.

Pete waited a few minutes before leaving for Number Four Barracks. He was afraid his mother might still be outside the barracks. His fears were unfounded and in just a few minutes more he was in the guardroom of Number Four Barracks. Pete noted that Number Four Barracks was considerably smaller than Number Two. An orderly of the guard went to the center of the quadrangle and shouted in the direction of T Company: "Mr. Swanson, T Company, report to the guardroom. You have a weekend visitor." This hollered message was repeated several times and met with derisive laughter and remarks coming from the direction of T Company, things like, "Aw right, Swanson. How'd you get so lucky? Been kissin' up again, huh?"

It took about five minutes for Swanson to appear, but it seemed much longer to Pete. Swanson introduced himself and said, "let's go up to my room for a few minutes, so you can put your things up." Swanson's room was on the top floor, the fourth gallery. On the way up, Pete noticed Swanson wasn't holding his chin in while on the galleries, nor was he moving fast like all the other freshmen. Swanson explained: "a knob with a weekend visitor is granted at ease for the weekend," he said. In the room, Swanson said, "my roommate's on weekend leave, so you can sleep in his bunk." The room's bunk beds had mattresses about an inch and a half thin, full of lumps, with weak looking springs.

"You guys sleep on those?" Pete asked incredulously.

"Oh, yeah, you're in the lap of luxury," Swanson said. "New mattresses with box springs are supposed to be on order. If you come here, don't count on them arriving until after you've graduated."

Pete looked about the two man room. Spartan. Tiny. In addition to the bunk beds, there were two small wooden desks, two wooden chairs, two wooden book shelves, and two metal lockers, which Swanson said were called presses. There was a sink in the front corner of the room behind the door, above which hung a mirror, and a steam radiator beneath the single window. That was it, other than a row of hooks on one wall, from which hung an array of clothing and other items.

"Where's the phone?" Pete asked.

"Pay phones down in the guardroom, and over at Mark Clark Hall."

"TV?"

"Swanson laughed, a loud guffaw. "Not allowed. We do have radios and stereos," he brightened.

"Air conditioning?"

"In your dreams. We do have heat." Swanson pointed to the radiator.

"I don't know that I was expecting the accommodations to be this . . . rustic," Pete said, searching for an appropriate word.

"Yeah, well, if you come here, this is what you get," Swanson said. "Plus, you get the shit kicked out of your ass the whole first year."

"Where you from?" Pete asked.

"Upstate New York."

Pete had noted the accent. "Didn't think you were from the South," Pete said. "Why'd you come here?"

"My old man's career army. A West Pointer. He was disappointed I couldn't get an appointment, so he sent me here as the next best thing."

"You gonna be army, too?"

"Haven't decided yet, but it's a possibility." Swanson opened his desk drawer, pulled out a pack of cigarettes and lit up. He inhaled, blew out a stream of bluish smoke, and said, "a bunch of us usually go out drinking on Friday nights. General leave. You're invited."

Before Pete could answer, the door to the room flew open and three freshmen cadets and another individual dressed in civilian clothes, whom Pete took to also be a weekend visitor, bounced in. Introductions were made all around. "Where you guys been?" Swanson asked.

"I keep tellin' ya, it's ya'll, Swanson," one of the other cadets said. "You're in the South now."

"Whatever," said Swanson. "I was just inviting Pete to come with us. Is your visitor coming?"

"I'm in," the other visitor said.

"Me, too," said Pete, who had never as much as tasted an alcoholic drink in his life. He wasn't about to admit that. They were all underage. Pete was wondering where the drinks were coming from.

"Jim's bringing the car around," someone said.

"Let's go do some serious drinking," said another. The two cadets who weren't hosting weekend visitors went on ahead, chins pulled in, forearms held in to their sides and parallel to the ground, double timing along the outside perimeter of the galleries and squaring their corners. The two weekend visitors with their two host cadets strolled leisurely behind. On the ground floor they passed the other two cadets, who had been stopped by an upperclassman and were being made to do pushups.

Pete and Todd, the other weekend visitor, stared as they passed. "I thought it was general leave," said Todd.

Jennings, Todd's host cadet, replied, "for a knob, general leave doesn't begin until you sign out in the guardroom and make it through the front sallyport."

Jim turned out to be the largest cadet and one of the biggest humans Pete had ever seen. He was waiting for them on the sidewalk outside the barracks, standing next to a 1950 Ford coupe parked in the street. Pete wondered how they found uniforms to fit him. He also wondered how he passed the physical exam for entrance to the Citadel. Pete estimated he was about six and a half feet tall and over four hundred pounds. Seeing Pete and Todd looking at Jim, Swanson said, "believe it or not, he's lost weight since he's been here."

"Where are Danny and Dave?" Jim asked, referring to the two cadets last seen doing pushups inside the barracks.

"They're coming," said Todd, "but there's been a slight delay."

Ten minutes later Danny and Dave emerged from the sallyport, both a little sweaty, but showing no other signs of their recent exercise. They all piled into the Ford, Danny up front with Jim, the others in the back. Due to the size of the driver, only two could fit in the front. The left side of the car went down when Jim got in. Pete wondered the tires didn't pop. Five somehow managed to squeeze into the back seat, Pete and Todd sitting on laps, and they were off.

The Beatles had appeared on TV on the Ed Sullivan Show two weeks earlier, and Beatles mania was in full force in America. No sooner were they off campus than the five cadets removed their garrison hats, part of their uniforms, from their heads, and replaced them with Beatle wigs amidst great hilarity and celebration. Pete thought they were acting like kinder-garteners instead of college students, but he had to admit they seemed to be having fun. Talking to Todd and Pete, Swanson said, "sorry we don't have wigs for you guys. Guess your hair's long enough as it is."

"You guys do look better with hair," Todd said. "I love the Beatles," he added.

"How about you, Pete?" Swanson asked. "What do you think of the Beatles?"

Pete remembered a conversation he'd recently had with his girlfriend Jennifer who'd said she thought the Beatles were best suited for preschool-ers. Pete agreed with Jennifer, whom he thought was quite sophisticated, but he wasn't about to rain on anyone's parade, especially not on a bunch of Citadel knobs in search of hair and fun wherever they could find it. "I think they're great," he said. "Long hair is definitely in."

Someone suggested that they needed to get some food before they started drinking. Big Jim, the driver, instantly agreed and headed for the nearest fast food type drive-in place on Rutledge Avenue. Called the Piggy Park, the place was famous for its barbeque, cheeseburgers, and onion rings. Big Jim downed two barbeque sandwiches, a cheeseburger, an order of French fries, an order of onion rings, and a chocolate milk shake. The others were done with eating and ready to get to the serious drinking long before Jim was finished. Finally, Jim dipped his last onion ring in ketchup, consumed it with a lip smacking flourish, let out a loud belch, and an-nounced, "on to Rabun's."

Rabun's Tavern had been a favorite of Citadel cadets for several gen-erations. Though from Charleston, Pete wasn't into the drinking scene and had never heard of it. Located on upper King Street near the Cita-del, the place was frequented by cadets, blue collar workers, and a few middle management businessmen types. Draft beer was served up in ice cold, frosted glass tankards. The first round was ordered up by Swanson. Thinking *here goes nothing,* Pete put the glass to his lips and sipped gin-gerly. Pete had only taken a few sips when the second round was ordered. At round three Pete's glass was still two thirds full. "Geez, you drink like a girl," Swanson observed. "If you're coming to the Citadel, you'll have to learn to drink." Pete noticed Todd was having no trouble keeping up. He was astounded they had been served. "Charleston's a wide open town," Swanson explained. "Citadel cadets can drink all they want. No questions asked."

"How about me and Todd?" Pete asked. "We're not in uniform."

"It's okay, you're with us," Swanson said.

The group decided to move on to Big John's on East Bay Street. Pete had heard of Big John's, but he had never been there. Its owner Big John Canady was a former lineman for the New York Giants of the NFL, and was a revered figure in Charleston. Pete was thrilled to be there, but he remained cautious about his beer drinking, ordering one beer the whole time he was there and taking only a few very small sips, while his companions drank so many Pete lost count.

Big John's was a much larger place than Rabun's and it was packed, including lots of cadets, many of them, like the group Pete was with, wearing Beatles wigs. As the evening wore on, Pete's group became louder and louder and more and more raucous. They began singing Beatles songs, in particular *Love Me Do, She Loves You,* and *I Want To Hold Your Hand.* Pete was having a ball. He found himself becoming a Beatles fan. He was learning the lyrics. He realized he might be the only sober one among the group who'd ventured forth from the Citadel in the ancient Ford coupe.

At about eleven fifteen Big Jim announced it was time to head back to the barracks. His words were only slightly slurred. Pete must have looked worried, for Swanson turned to him and said, "don't worry, he's okay to drive. He's our permanent designated driver. Never failed to deliver us safe and sound. No matter how much he's had to drink." They all crammed back into the Ford. Pete was plenty worried.

Instead of driving directly back to the Citadel, Jim detoured through Hampton Park. He stopped at the zoo and the cadets, except for Jim, got out and disappeared into the night. Todd and Pete looked at each other. "What's up?" they both asked Jim.

"They've gone to piss on the lion," Jim said. "Citadel tradition. All knobs returning to campus after a drinking spree are expected to urinate on the lion from time to time. Makes him really mad. You'll hear him in a minute."

"Not that old lion!" Pete exclaimed. Pete was familiar with the Hampton Park lion. "That's cruel. He's too old."

"I agree," said Jim. "That's why I didn't go."

"But you're an accomplice," said Pete.

"I have to see this," said Todd, starting to get out of the car.

"No," said Jim. "You're just a weekend visitor. Stay here. Next year, when you're a knob, you'll have your chance."

Just then there was a tremendous lion roar. ARRAGH. It was probably their imagination, but it seemed so close, the car seemed to shake. The first roar was followed by another, not as loud, and then a third, more of a cough than a roar.

"That old lion sounds sick," said Pete.

"He is," said Jim. "Sick and old. This tradition may not last much longer." Swanson, Jennings, Dave, and Danny suddenly appeared out of the dark, running toward the car, giggling and drunk, still zipping up.

"That's one mad cat," Dave said.

"You'd be mad too if you got pissed on over and over every Friday and Saturday night," said Jennings.

"It's not as bad as being shit on every day as a knob," said Danny.

Jim parked the Ford on a side street off campus about two blocks from Lesesne Gate. "Ten minutes till midnight," Jim said. "We'll have to hustle." They ran all the way to the barracks and made it with about a minute to spare. General leave ended at midnight. Freshmen weren't allowed cars on campus. Jim, like Pete, was from Charleston. Every Friday Jim's parents brought him the car for his weekend use, parking it off campus on the same street.

That night Pete slept the sleep of the dead. He dreamed. He dreamed of Big John's, drunken knobs, the Beatles, and coughing lions in Hampton Park. He awoke with a start at six A.M., the sound of reveille, blown by an unseen bugler, reverberating in his ears. Weekend visitors and their cadet hosts did not have to meet the breakfast formation. They followed the marching companies to the mess hall where several tables were set aside for them. The food was bad, the clamor of the mess hall worse. Meal times clearly were not happy times for knobs.

The Saturday schedule for weekend visitors was a full one. First up after breakfast was a complete tour of the campus, followed by a meeting with a faculty advisor from the department the prospective cadet had indicated on his application was his probable major. Pete didn't have a clue what he wanted to study, so he had put down premed, which would please his dad. The main thing he took from this meeting was that all Citadel professors wore uniforms to class and were members of SCUM, which stood for South Carolina Unorganized Militia. Then it was back to the mess hall for another delicious meal and more clamor. In the afternoon each visitor had a one on one interview with a tactical officer from the commandant's department.

Pete's interview was with a Major Kirkland. On College Day Pete had not gotten the name of the air force officer whose talk had first interested him in the Citadel, and he was flabbergasted when he recognized his interviewer as the same officer. The very same. Pete took it as fate, a sure sign he was destined for the long gray line. The interview went well. Pete told the major of their College Day encounter. The major was pleased. Pete was unsure if the major was most pleased with himself or with Pete, but he told Pete he was sure he'd make a formidable member of the long gray line, whatever that meant.

That evening Pete had expected another sojourn in the Ford coupe and another round of bars, but it turned out Big Jim had a date, so transportation was problematic. Pete surmised some Charleston girls must love going out with cadets, even morbidly obese ones. Maybe both of them were cat lovers. Swanson suggested a quiet evening at the movies at Mark Clark Hall. It was free. A war movie was playing, what else? *Von Ryan's Express,* starring Frank Sinatra.

Next morning Pete's mom and dad picked him up as promised and his initial encounter with the long gray line was concluded. Pete told them he was more certain than ever that the Citadel was the place for him. He had missed Jennifer. That week at school he told her the same. Later that week the seniors received their yearbooks. The next week Pete gave his book to

Jennifer. She kept it a week and returned it to him with one of those long, full page epistles in which she expressed both her love and her dismay he wouldn't be joining her at Carolina. She wished him well as a future member of the long gray line. This gave Pete an ominous feeling. He wrote a short, few lines in her yearbook in which he assured her of his undying love and devotion.

Pete and Jennifer dated all that summer, a summer in which Pete studied *The Guidon,* worked out so he could be in the best possible physical condition, spit shined shoes, polished brass, and prepared himself as best he could for the plebe system. At the end of the summer they both went off to their chosen schools, both knowing their relationship was unlikely to last, but neither speaking about it. The relationship sort of died on the vine. For his part, Pete regretted it, but in the grand scheme of things it was but a small disappointment. At the Citadel Pete learned how to handle happiness and disappointment, success and failure, victory and defeat. He wears the ring, a member of the long gray line.

ECHO TAPS

The plebe system administered to freshmen at the Citadel in the 1960s was hard, tough physically and mentally. War was raging in Vietnam. At other college campuses across the country students were protesting with antiwar rallies, which sometimes turned violent and ugly and made national headlines. Not at the Citadel. At the Citadel all was calm, serene, and peaceful. Except in the barracks. No antiwar sentiment. War was glorified. Cadets looked forward to graduating and going off to fight for God and country. Maybe it was the cruelty inflicted upon them in the barracks their first year that made them determined to mete out worse than they got once they became upperclassmen, and made them eager to be a part of the real military once their Citadel days were over. Whatever it was, knobs who survived the grueling punishment of that first year, so the theory went, were transformed into Citadel men, men true to their alma mater, men who were enlightened citizens and courageous, loyal soldiers, soldiers willing to fight and die.

One such Citadel man was Sean Mitchell. Sean was from Savannah, Georgia, as was Pete Creger's roommate Bo Warner. Sean and Bo grew up on the same street in Savannah. Sean was two years older. He and Bo's older brother Bobby, who had the good sense not to come to the Citadel, were best friends. Bo, Bobby, and Sean all went to the same military high school in Savannah. After high school Bobby decided he'd had enough of the military and he went to a normal college, the University of Georgia. Sean and Bo, though, were eaten up with the military. They both came to the Citadel.

Had it not been for Bo and Sean, Pete never would have made it through freshman year. Bo came to the Citadel prepared. He knew all about the military stuff. He knew how to shine shoes and brass. He knew rifle manual. He knew how to march. He had the right attitude. He was in great physical shape. The plebe system was almost like water off a duck's back for him. All he knew he imparted to Pete. The plebe system was much harder for Pete, at times unbearable. He hated all upperclassmen, except for Sean. Sean showed Pete upperclassmen were human after all, that the plebe system was just a game, perhaps the most important lesson of all. Had Pete not learned that lesson from Sean, he wouldn't have made it at the Citadel.

During Pete and Bo's freshman year, Sean was a junior. Pete and Bo were in F Company, foxtrot in the phonetic alphabet. Sean was a platoon sergeant in E Company, echo in the phonetic alphabet. When his little brother Bo enrolled at the Citadel, Bobby Warner, filled with horror stories about the place from his best friend Sean Mitchell, extracted a solemn promise from Sean that he would look after his little brother. Sean was true to his word, though Bo needed little looking after. Pete benefited more than Bo. Pete needed looking after.

Pete and Bo had been at the Citadel only a week the first time Sean came to their room to check up on Bo. Classes had not started. Pete and Bo, along with the other F Company freshmen, had barely managed to crawl along the gallery back to their room following a sweat party. They were exhausted after running in place, performing pushups to the limits of their endurance, and being yelled at until the upperclassmen's voices nearly had given out. They were lying on the floor of their room, too tired to get up, wipe the sweat from their bodies, and fall into their bunks. It was around ten o'clock at night and they had been back in their room about ten minutes. Pete was lying closest to the door and had just told Bo he didn't think he could do this for nine months when suddenly the door was flung open and an upperclassman stormed into the room. They didn't yet know the faces of all F Company's upperclassmen. They hardly knew each other's faces. As he had been taught, Pete jumped to his feet, assumed the brace position, and yelled, "ROOM, A-TEN-SHUN."

Instead of jumping to his feet and bracing beside his roommate, Bo, who at least had lifted up his head, let his head drop back to the floor and started laughing. He laughed so hard Pete thought he was going to choke. Pete continued bracing. Bo was still laughing when, to Pete's surprise, the unknown upperclassman went over to him, pulled him to his feet, and the two of them embraced. "Thought it was a good time to check on you," the upperclassman said. Turning to Pete, he said, "at ease. Relax." Pete relaxed his chin, but was wary.

Bo made the introductions. "Sean's a friend, my brother's best friend," he said. "We're both from Savannah."

Sticking his right hand out to Pete, Sean said, "glad to meet you." Pete shook Sean's hand. He seemed a regular guy. It was pretty clear he and Bo were good friends. They had the common bond of Savannah, the same high school, the love of everything military, Bo's brother, and now the Citadel.

Seeing the two of them carrying on together, Pete thought they acted like they hadn't seen each other in years. How long could it have been? A few weeks? Pete had to admit this past week, the first week at the Citadel, had seemed like forever. The thought of the year's end stretched on interminably. An eternity. Sean nodded his head in Pete's direction. "How about this guy?" he asked. "Does he belong here? You two get along okay?"

Bo endeared himself to Pete on the spot by saying without hesitation, with apparent honesty, "it's only been a week, Sean, but yeah, he's an okay guy. He puts out. We're getting along fine."

"Good," Sean said, speaking to both Bo and Pete. "It's important to have a good roommate. You'll grow close to all your classmates, but especially your roomie, but the chemistry has to be right. If the two of you have that, you'd be amazed how much help you can be to each other."

Pete wanted to say something, but refrained from doing so. After all, Sean was Bo's friend, not Pete's. He was fraternizing with Bo, not Pete, and he was an upperclassman. Freshmen weren't supposed to speak to upperclassmen without first asking permission, unless answering a question posed to them. Pete had yet to make a statement to any upperclassman who hadn't asked him a question and Sean hadn't asked him a question. He was Mr. Mitchell to Pete and the situation was awkward.

Pete must have looked like he had something on his mind, because Sean asked, "do you want to say something, Pete?" Upperclassmen didn't call freshmen by their first names. Sean went on, speaking to both of them again. "Okay, let's get something straight. Whenever I'm in this room with either of you, or both of you, and we're alone, the plebe system isn't in effect, and the three of us can act human to each other. If there's someone else in here with us, either another knob, or another upperclassman, then it is in effect. Both of you revert to being knobs. I treat you as knobs and I'm an upperclassman to you, your superior in every way. The same goes for outside on the gallery, or anywhere in the barracks, or anywhere else on or off campus, unless we happen to be alone together, but even then, outside this room, we have to be careful. Understood?"

Bo and Pete nodded they understood and agreed. "Okay, then, Pete," Sean asked, "what is it?"

"I was just going to say I haven't been any help so far to Bo, but I'll try to be. But he sure has been a big help to me. I feel lucky to have a roommate who's been to a military school and knows all this military stuff."

Sean smiled. "That's good," he said. "Both of you keep putting out, and you'll both be fine. My visits will be short, but I'll make them as often as I can, every few weeks or so. Anytime I'm here and there's any kind of problem, let me know and we'll talk about it."

"Thanks," Bo said. "That means a lot." Pete felt even luckier being Bo's roommate.

True to his word, Sean Mitchell was a frequent visitor to Bo and Pete's room during their long and difficult freshman year. Sometimes he came during evening study period, sometimes after it ended at ten thirty but before lights out at eleven. Once he was in their room when the bugler began playing taps. He didn't leave until the bugler was done, and before leaving he said, "God, I love that. It's my favorite."

Bo said, "it's not mine, but I like hearing it because it means I can crawl into the rack and get some much needed sleep, that is if all those asshole upperclassmen, present company excepted, would stay the hell out of our room and quit harassing us."

Sean smiled and said, "knobs are harassed for their own good. It's the system. It's what'll turn even puny little knoblets like the two of you into Citadel men."

Pete said, "these two future Citadel men could do with less harassment and more rest." After Sean was gone, as they lay in their bunks, Pete asked Bo, "do you think Sean really believes it's all the upperclass harassment, the system, that turns knobs into Citadel men?"

"Oh, he believes it all right," Bo replied. Pete wasn't all that sure he wanted to be one.

The more Pete saw Sean Mitchell the more he liked him. Sean would come by the room after bad sweat parties. Though Bo and his brother Bobby were Sean's special friends, Sean was interested in Pete, too, just because Pete was Bo's roommate, classmate, and friend. Pete began to see there really was something very special about the Citadel.

One of the things that intrigued Pete about Bo and Sean was that their love for the military began when they were kids. They told endless stories about playing war and guns out in the fields and woods near their homes in Savannah when they were growing up. Pete supposed most small boys became infatuated with uniforms and all that went with them. Pete played his share of war games as a kid, but he got over it. He grew out of it. Bo and Sean and others like them never did.

From all Pete could gather, Sean must have been an exemplary knob. There was no doubt that Bo was. Pete, militarily, made do. He survived. The most notable thing about him as a knob was that he was Bo Warner's roommate. The gung ho types wondered how Bo put up with Pete. Sean had been a corporal in E Company his sophomore year. His sophomore year Bo, too, was a corporal. No one was prouder of Bo than Sean, who that year was a first lieutenant and E Company executive officer. Pete started the year as a private, happy to be an upperclassman at last.

Bo and Pete saw a lot of Sean their sophomore year. They were upperclassmen and were on a first name basis with Sean, with no fear of reprisal. Sean still visited their room and they could go to E Company area. That year, unlike freshman year, flew by and the next thing Pete and Bo knew they were juniors. Bo was a platoon sergeant in F Company and

Pete, somewhat to his surprise, was a squad sergeant. Sean Mitchell had graduated and was in the real military, a second lieutenant in the marine corps, soon to be deployed to Vietnam and the real war. Bo got a letter from him just before he left for the war. He was excited about the prospect of winning medals. When Bo read the letter out loud to Pete, Pete thought *he still thinks it's a game.* Six months later Sean was dead.

Bo and Pete knew of Sean's death before anyone else at the Citadel. Bo received a phone call from his mom, who had learned of it from Sean's mom, who had come to her house in person to tell her. The two of them cried together in the Warner living room. Sean's dad was too distraught to talk about it. Women are always stronger. Bo's mom broke down again on the phone telling Bo about it.

Pete was in their room when Bo came in, tears streaming down his face. It was a while before Bo was coherent enough to tell Pete what was wrong. Bo was granted a special leave from the Citadel to attend the funeral in Savannah. Pete applied for leave too, but was turned down. The Citadel policy was to grant leave only for deaths in the family. Bo was granted special leave due to the closeness of the two families. Pete didn't qualify.

Official word of Sean's death in Vietnam reached the Citadel the day Bo returned from Savannah. That evening at lights out, eleven P.M., the voice of the day's officer in charge came over the PA system in each of the barracks. He said there would be a special announcement from the school's president, General Marcum. The general announced to the corps of cadets that word had been received that Marine Corps Second Lieutenant Sean Mitchell, the past year's executive officer of Echo Company, had died from wounds received in combat in the republic of South Vietnam. For heroism in the battle that had taken his life, Lieutenant Mitchell posthumously was awarded the Silver Star, one of our nation's highest honors for bravery under fire, second only to the Congressional Medal of Honor. All cadets, including freshmen, who were given at ease, were ordered to stand on the galleries outside their rooms, heads bowed in a moment of silent reflection, followed by the playing of echo taps, in memory of Lieutenant Mitchell.

Pete and Bo stood together on the gallery outside their room. They bowed their heads. It was a dark night in early spring, a cool night with a slight breeze. The galleries were crowded, but darkness and silence enveloped the barracks like solemn, black draperies. The general's imposed quietness ended with the plaintive, metallic, brassy notes of the first bugler, stationed in the center of the quadrangle of Number Two barracks, and followed by the echo of the second bugler, unseen, somewhere in the distant darkness of the night: "Da-Da-Da . . . Da-Da-Da . . . Da-Da-Da . . . Da-Da-Da . . . Da-Da-Da-Da-Da-Da . . . Da-Da-Da . . . Da-Da-Da-Da-Da-Da . . . Da-Da-Da."

A change came over Bo Warner. Not that he didn't carry out his duties as a platoon sergeant in F Company. He did. But he did it differently. He was still firm with the knobs, but not harsh. He scarcely raised his voice to a knob the rest of the year. There were only six weeks left in the year and they would be seniors. For the coming year Bo was offered the position of cadet captain, F Company commander, but he refused it. Something unheard of. "It wouldn't be right for me to ever outrank Sean," he said. For a while it looked like Bo was going to be a senior private. Finally, he accepted the rank of first lieutenant, F Company executive officer, the same rank held by Sean his senior year in E Company. He didn't rack a single knob the entire year. Pete and Bo's room became a knob haven, a place where knobs could have an occasional few moments of respite, recover their equilibrium, and resolve to carry on.

Sometime that senior year the new Bo and Pete discussed fleeing to Canada to avoid going to war, but they both knew neither of them would do it. As it turned out they didn't have to. As they neared graduation, the army announced a new policy. They didn't understand it, but they didn't argue with it. The army said there was an overabundance of second lieutenants serving in Vietnam.

Therefore, for those who already had a commission to serve in the army upon graduation from college, but who wanted to go to graduate school, the army would defer your service until completion of all graduate studies. Bo and Pete jumped on it. By the time they completed Ph.D.'s, the war was over. They both only had to serve six months active duty, followed by three years in the reserves. They finished up their army careers as second lieutenants, neither outranking Sean Mitchell.

Sean was twenty two when he died serving his country. His Silver Star is displayed in the Citadel museum, donated by his parents. The playing of echo taps in the barracks in memory of fallen Citadel graduates became a school tradition.

F TROOP

From its founding in 1842 the Citadel has been steeped in tradition. There have been changes through the years, some major, others minor, but the basics of the military and the plebe system have remained the same. When Pete Creger and the other members of the Class of 1968 began their Citadel training in the fall of 1964, there were no black cadets. Neither were there women cadets. The first black cadet appeared on campus in the fall of 1966. Women did not arrive until the 1990s. In the 1960s there were seventeen companies in the corps of cadets. The number of companies has increased. In the mid-1960s F Company began its own tradition. F Company is no longer called a company. It's called a troop. F Troop. The origin of the name change is forgotten. This is the story of how the tradition began.

On September 14, 1965, a new comedy show premiered on television. The event passed largely unnoticed at the Citadel. The show wasn't a big hit. It lasted only two seasons, the first filmed in black and white, the second in color. A few weeks earlier Pete Creger, Squeaker Dorfner, and the other members of the Class of 1968 had returned to the Citadel to begin their sophomore year. Their numbers were severely diminished. Many left during the rigors of knob year. Some finished the year, but opted not to return. The Citadel wasn't for them. The returning remnant was proud and excited.

They were proud of their previous year's accomplishment and excited to be upperclassmen. Few had heard of the new TV show. None could have foreseen the events of the coming year, nor the show's impact on F Company. F Company had just experienced, arguably, its finest hour. The year before the Class of 1968 arrived on campus F Company had excelled in every area of military life and had won the coveted Commandant's Cup as the best overall company in the corps. Two F Company freshmen that year had placed first and second in the Star of the West competition for best drilled cadet. The competition was named after the *Star of the West,* a Union ship dispatched by President Abraham Lincoln to resupply Fort Sumter in the days preceding the start of the Civil War. The ship turned back after being fired on by Citadel cadets as it approached Charleston harbor. Citadel historians consider those shots, not the bombardment of Ft. Sumter, which occurred weeks later, the first of the war. The company also stood out in the weekly retreat parades held each Friday afternoon, winning more parades and accumulating more points toward the cup than any other company. The company was named "most disciplined," a distinction earned by receiving the fewest demerits and punishment orders. That year F Company was the hands down winner of the best company award.

Winning the award as best company was prestigious. There was the cup itself: ornate, large, double handled, silver, displayed on a glassed in shelf beside other trophies inside the front entrance to Mark Clark Hall. Engraved on the front of the cup were the words "Commandant's Cup, Awarded Annually to the Best Overall Company in the South Carolina Corps of Cadets." Next to the cup was an ever expanding wooden plaque with engraved silver tags. The tag at the top read "Each Year the Company Awarded the Commandant's Cup Serves the Following Year as Honor Company." Beneath that tag were smaller ones naming the year, the company, and the company commanders.

Having won the award the previous year, F Company set a goal of winning it again. No company had ever repeated as honor company. A particularly grueling plebe system resulted for the Class of 1968 in F Company as a part of that effort. The goal was achieved. The previous year's runner up in the Star of the West won the competition and a F Company freshman, a member of the Class of 1968, came in second. The company again excelled at parade and in the area of discipline. F Company served as honor company two consecutive years. Within the company, however, there were dissenters, those who did not want a threepeat. Being honor company carried with it not just prestige, but additional responsibilities and duties. Honor company served as the honor guard, welcoming all visiting dignitaries to the campus. That meant being super shined up all the time, being super drilled all the time. Some thought being honor company wasn't all it was cracked up to be. F Company's standard of excellence at honor guards began to slip.

Worse than that, discipline began to fail. By the end of first semester of the Class of 1968's sophomore year, there wasn't even a glimmer of hope of F Company being honor company three years in a row. Those who were glad, who'd had enough, were in the majority. Morale hit rock bottom. When things couldn't get worse, they did. Two seniors were accused of hazing. The allegations were true and were among the worst incidents of physical brutality perpetrated upon helpless freshmen by out of control upperclassmen in the history of the school. The accused were roommates and the hazing occurred in their room in the barracks. As punishment one was expelled. The other was given a lesser sentence. Six months restriction and one hundred twenty tours.

A punishment tour had to be walked on the quadrangle of Number Two barracks. No cadet was allowed to graduate with unwalked tours. The final semester that year the unexpelled miscreant could be seen every day on the quadrangle, alone with his rifle, a silent, sad sentinel doggedly performing his punishment, a reminder to all of F Company's fall from grace.

There was talk F Company would lose its designation as honor company. There were those who wouldn't have minded, an indication how bad things had gotten. That didn't happen. What did happen may have been worse. F Company's popular, respected company commander, Cadet Captain Joseph Blackaby, was removed as company commander. Busted down to private. Officially, his offense was listed as "failure to maintain discipline."

The well-liked company executive officer, Warren Henley, was passed over. More resentment. No matter who became the new company commander, he would be in charge of a company on a downward spiral. An

impossible, thankless job. Elliott Johnson, one of F Company's first lieutenants and a platoon leader, was promoted to captain of a company in
full-blown disarray. Johnson looked like a good choice. Impeccable military bearing. Unquestioned leadership. But, too much of a disciplinarian.
F Company was more in need of inspiration than strict discipline. Johnson's strict, stern style didn't go over well. He tried hard, he did his best,
but F Company didn't respond to him. He had a difficult time as company
commander.

Enter *F Troop*, the new television show. Later, Pete Creger would say he
was the first one to become a fan and to spread the word about the show
and its similarity to F Company's situation. Whether or not his claim was
accurate, he was certainly among the first to start calling F Company "F
Troop," after the show. The television series was about a dysfunctional
cavalry troop stationed at the mythical Fort Courage, Kansas, after the
Civil War in 1865. It starred Ken Berry as Company Commander Captain
Wilmot Parmenter, whose comedic ineptness in attempting to maintain
discipline and order amid the antics of his wayward soldiers paralleled
those of Elliott Johnson to restore the Citadel's F Company to its former
glory as honor company. Ludicrous in the extreme. F Company's finest
hour was over. Laughter was not the best medicine, it was the only medicine. Squeaker Dorfner was the Class of 1968's acknowledged leader in F
Company. He was company clerk and guidon corporal. As such, he carried the company guidon in front of the company at parades, marching
beside the company commander with the guidon, a small banner or flag
attached to the top of a long pole and emblazoned with the company insignia F. Squeaker latched onto the concept that F Company had become
like F Troop. He came up with the idea of changing the wording on the
company banner to *F Troop*, and so F Troop was born. It was a difficult,
prolonged birth.

First a banner with the *F Troop* wording had to be procured. That
turned out to be the easy part. Then the whole company had to be in on
it. New company commander Elliott Johnson was none too happy about
being compared to Captain Wilton Parmenter. Squeaker persuaded him it
would be good for company morale. Johnson wasn't too sold on the idea,

but he agreed some levity would be a good thing. There was no debate about whether or not to seek the approval of the school administration. Squeaker and Johnson insisted on complete secrecy. There must be no leaks to the administration. Corps Day of that year was chosen for the debut of the new F Troop guidon flag. Corps Day, held annually to celebrate the birthday of the corps, is one of the school year's biggest weekends. It is always held near the end of March, near the end of winter, the beginning of spring. That year F Company, soon to be F Troop, was badly in need of spring and a new beginning. Corps Day, like the other big weekends at the Citadel, Parents Day, homecoming, and commencement, featured a retreat parade on Friday afternoon and a second parade, a review of the corps, on Saturday morning.

Knowing Major Gillespie, F Company's tactical officer, would be lurking around inside the barracks as the companies assembled on the quadrangle, Squeaker kept the folded F Troop flag hidden away inside his full dress blouse. The moment of truth would come once F Company marched through the sallyport to the staging area between first and second battalions. Once outside the barracks, in the moments before F Company marched onto the parade ground, Squeaker would have time to make the switch. On that glorious Friday afternoon of Corps Day, 1966, amid bleating bagpipes, beating drums, blaring bugles, shouted commands, and the tromp, tromp, tromp of marching feet, a new Citadel tradition was born.

Squeaker made the switch. The cadets of F Troop marched by, past throngs of visitors, some standing, others seated in chairs, or on the bleachers in front of the barracks, onto the parade ground, their new guidon flag fluttering thrillingly in the cool March wind. F Company no more, but F Troop. No one seemed to notice the new flag, a good thing. Once out on the field, the parade wouldn't be disrupted to remove an offending flag. The chatter within the ranks, always abhorred by cadet officers, but seldom wholly silenced, snowballed into quiet, mirthful laugher. Elliott Johnson, to F Troop's delight, did not attempt to quell the noise, but joined in. He was enjoying himself.

Once F Troop was aligned in its proper place on the field, going through the manual of arms with the other companies, there was little chance of detection. The distance across the parade ground to the reviewing stand was too great, even for the most penetrating observer. The officers front was a different story. In this maneuver the officers of all the companies, accompanied by the guidon bearers, formed a parallel line, marched up to the reviewing stand, and performed an impressive salute before the assembled crowd, the officers with their swords, and the guidon corporals with the company guidons. The smiles on the faces of Squeaker and the officers when they returned showed all was still well.

Everyone was amazed the F Troop guidon so far into the parade was undiscovered. Everyone knew that soon after the regimental adjutant gave the order "PASS IN REVIEW," the F Troop flag at last would be exposed to full view. No possibility of escaping notice. In executing the order each company marched in turn past the reviewing stand. With the order "EYES RIGHT," the guidon corporal saluted by first raising the guidon into the air and then bringing it back down and holding it parallel to the ground, fully unfurling the flag so that all those watching knew which company was passing by. The plan was not to avoid detection, but to avoid capture. Detection was the greatest part of the fun. The laughter began in the crowd as soon as F Troop began its eyes right. All of F Troop was smiling, though not laughing. Just past the reviewing stand each company in turn made a right turn and marched off the parade ground and returned to their barracks, the end of the parade. The laughter followed F Troop all the way back to the barracks. So did Major Gillespie. He wasn't laughing. He was walking fast, following F Troop, frowning, and shouting, "Mr. Johnson, I want to see you!" Squeaker, as planned, had broken ranks long before reaching the barracks. The escape plan. He ran at full speed into the barracks ahead of the troop. By the time the troop, joined by Major Gillespie, stood inside the barracks awaiting dismissal, he had switched the flags back, hidden the F Troop one, and stood in his proper place with the guidon, breathing hard, but grinning harder.

The major walked over and stood by Squeaker and Johnson. The proper F Company flag was in its place atop the guidon pole, visible to all. The major addressed Elliott Johnson. "Mr. Johnson," he asked, "did you have a part in this?"

Not answering the question, Johnson replied, "sir, I'm sure Mr. Dorfner was just having a little fun on Corps Day."

"This isn't like you, Mr. Johnson."

Squeaker spoke up. "Sir, have you seen that TV show, *F Troop*? It's a pretty funny show."

"Yeah, I've seen it." Gillespie smiled without meaning to. "This isn't Ft. Courage."

"No, sir. It's the Citadel, sir," Squeaker popped to and stood stiffly at attention, almost in a brace.

"I don't know what you've done with that other flag and I really don't want to ask. I don't want to see it again. Understood?"

"Is that an order, sir?" Johnson asked.

"Consider it a suggestion. A strong suggestion. If it becomes necessary to make it an order, this entire company is in shit. Deep shit." But as he said this, there was that smile again. Major Gillespie walked away. The whole company had heard the exchange.

That evening was a busy one. There was a formal dance, which the Citadel called a hop. Hops were held on the Friday evenings of big weekends, the Corps Day hop being the last one of the school year. A Citadel tradition. Full dress uniforms. The girls dressed to the nines in formal evening gowns. Jewelry and corsages. A big name band. A lot of preparation went into it. Even so, before picking up their dates Squeaker and Johnson found time to discuss the meaning of Gillespie's smiles. The Citadel was not about anything if it was not about time management.

Gillespie had said he was only making a suggestion. The smiles seemed friendly enough, albeit accompanied by dire warnings. Was he secretly with them? Could he be pushed a little further? Was there enough wiggle room for the F Troop banner to be displayed at least one more time? At the Corps Day review scheduled the next morning at 11 A.M.? Squeaker thought so. Johnson, a senior, didn't want to do anything that might jeopardize his graduation. As far as Johnson was concerned the F Troop flag had made its first and last ride. Discussion over. Squeaker left Johnson's room, the allotted time for their dialogue up, saying, "we'll talk about it some more at the hop." Johnson groaned. He admired Squeaker's persistence, but he could be a pain in the ass.

Elliott Johnson had already won accolades as a distinguished military student. He had a contract to accept a commission as a second lieutenant in the army upon graduation. He was engaged to be married and the wedding was to take place in the Summerall Chapel the afternoon of his Saturday morning graduation from the Citadel. All he needed to make it all happen was his diploma in hand and he'd be damned if he was going to let an obsession with a silly TV show ruin all that. Johnson and his fiancé Marilyn Harper had begun dating their freshman year in college, he at the Citadel and she at Columbia College, an all-girls school. They became engaged their sophomore year.

The two of them favored single gender education and had decided their children would definitely attend their parents' colleges. Not in their wildest dreams could either of them imagine that the Citadel, by the time their children would reach college age, would be coeducational. They had attended every hop together during Elliott's four years at the military school, and this would be their last.

This was a very special time for them, a time to remember, a few short months away from the end of their college careers and the real beginning of their lives together. This was a special evening, made more so by the appearance at this hop of one of their favorite singing groups, Frankie Valli and the Four Seasons. True, some of the Four Seasons' music was more for standing and listening than for dancing, better suited for a concert than a Citadel hop, but it didn't matter to Elliott and Marilyn. They loved to do both.

Marilyn could tell Elliott was more than a little distracted. Probably over the goings on in F Company, she thought. She had agonized with him over the hazings, his friend Joe's being removed from command, and his own decision to assume command. He had loved his role as a platoon leader; and there was so much more to running a company, especially a top company now beset with difficulties. It didn't help that early in the evening they had run into Joe and his date. Marilyn was aware that in addition to his troubles in F Company, certainly not his fault, Joe and his longstanding girlfriend, a girl Marilyn knew, had recently broken up. The moment seemed awkward. Joe and his date appeared to be enjoying themselves, but Joe seemed cold toward Elliott, the classmate camaraderie lacking.

Minutes later the Four Seasons began singing "I've Got You Under My Skin," definitely a standing and listening number. Elliott stood behind Marilyn, his arms wrapped around her waist, his hands clasped together in front. They nuzzled each other and swayed with the music. Being young and in love was a wonderful thing. Glancing to her left Marilyn noticed Joe and his date, whose name she couldn't remember, standing near but not close together. She was a little saddened for Joe. She wished Joe and Ginger were there together. Even in the dim light she could see the slightly darkened coloration on the shoulders of Joe's full dress blouse outlining where his captain's stripes had been removed. She wondered if Elliott had noticed.

Elliott had noticed. It bothered him. He wished he was back in charge of his platoon. As the tune ended he became aware of Squeaker hurrying in his direction, his cute little date, whom he held by the hand, struggling to keep up. Squeaker was being his aggressive self. Not now, Squeaker, Elliott thought. Squeaker politely introduced his date. Then, mouth firmly set, he said, "Major Gillespie's here with his wife. Let's go talk to him."

"About what?" Elliott let his irritation show. It didn't faze Squeaker. "You know what."

"This is not the place, Squeaker. Once was fun. We got away with it. No need to . . ." Before he finished the Four Seasons were in to "Walk Like a Man," and his words were drowned out, the music too loud to talk and be heard.

As soon as the song ended, Squeaker pulled Elliott aside. He spoke softly, so as to be heard only by Elliott. "C'mon, Elliott," he almost whispered. "You're the company commander."

"That's right, I am. We're not doing it again. That's an order!"

Flustered, the words to the song drumming in his head, Squeaker came out with, "be a man, Elliott." He regretted it the moment the words were out of his mouth.

Elliott's face flushed red. "You're getting under my skin," he retorted angrily.

At that moment Major Gillespie and his wife walked up. Introductions were made as the band struck up "Sherry," after which they took a break, making talk easier. The major brought up the topic Squeaker wanted to talk about. "I was telling Mrs. Gillespie about the caper this afternoon," he said. "I wish I had been there," Mrs. Gillespie lamented. "I'll be there in the morning. Can you boys do it again?"

"No, dear, they can't," the major said. "It's beneath the dignity of the corps."

"It is the corps' birthday, sir," Squeaker said imploringly. Elliott glared at him.

"You two gentlemen know very well what I said this afternoon," the major said, taking his wife by the arm and steering her away.

"Yes, sir," Elliott said.

Mrs. Gillespie looked back over her shoulder as she was being led away, and Squeaker said to her, "I believe it was only a suggestion, M'am." She smiled and winked at Squeaker. She turned her head around and looked up lovingly at her husband. The two of them strolled off arm in arm. "Did you see that?" Squeaker asked.

"Yeah, I saw it," Elliott said. "As you reminded me a few moments ago, I'm the company commander and I'm making the major's suggestion an order."

The next morning outside the barracks Squeaker waited until the last possible minute, just before the company marched onto the parade ground, before making the switch. F Troop swaggered onto the field. Elliott Johnson was beside himself, but Squeaker had acted so deftly that the deed was done, the parade begun, and there was nothing he could do about it. During eyes right Squeaker spotted Mrs. Gillespie in the stands. She was beaming. She waved a white handkerchief. Squeaker thought he heard her shout, "yeah, F Troop!" The crowd began applauding. Others began chanting, "F Troop, F Troop, F Troop." Over and over. The company took it up. They entered the barracks shouting it again and again. Inside the barracks, standing in ranks waiting to be dismissed, they continued with the chorus, louder and louder, "F Troop, F Troop." Elliott Johnson tried to quiet them before dismissal. He finally gave up, gave the order, "company dismissed," and walked off.

As he walked off, he was confronted by Major Gillespie. "I had nothing to do with it, sir. It was all Mr. Dorfner. He made the switch at the last minute, as we marched onto the field. There was nothing I could do."

"You're the company commander. You're responsible."

"Yes, sir," Elliott said disconsolately. Then, he brightened. "Mr. Dorfner disobeyed a direct order from me."

"Where is he?" Major Gillespie asked, looking around.

During the din, Squeaker had put his latest escape plan into action. He had whipped the F Troop flag from its pole and handed it to his classmate Pete Creger. Pete stuffed it into his full dress blouse and waited for the dismissal order. As soon as it was given, he bolted from the barracks. At that very moment he was half way across the parade ground, still in his full dress uniform, headed to the office of the chaplain, Colonel Sydney, in the rear hallway of Summerall Chapel. Squeaker was in his room, the F Company banner back in place on the guidon, when Cadet Captain Elliott Johnson and Major Gillespie stormed in.

"Okay, Mr. Dorfner, cute," Major Gillespie said, irritation in his voice, but a smile breaking out on his face. "I will say Mrs. Gillespie enjoyed it. She did say she sort of encouraged you. You added to the birthday celebration. Now, hand over the flag that says F Troop and that'll be the end of it."

"The crowd seemed to like it, sir."

"You're stalling, Mr. Dorfner. Hand over the flag."

"I don't have it, sir."

"Where is it?"

"I gave it to one of my classmates."

"Which one?"

"Mr. Creger, sir."

"You mean sweet potato Creger?"

"Yes, sir. That's him."

Freshman year Pete Creger had been struck in the head and knocked unconscious by a sweet potato thrown by Colonel Sydney during his famous sweet potato sermon in Summerall Chapel, another Citadel tradition, one that Creger's injury had put in jeopardy. Everyone knew the story.

Cadet Creger and Colonel Sydney had formed a special friendship. Major Gillespie had a vague feeling that Cadet Dorfner's giving the F Troop flag to Creger had some design behind it, but he couldn't fathom what it was.

"Well," Major Gillespie said, "let's get Mr. Creger and the flag in here right now. Go get him! Tell him to bring me the flag!"

"Mr. Creger's not in the barracks, sir."

"Where is he?"

"He's taken the F Troop flag to Colonel Sydney. The colonel's agreed to keep it for us over at his office in the Summerall Chapel. For safekeeping, sir."

"Oh he has, has he?"

"Yes, sir. He has."

"Mr. Johnson, did you know anything about this?"

"No, sir. First I've heard of it, sir."

Squeaker said, "we're acting under direct orders of the colonel, sir. He did say he'd be happy to talk to you about it." The major frowned. "That is, if you have any questions, sir."

"Oh, I've got lots of questions," the major said. Then, his face breaking into a grin, he turned to Elliott Johnson and said, "write this man up for a DDVO."

"A DDVO, sir?"

"Direct disobedience to a verbal order." Elliott didn't say anything, but he wore a puzzled look on his face. "Didn't you tell me you had given Mr. Dorfner a direct order not to fly the F Troop flag today?"

"Yes, sir. I did, sir."

"Then write him up. That's an order."

Elliott wrote it up. On the following month's delinquency list there it was: "Dorfner . . . DDVO . . . 5 demerits." They were the only demerits Squeaker received all year, and the only punishment anyone received related to the flying of F Troop on the company guidon.

A meeting was held between Colonel Sydney, Major Gillespie, and General Rubino, head of the commandant's department, the ruling authority for all things military at the Citadel. Several more meetings were held, one with General Marcum, president of the college. The matter went before the board of visitors, the Citadel's trustees. Right before graduation that year a decision was reached to allow F Company to continue flying the F Troop guidon. As the companies were forming up for the commencement parade, the final parade of the year, Colonel Sydney came into the barracks and presented the F Troop guidon flag to Cadet Captain Johnson, who in turn handed it to Cadet Guidon Corporal Dorfner, who affixed it to the company guidon. At that moment F Company officially became F Troop.

F Troop the television show aired a total of sixty five episodes over two seasons, the final one on April 6, 1967. Many shows live on in syndication, but not *F Troop*. It lives on only at the Citadel. In early September, 1966, Charles Foster became the Citadel's first black cadet. The administration originally planned to assign him to F Company, back in its glory days when it was by far the best company in the corps. Had F Company still been the best company in the corps, the administration never would have allowed the name change to F Troop. The Citadel's F Troop shared more than a name with the F Troop of Ft. Courage, Kansas. They were a bunch of bumblers, not to be entrusted with the first black cadet. Charles Foster was assigned instead to G Company. He survived and graduated with his class in 1970, the first black graduate.

By the time of Charles Foster's graduation, *F Troop* the TV show was well on its way to oblivion. The last of those who had been at the Citadel when F Company became F Troop graduated the year before Charles. The name F Troop remains well entrenched, a tradition that lives on.

In a final bit of irony, Emily Johnson, first born child of Elliott and Marilyn Johnson, despite the protests of her parents, both of whom still believed in single gender education and wanted her to go to Columbia College, enrolled at the Citadel and was assigned to F Troop. She followed in her father's footsteps as F Troop commanding officer and graduated in 2003.

THE HAND OF GOD

P ete Creger's friend Joe Nolan, when the two of them were still knobs at
the Citadel, once remarked to Pete, "this place doesn't make a man out
of you, it just proves you already are one." Most cadets at the Citadel hated
the place while they were there and loved everything about it once they'd
graduated. They were bonded together for life. Perhaps that's the greatest
thing the Citadel did for them.

Kyle Gallagher, Joe Nolan, and Pete Creger all started out as premed
majors. That's how Kyle and Pete first met Joe. The three of them were in
the same chemistry class that first semester. Kyle and Pete already knew
each other. They were in the same company. Joe was in another company
in another battalion. At the beginning of the year the department head
gave all the freshmen premed students a pep talk. He told them that one
hundred percent of the Citadel premed graduates the department recommended for entrance into medical school were accepted. What he didn't
tell them, and what they found out later, was that the department on average only recommended three a year.

That first semester Pete had the third highest grade in the chemistry
class, a C+. Joe had the highest grade, an A, and Kyle the next, a B. All the
rest were D's and F's. Two and a half years later Pete saw the handwriting
on the wall, and midway through his junior year he transferred to the
English department. At the beginning of junior year Joe was transferred
into the same company as Kyle and Pete.

Around the time Pete transferred to the English department, Joe and
Kyle began preparing for the MCATS, the medical college aptitude test.

Six weeks before the scheduled date of the test Joe became very ill. He went to the Citadel infirmary, which had a notoriously poor reputation, and was avoided by cadets whenever possible. The nurses there thought he had the flu. They gave him aspirin for fever, told him to drink lots of liquids, and to stay in bed for a few days.

Two days later Kyle and Pete paid him a visit in his room. He was worse. Pale and weak. They became alarmed. They ran to the barracks guardroom, procured a stretcher, summoned two other classmates, and carried him to the infirmary. The nurses agreed he was very sick. They still felt it was the flu. Kyle disputed their diagnosis. "I'm a premed major," he said. "Flu's very contagious. How come no one else around here is sick? He needs to see a doctor."

"Well, Mr. Premed Major," came the reply, "we're going to keep him here, he'll certainly see the doctor, and we'll take good care of him. As to flu being contagious, the four of you could be the next to get it. Report back here the minute you have any symptoms."

The next day the four stretcher bearers, all symptom free, went to the infirmary together to check on poor Joe. He was even worse. Much weaker. Kyle asked if his parents knew he was sick. Did he want them to be called? In a weak voice, not much beyond a whisper, Joe said he didn't want to worry them, but yes, he thought it best to let them know.

Back at the barracks Kyle telephoned the Nolan home from one of the pay phones in the guardroom. Joe was an only child whose mother had never worked outside the home. Kyle and Pete hoped she would be home in the middle of the afternoon. Pete stood in the guardroom listening to Kyle's end of the conversation, glad Mrs. Nolan had been at home and it was Kyle, not him, making the call. Kyle did a good job explaining to Mrs. Nolan that Joe was sick in the infirmary, probably nothing too serious, but without ready access to a phone, otherwise he would have called himself, striking the right chord between *nothing to worry about* but *you need to check on him.*

That evening around ten thirty, just as evening study period ended, Kyle rushed breathlessly into Pete's room. "Come with me to the guard-room," he gasped. An orderly of the guard had just come to his room and told him he had a phone call in the guardroom from Mr. Nolan, Joe's dad. Kyle wanted Pete to come with him, for support, in case there was bad news of some kind.

Once again Pete stood in the guardroom listening to one end of Kyle's phone conversation. There wasn't much to hear. Mostly, "yes, sir . . . no, sir . . . I see . . . wow . . . that's awful . . . I'm so sorry . . . please keep us posted." Things like that. Kyle hung up the phone. He was shaken. Glum. He didn't speak.

"Bad?" Pete asked.

"Bad," Kyle said. "Acute appendicitis. Mr. and Mrs. Nolan didn't get here until early this evening. They went straight to the infirmary after Mr. Nolan got off work. They took one look at Joe and phoned their family doctor. They were lucky to reach him. He told them to call an ambulance and have Joe taken to the ER at Roper hospital. He met them there. He and the ER doctor consulted and agreed on the diagnosis. They called in a surgeon. Joe's in surgery right now. Going in, the doctors were concerned the appendix may have already burst. Mr. Nolan's already gotten a report from the operating room that the appendix was ruptured." Kyle stopped talking.

"Is he going to be all right?"

Kyle didn't answer right away. Finally, he said, "Mr. Nolan's very concerned. He's also mad as hell. If Joe makes it, he credits my phone call—us—with saving his life."

"Saving his life!" Pete exclaimed. "Surely it's not as serious as all that."

"It was, and it is," replied Kyle. "The only treatment for appendicitis is surgery to remove the inflamed appendix. If caught before the appendix ruptures, it's relatively routine surgery. If not, the surgery can be complicated. The inflammation spreads throughout the abdominal cavity, infecting the other organs. A condition called peritonitis. It can be very serious. Depending on how bad it already is, they may even have to sew him back up, pump him with antibiotics and fluids, and put in drains to get the infection down, and then go back in to remove the appendix."

Even given the gravity of the situation, Pete marveled at how much Kyle, a serious pre-med student, already knew. Surely, Mr. Nolan couldn't have relayed all that information. Incredulous, Pete exclaimed again, "you're saying Joe could die!"

"It's a definite possibility," Kyle said, sadly shaking his head. "He would have if he'd stayed at the infirmary." Becoming suddenly angry, Kyle shouted, "those bastards! Those dumbass bastards!"

"Maybe our concern did save his life," said Pete, sounding even more incredulous.

"I sure as hell hope he pulls through," said Kyle.

"If he does, how long do you think the recovery will be?" Pete asked Kyle.

"I don't know," Kyle replied, "but I think he'll be plenty sick for a while. He's going to be in the hospital a while. He's going to miss a lot of school."

"He could miss taking the MCATS," Pete said, as the thought of how disappointing that would be to Joe struck Pete and Kyle at the same time.

"I'd say he probably will," replied Kyle. "Even if he's out of the hospital in time, he'll probably want to put it off, since he won't have been able to study for them. He may even miss so much school that he'll miss this semester." For Joe not to graduate with their class was unthinkable.

Joe did pull through, much to everyone's relief. The scenario that Kyle Gallagher, that savvy future MD, described did play itself out. Joe did have to have a second surgery to remove his appendix, performed a week after the first one, and after being administered massive doses of high powered antibiotics and enduring the insertion of plastic drainage tubes. He was in intensive care another week after the second surgery. Following that, his recovery was slow, but sure. As the date for taking the MCATS approached, Joe was still hospitalized and it was obvious taking them was an absolute impossibility for Joe.

Two days before the scheduled test date Kyle walked into Pete's room in the barracks. "Pete," he said, "I really hate to do this to you, but I need to ask you for a favor, a big favor." Pete looked at Kyle. Kyle looked like a very unhappy camper. Pete had no idea what was coming. Kyle was Pete's Citadel classmate. It would be hard denying him a favor, big or small.

"Sure. What is it?" Pete asked glibly.

"Joe's dad has been bugging the hell out of me. He wants me to go to the hospital with him tomorrow to help talk Joe into going ahead and taking the MCATS now. I don't think it's a good idea. I think Joe should wait, but I can't tell his dad that. His dad's convinced himself I can get Joe to do it even though he hasn't been able to. I can't imagine why he thinks that. He's also convinced himself if Joe doesn't take the MCATS now, he never will, particularly if he loses this semester and falls behind in school. He's obsessed with Joe being a doctor. He says he's talked to Joe's doctors and even though they're not ready to release him from the hospital yet, they'll let him out long enough to take the test. I'm in a real dilemma. My heart's not in it. Joe's dad will see that. I need you to be there with me. Joe really is a smart guy. Maybe he would do all right if he took them now. I need you to do some of the talking too. Will you come to the hospital with me to talk to Joe?" When Pete didn't say anything, Kyle added, "as a favor to me?"

"I need a minute to think," Pete said. Kyle looked anxious. Gathering his thoughts, Pete said, "if you disagree with Joe's dad, you should tell him so. You shouldn't talk to Joe about it if you genuinely feel Joe would be making a mistake taking the MCATS now. It's Joe's life, not yours. I'll only go with you if you're going there to take your best shot at doing what Joe's dad wants you to do."

"But then I'd be doing what I think isn't best for Joe," Kyle protested.

"It's not your call. It's Joe's decision. Don't you think Joe's dad knows Joe better than you or me? Knows what Joe's capable of?"

"So you think Joe's dad is right?"

"No, Kyle, I'm not saying that. I don't know who's right. I'm saying in the end, right or wrong, it's Joe's decision, not yours, not his dad's, and certainly not mine. When I changed my major from premed to English, it was my decision, not my dad's, even though my dad wanted me to be a doctor every bit as much as Joe's dad wants that for Joe. The difference between me and Joe is that I really didn't care about being a doctor. Joe does. Who can say what's best for Joe right now? I do think Joe's dad, being his dad, is entitled to an opinion. You and I really aren't. I'll only go with you if you can set aside your own feelings and go there to support Joe's dad fully, one hundred percent."

"You're making this hard. I didn't think it was this complicated. I've already told Joe's dad I'll come. I guess I have to. I'll have to think about what you've said. If I want you to come with me I'll let you know before tomorrow." With that, Kyle left the room. Pete had no idea what he was going to do.

The next day Kyle came up to Pete and said, "We need to leave for the hospital to see Joe in about an hour. Sorry for the short notice. Can you come?" Pete knew Kyle wouldn't be including him on the trip unless he was going along with what Pete had told him.

On the way to the hospital there was an urgency in the air, as though they were on an important mission. When they walked into the hospital room, Mr. Nolan was already there, sitting on the side of Joe's bed. Joe still looked pretty sick, pale, washed out and wasted, almost emaciated. He had lost about thirty pounds. He acted normal, which was a good sign.

Mr. Nolan patted the side of the bed, indicating to Kyle he should sit there. Mr. Nolan got right down to business, telling Kyle he and Joe had been talking about the MCATS. Joe said he wasn't up to taking them. Kyle jumped right in, urging Joe to reconsider in a sincere, encouraging voice, telling him although a lot of students busted their balls studying for the MCATS, he had it on good authority it really wasn't necessary. He said he was sure Joe could handle it easily. He then turned plaintive, telling him what a shame it would be if he let his illness get him down, and how he would regret it if he didn't go forward as though his illness had never happened.

Joe protested firmly, saying he had missed so much school this semester he'd never catch up. Mr. Nolan said, "no, Joe, I've talked to all your professors. They all think highly of you and to a man have told me they'll give you all the help you need to make up the work. "

"It'll be too hard, it can't be done," said Joe. "I haven't even been released from the hospital."

"How'd you like to get out of here today, Joe?" Mr. Nolan asked.

"You know the answer to that. I've been ready."

As if he had been standing outside the room in the hallway waiting for his cue, a doctor walked in.

He was wearing a stethoscope around his neck and had that doctor air about him. He placed his hand on Joe's forehead, popped a thermometer in Joe's mouth, felt Joe's pulse, listened to Joe's heart and his breathing with the stethoscope, removed the thermometer, went to the end of the bed, picked up Joe's chart, and scribbled something on it. Apparently he was the head doctor on Joe's case. He looked up from Joe's chart and said, "Joe, I hear you've got an important test to take tomorrow." Joe didn't say anything. The doctor went on. "The staff has conferred. Initially, we thought you should stay here another four or five days, to rest and regain your strength, but you've come along better than expected. We're discharging you this afternoon. Go home, take that test tomorrow. After that, stay home another week before reporting back to the Citadel. Those are doctor's orders."

As he left the room, the doctor turned back to Joe and said, "good luck on the test, not that I expect you'll need it. You'll do fine." Turning to Mr. Nolan, he said, "I'll leave written instructions at the nurses' station. Call my office for a follow up appointment. Any questions before you leave the hospital, the nurses will know where to find me."

Joe was a happy boy. He threw back the bed covers and sprang from the bed. He went to the closet and looked in, expecting to find his clothes there, but all he found were the pajamas he'd been wearing when he was transported to the hospital. He told his dad, "I don't have any clothes."

"Your mom's on the way here," Mr. Nolan said. "She's bringing 'em." Joe smiled and went to his dad and gave him a hug. "You gonna take that test tomorrow?" Mr. Nolan asked.

"I don't know," Joe said. "I'm thinking about it."

On the way back to the barracks Pete asked Kyle if he thought Joe would take the MCAT the next day. "I think he will," Kyle said. During the time at the hospital with Kyle, Joe and his Dad, other than saying hello and goodbye, Pete had scarcely said a word. He had sat in a corner. A spectator.

Both Kyle and Joe took the MCATS the next day. Pete spoke to both of them afterward and they both said it was hard and long, but they felt reasonably good about it. True to their word to Joe's dad, all of Joe's professors helped Joe make up his missed work and he did not fall behind his class. There was a rumor, unsubstantiated, that Joe's dad had threatened the Citadel with a lawsuit if Joe didn't graduate with his class. Both Kyle and Joe made the dean's list that semester. As for Pete, he made gold stars, even better than dean's list. He'd found his niche in the English department. He started thinking about taking the GRE. Maybe graduate school. Maybe a Ph.D. It didn't make his dad any too happy. "You'll just wind up a damned old English teacher," his dad complained.

Senior year dawned. Joe's brush with near death was forgotten. Pete, Kyle, and Joe worked hard on their academics. Joe and Kyle often studied together. Pete was glad to have left the days of musty chemistry labs and the odor of formaldehyde behind. That winter, the winter of senior year, was a cold one. In mid-January Charleston was hit hard by a fierce snow and ice storm, an extreme rarity for the coastal south. Joe's dad fell victim to a freakish accident. Getting out of his car in the paved driveway of his home, he slipped on a patch of ice, fell backwards, and hit the back of his head hard on the concrete. He died. Killed instantly.

Kyle and Pete wondered "what else bad can possibly ever happen in Joe Nolan's life?" The image of Joe's dad sitting on the edge of Joe's hospital bed became forever etched in their memories. The senior class of their company, twenty of them, gathered in Kyle's room. They walked together to Joe's room to offer condolences. They considered themselves men. They came to Joe one at a time and each told him how sorry he was. Some shook his hand. Some hugged him. Kyle and Pete were the last. Pete grasped Joe's right hand in both of his own, looked into his eyes and tried to speak. Seeing the sorrow there, words would not come. Pete felt Kyle's arms encircling them both. The three friends stood together in silence. The others stood in silence too, and quietly began moving from the room, leaving the three alone. When the others were out of the room, Joe began crying. They did not speak. Pete tried again, but the words would not come. He left the room, leaving Joe and Kyle together. Pete felt defeated, an English major now, a man who intended to spend his life among words, with no words of comfort for his friend.

The funeral was held at the First Baptist Church, where the Nolans were members. The preacher, near the end of his remarks, trying to explain the unexplainable, said, "None of us can understand God's purpose in this tragedy, but He has a purpose. God is in control. His hand is in everything. It is the hand of God." Joe's dad had been in the army in World War II. He was buried with full military honors, an honor guard carrying the flag draped coffin, a squad of riflemen saluting with fired volleys, and two buglers, one near, one far off, playing echo taps. Lastly, the flag was removed from the coffin, folded, and given to Joe's mom. Joe's dad was forty-six years old.

Joe, Kyle, and Pete graduated that spring. Citadel men now. Joe and Kyle, with the recommendation of the Citadel's premed department, were accepted into medical school and became doctors, Joe a surgeon in another southern state and Kyle a family practitioner in Charleston. Pete obtained a Ph.D. in English literature and became a professor at the Citadel. He lived among words.

The three friends kept in touch for many years. Kyle and Pete more so than Joe, since Joe was in another state. Joe kept in touch with Kyle more than Pete. The medical thing. The Citadel has class reunions every five years. They're a really big thing. The three friends have attended most of them together; they've had some really great times. Joe won't be attending the next one. Kyle and Pete will miss him.

Sometime after the last reunion, Joe, a renowned surgeon, accepted an invitation to speak in Charleston at a medical symposium. Kyle decided he'd like to hear his friend's talk, and invited Pete, though not a medical man, to attend with him. The three planned lunch together after the speech and before Joe's flight out that afternoon. The speech was on some new surgical technique, above Pete's comprehension. The other doctors seemed impressed. Near the end, in midsentence, Joe paused. A funny look came over his face. There was a glass of water on the podium. Joe picked it up and took a swallow. Then he collapsed forward across the podium, pitching the glass into the front row of the audience before rolling to his left onto the floor. None of the doctors could do anything for Joe. Kyle and Pete were near the back, so it took them several minutes to reach Joe's side. By the time they got there the others who had reached him first were saying he was dead. Probably dead when he hit the podium, before he rolled onto the floor. Dead of a sudden, massive heart attack. Dead at fifty-three, seven years older than his dad when he died. One of the doctors who pronounced Joe dead, who had been sitting in the front row and was among the first to reach him, described it this way: "it was as though a giant invisible hand, the hand of God, reached down from heaven, grasped him across the chest, and squeezed the life out of him." Kyle and Pete thought of the words of the preacher at the funeral of Joe's dad, thirty years before. Both men of faith, they couldn't understand it anymore at that moment than they could thirty years ago. Sometimes it sets them to wondering. Is God's hand in all wars, all famines, all disasters, all sudden deaths, all things big, all things small? Sometimes, God, what are you thinking?

COMMAND DECISION

G uard duty at the Citadel was a pain. For most of his cadet career Sammy Graham was a private, but for reasons inexplicable to him about midway through his senior year he was elevated to the lofty position of second lieutenant, becoming Cadet Second Lieutenant Sammy Graham. Some gung ho types liked guard duty, but so far as Sammy was concerned the worst, the absolute worst, position of all on the daily guard detail was JOD, junior officer of the day, second in command of the entire detail. The first in command was the OD, officer of the day. The only real duty of the JOD, the biggest pain of all, was to patrol the campus at night, from dusk till dawn, in a jeep making sure all was quiet and in good order. The JOD was always selected from among the second lieutenants. Call him nonadventurous, but from the day he was commissioned second lieutenant, Sammy lived in dread of serving as JOD. He couldn't imagine anything eerier, spookier, than driving around campus all night, especially in the dark hours past midnight, alone, the only one on campus not asleep.

Sammy heard about the posting of the new guard detail before he saw it. At least ten of his friends came up to him and asked, "hey, Sammy, ya seen the new guard roster yet?" None of them mentioned he was on it, nor his assigned duty, but he knew. He kept putting off going to the company bulletin board for a look. When he finally stood before the board, scanning for his name on the white, thumb tacked list, he held out a forlorn hope he might only be an OG, officer of the guard, in command of the guard detail in one of the barracks. The OG was required to sleep overnight in the barracks guardroom, but he didn't have to stay up all night driving around in an open jeep. It was not to be. It was there in black and white, Sammy Graham, JOD. The miserable task lay before him. To make matters worse, it was mid-April and the college baseball season was underway. The Citadel had a home game scheduled the evening of his JOD duty. He and his two roommates, who shared an alcove room, had planned to go. He would miss the game. In Sammy's four years at the Citadel the two major sports teams, football and basketball, had yet to manage a single winning season, a futile record of athletic ineptness. The baseball team, on the other hand, was a different story. A winning record every year. Conference contenders. This season was no exception. Sammy and his roommates were big fans. They seldom missed a game.

The OD and JOD always exchanged keys to the jeep in the mess hall during the evening meal. The meal over, the OD left the mess hall off duty until the following morning, and the JOD left the mess hall, climbed into the jeep, and began his long, boring night patrol. That evening as Sammy was handed the keys to the vehicle, he caught sight of the OC, the officer in charge, and on the spur of the moment an idea formed. It was a what-the-heller, a no-harm-in-asking sort of thing. He didn't really expect it to work. The OC was a regular army officer stationed at the Citadel as a military science professor and assigned to one of the companies as a tactical officer. He was required to pull guard duty too. While on guard duty, he was the one really in charge of the campus, followed by the OD and the JOD, at that moment, Sammy Graham. The OC that night was Colonel Kirby, a pretty decent guy.

Sammy approached Colonel Kirby as he was leaving the mess hall and the two of them strolled outside together. As they reached the jeep parked beside the mess hall, Sammy said, "Colonel, I'll make an initial patrol of the campus now. Make sure everything's in proper order."

"That's fine," the colonel said. "Carry on."

Then, before getting in the jeep, Sammy asked the big question. "Colonel, if everything's in good and proper order, do you suppose it'd be all right if I attended the ball game this evening?"

The OC looked at Sammy a little funny. Sammy assumed he hadn't expected such a ridiculous question. Guard duty at the Citadel was serious business. The OC surprised Sammy by stating, very seriously, a stern military expression on his face, "you're in command. Why don't you make a command decision?" He walked off without another word. Sammy didn't know what Colonel Kirby would consider the correct "command decision." Who was he kidding? JOD's didn't attend baseball games. On the other hand, he certainly was saying the decision was Sammy's. Maybe the colonel would be disappointed if he didn't go. The game didn't start until eight P.M., a late start. Sammy mulled it over while driving around campus. At seven thirty he parked in front of Number Two barracks and went up to his room. His roommates were getting ready to leave for the game. "How'd you like a ride to the game?" Sammy asked.

It was cool, driving his roommates to College Park in the jeep, a tight squeeze, but a lot of fun. It might have been a first. Sammy had never seen another OD or JOD driving around with passengers. Sammy didn't make the "command decision" until he reached the parking lot. He parked the jeep and walked into the stands with his roommates. One of them asked, "are you sure you should be doing this?"

"I'm the JOD," Sammy said. "I spoke to the OC about it and he said it was my decision. I'm in command, so here I am."

The first person they saw, sitting in the stands as they walked in, was Colonel Kirby. He looked at Sammy and said without smiling, "I see you made a command decision."

"Yes, sir. I did. Command is great. It should be a great game." Sammy hoped he didn't sound too flippant.

"I hope so," the colonel replied, still unsmiling.

It was a great game. A really great game. One of the best ever, depending on your perspective. If you liked pitcher's duels. If you were a student of the game and your interest hung on every pitch. If not, it might have been a little boring, but no one could have been bored by the finish. The opponent was Springmont College, one of those small schools in the mountains of western North Carolina. A nonconference game. A game of no real importance. Except every game is important. Springmont, like the Citadel, had a fine baseball program. They always fielded a winning baseball team. They were no pushover. The Citadel had played them for a number of years, two games per season, home and home. The Citadel had already played them once that season and had managed a two run win in the mountains. A sweep of the season series was on the line.

Things were looking good until the Springmont half of the ninth inning, the top of the ninth. Up till then the Citadel led 2–0. It had been a beautifully pitched game. The hitting star had been Jerry Cromwell, the tall, lanky, left handed Citadel first baseman. He had scored both of the Citadel's runs, the first on a solo home run in the first inning, pulled down the first base line, just fair, and just over the short right field fence, only three hundred ten feet from home plate. Leading off the fourth inning, Jerry had tripled in the gap between center field and right field, a line drive that landed between the outfielders and rolled to the wall, nearly four hundred feet from home plate. They thought he might have had a shot at another home run, this one an inside the parker, but the third base coach held him up. The next batter hit a towering drive to deep center and Jerry scored easily on the sacrifice fly. The 2–0 score held up until the ninth. Until then the real star of the game had been the Citadel's little left handed pitcher Matt Holcombe, who had fired a nifty two hitter through eight innings, keeping the Springmont batters off balance with a slow curve and a hard to hit change up.

In the ninth Matt walked the first two hitters and was lifted for a reliever. It looked like a good move when the new pitcher, Jay Holland, struck out the first hitter he faced and got the next one on a long fly to center. Both runners tagged up and advanced a base. No one was worried. There were two outs. Only one more needed. It wasn't to be. The next hitter singled sharply up the middle and both runners scored. Tie ball game. Too bad, especially for Matt, who had a no decision after eight plus excellent innings. The next batter grounded out. The Citadel failed to score in the bottom of the ninth and the game headed into extra innings.

There was a fairly large crowd on hand for a weeknight ball game, but the hour was late and a lot of them left. Sammy had nothing to do but drive mindlessly around campus in a jeep. He stayed, his roommates, too. The game went fifteen innings. Colonel Kirby stood up and stretched after the eleventh, said good night, and left. He didn't mention Sammy's command decision. There was plenty of excitement throughout the extra innings. Both teams threatened multiple times, but there was no more scoring until the fifteenth. By then the crowd consisted of Sammy, his two roommates, and about a dozen others. As the innings kept going by, they kept thinking the game might be stopped because of the late hour, and called a tie. In the top of the fifteenth Springmont scored a run and led 3–2. Pretty deflating.

The first batter up for the Citadel in the bottom of the fifteenth was the light hitting shortstop, the number nine hitter in the order. Coach pinch hit for him. The pinch hitter hit a ball hard, a sinking line drive right at the Springmont third baseman, who got in front of it, almost caught it, almost trapped it at his shoelaces, but the ball scooted away from him. He scooped it up and fired to first. A close play, hard to tell if the runner was safe or out, but the umpire called him out. The crowd was down to only a few, but the boos were long and loud. One out. Nobody on.

The Citadel was back to the top of the lineup, but it wasn't looking good. Jim Blake was not the usual type leadoff man. Also a football player, he was powerfully built and known for making contact and rapping out doubles, so Coach liked him in the leadoff spot. Jim hit a ball as hard as a ball could be hit, a high drive to straightaway center field. Had the ball been hit to any other part of the park, it would have been a home run and the game tied, but College Park was four hundred and ten feet to dead center.

Sammy thought the Springmont center fielder couldn't possibly catch up to it, but somehow he did, making a fantastic over the shoulder running catch, a la Willie Mays. Unbelievable. Two outs. Nobody on. Not much hope left.

Down to the last batter. Roy Jennings. Scrappy, hard hitting second baseman. Roy hit a ball identical to the inning's first hitter. Again, a sinking liner to the third baseman. Again, a near catch, a near trap, the ball scooted away again, again was picked up, and again fired on a line to first. The same play. Another close play. Hearts sank. A different result! The umpire called him safe. He probably feared for his life. Wild cheering. Still hope. Two out, but a man on base.

The next batter was Jerry Cromwell. Momentary hope, but they'll probably walk him. In addition to his homer and triple, Jerry had singled in his third trip to the plate. Sammy had lost track of the number of his other at bats, but every other one had been a walk. There was a conference on the mound, the Springmont coach and the entire infield. The umpires had to break it up. A reliever was warming up. Sammy never knew nor cared why the reliever wasn't brought in nor why they pitched to Jerry, but they did. Maybe they thought the percentages were with them and they could get him out one time. It didn't happen. Jerry was thrown one pitch and he parked it over the right field fence. Way back. A two run homer! Citadel won! 4–3. Bedlam. No one wanted to leave, even though it was past two A.M. Sammy heard the Springmont coach congratulate the Citadel coach and say, "that's the way to win 'em." It sure was.

Sammy drove the jeep back to campus and gave his two roommates a victory ride around the parade ground before dropping them off at the barracks. He spent the rest of the night, a much shortened night, alone, patrolling the campus, replaying the game in his mind. He handed over the jeep's keys to the OD in front of Number Two barracks at six fifteen as the sun was rising and reveille was sounding. He didn't tell the OD he'd been to the game. He probably would not approve, but as far as Sammy was concerned, his first command decision was a shining success.

I WEAR THE RING

"I wear the ring." Poignant words. The opening line of Pat Conroy's classic novel about the Citadel, *The Lords of Discipline.* Read and loved by all Citadel graduates. Conroy, Citadel class of 1967. Conroy and his novel. Both once banned from campus, now embraced. That great line is followed by this one, equally meaningful: "I wear the ring and I return often to the city of Charleston, South Carolina, to study the history of my becoming a man." Before Conroy another writer, Calder Willingham, penned another novel about the Citadel. Titled *End as a Man,* it too was banned from the Citadel campus. So far as is known, neither the book nor its author have ever been embraced by the school. You see, Willingham does not wear the ring. He attended the Citadel but dropped out during his freshman year. He didn't make it. Conroy, though, at least in part, dedicated his book to Willingham. In Conroy's dedication are found these words: "And to the boys who did not make it."

Most, but not all, Citadel graduates return to the city of Charleston, and to the Citadel quite often, at least as often as they can. They are drawn there by their common bonds of the city, their four years at the school, their lifelong friendships, and their lifetimes of wearing the ring. Ask any Citadel graduate to name his most treasured personal possessions, and his Citadel ring will be at or near the top of his list. When women were first admitted to the Citadel, a few overzealous, indignant alumni threatened to return their rings to the school, but they were just posturing. They didn't mean it. None committed the act. They got over it. They still proudly wear the ring.

Some of the boys, now old men, who made it through that first year, but for one reason or another never graduated, who don't wear the ring, also migrate to Charleston and the Citadel regularly. They even attend class reunions. They are welcomed and affirmed every bit as much as those who wear the ring. Their common bonds are not just the terror of that first year, nor just the achievement of surviving it, but the close, unbreakable friendships forged while they were there, and the shared camaraderie of the years. Not so the ones who quit. Few of them are ever heard from again. Rather than disdaining them, to the contrary, those who wear the ring honor them with fond remembrance, as Conroy did in dedicating, in part, *The Lords of Discipline* to them.

One of those who didn't make it was Dan Gilbert, a gentle, too-sensitive boy from the South Carolina upcountry. I remember sitting with him, along with several classmates, in the knob canteen adjacent to Mark Clark Hall between classes on a warm late September morning, listening to him lament. We had been at the Citadel less than a month. Dan had large, brown, sad eyes, made sadder by the agony of endurance. He was a fine, handsome boy at his wit's end. In a voice filled with pain, he said, "I can't take it anymore. This place is killing me. If I stay here, I'll go crazy." We believed him. He appeared on the verge of a mental breakdown. It wasn't the demanding physical regimen of the Citadel that did him in. That he could handle. It was the unending verbal abuse, the constant shouting, the haranguing obscenities, the foul cursings that were a part of everyday Citadel life, that unhinged him. He left that day, never to be seen or heard from again. I wear the ring, but I remember Dan Gilbert.

Another was Art Cardenale, a strong, wiry boy from Texas, with a surprisingly strong southern accent. I can still picture him pumping out pushups and hear him counting them out in his deep south voice: "one suh, two suh, three suh . . ." He couldn't adjust to the military. Bobby Hankins, who wears the ring, thought Art was Citadel material. He tried to talk him out of leaving. Art told Bobby he couldn't get the knack of spit shining shoes or polishing brass. "My shoes and brass look like shit and I'm catching hell for it," Art said. Bobby told Art he'd help him. Art agreed.

Bobby spent several hours one afternoon shining Art's shoes and brass. When Bobby finished Art's shoes looked like glass, his brass like mirrors. The next day Art quit. Bobby was furious. None of us saw or heard from him again. Today Bobby understands. Like me, he wears the ring, and remembers Art Cardenale.

Lenny Noftsker fell into that category of boy who never should have been at the Citadel. A large, overweight boy from California, the place scared the living hell out of him. He was known to hide in his room to avoid sweat parties on the galleries. The upperclassmen always found him and dragged him out of his room, which made matters even worse for Lenny. Some knobs, more from laziness than anything else, but also to avoid trouble on the galleries while going to the latrine, would pee in the sinks in their rooms. Lenny did it all the time. As gross as it was, his roommate tolerated it. Lenny was genuinely afraid to go to the latrine. One day he took it too far. He shit in his drawers while alone in his room and placed the shit filled underwear in his laundry bag which hung on a peg on the wall. His roommate couldn't help smelling it. Lenny confessed to the deed. The roommate went berserk and reported it to his squad sergeant. "I refuse to room with that grodo anymore," the roommate said.

"Don't worry, you won't have to," said the sergeant. Lenny was given his own private sweat party. The sweat party to end all sweat parties. Lenny didn't so much quit the Citadel; he was driven out. He was never seen nor heard from again. Those of us who wear the ring wish Lenny well. We hope he succeeded somewhere else. We're glad Lenny doesn't wear the ring. We wear the ring, but we remember Lenny Noftsker. We wish we could forget him, but we can't.

Another who didn't make it was a nice, quiet boy named Emil Rodriquez. We all thought he was doing fine, but suddenly he was gone. He left right after Dan Gilbert. Must have quietly decided the Citadel wasn't for him. Dozens of them left that way. That first week they dropped like flies. After that, two or three a week for a while. Some didn't return from Thanksgiving. Still more didn't show back up after the Christmas holidays. Of the forty-five who began the year in F Company, only nineteen were there at the end of the year. Four years later, fourteen of us graduated. We wear the ring.

I remember the five who finished the first year, but who never wore the ring, as well as I remember the ones who wear it, but for different reasons. One was my roommate freshman year. He was as sharp militarily as any knob in the company, but his parents had made him come and he hated the Citadel. All of us said we hated it that first year, but when he said it, he really meant it. No one was surprised when he didn't return for sophomore year. He wasn't well liked. I may be the only one who isn't glad he never wore the ring. My roommate sophomore year didn't return after that year. No one knew why. Not sure, but he may have flunked out. I was beginning to have a complex. Was rooming with me fatal to a Citadel career? Only to those two plus one more as it turned out. All three of my other roommates, close friends to this day, like me, wear the ring.

Jack Zwiller is the most memorable of the boys who completed the first year, left well before graduating, and whose whereabouts remain unknown. He was from New Jersey. By comparison, most of us southern boys were innocents. Not that any of us were all that innocent. Jack, though, was a real sophisticate. A chain smoker and heavy drinker at eighteen. Impressive to the adolescent mind. He introduced a great many of us to the pleasures of alcohol. His favorite watering hole in Charleston was the Piano Bar in the Swamp Fox Room at the Francis Marion Hotel on King Street. The Swamp Fox Room became an after parade Friday tradition thanks to Jack, a tradition that continued long after he was gone. Cold draft beer and mixed drinks: rum and coke, gin and tonic, whiskey sours, scotch and soda. Progressive learning. Jack taught many of us to drink. He is properly remembered for this one accomplishment alone, but there is much more to his story.

One afternoon soon after the second semester of knob year had begun, while taking a shower, Jack suffered an epileptic seizure. No one knew what it was at the time. I wasn't there to see it, but those who were said it was frightening. One minute he was upright. The next he was lying on the shower floor, limbs trembling, head thrown back, eyes rolled up, tongue, thankfully, hanging out of his mouth, not swallowed. Someone ran from the shower to the gallery, wet and dripping, and called to the guard room for a stretcher. By the time it arrived the worst was over: Jack was conscious, sitting on the shower floor dazed, but coming to himself. He protested being put on the stretcher and taken to the infirmary, but those who witnessed the event were scared, and insisted. Jack continued to object.

Someone called for the company commander. He took one look at Jack and ordered him to get on the stretcher. He was taken away, naked and wet, covered by a towel. Jack was kept in the hospital several days. Rumors were rampant. Epilepsy suspected. If so, was this his first attack? Had to be, otherwise, what was he doing at the Citadel? Wouldn't having such a medical condition disqualify you from attending the Citadel? If this wasn't his first attack, then he had to have lied about it on his application. Everyone assumed this was the end of his Citadel career. But it wasn't. Out of the hospital, the diagnosis of epilepsy confirmed, Jack was close mouthed. His roommate remembered Jack took a little white pill every morning. Jack claimed it was some kind of vitamin and his roommate forgot about it. Until now. Now he couldn't remember Jack taking it recently. Could it be a preventative Jack for some reason had stopped taking?

Whatever it was, nothing happened to Jack. He remained at the Citadel. Life went on. Knobs, including Jack, continued to be racked without mercy. Some of us joked that if we were upperclassmen, we'd be afraid to rack Jack. He might have another attack, die, and we'd be charged with murder. A month later Jack had his second seizure. I witnessed this one. It happened at a formation on the quadrangle, while he was bracing, as all knobs are required to do. He went down like he'd been shot.

There was a loud "cra-ack" as his head hit the concrete quad. I was one of four knobs ordered to hustle him to the infirmary on a stretcher. By the time we got him on the stretcher the spasmodic jerking of his legs had stopped, but he was still out cold, stiff as a board. We thought he'd probably killed himself. It was terribly upsetting. We were sure this was the end of Jack at the Citadel.

Not so. Jack stayed on. He continued his torrid drinking. He assured us he was okay, but we couldn't help wondering. Now we all knew for certain he took pills for epilepsy. Should a person take that kind of medication and drink as much as Jack did? The third attack came almost at the end of the year. Jack and I and one other F Company classmate were in the same math class. The three of us stayed up practically the whole night studying together for the final exam to be held the next day. At breakfast formation early the next morning there again was a loud "cra-ack," the sound of Jack's head bouncing off the quad. This time I wasn't forced into stretcher bearer duty. I had an exam that morning. Two hours later, during the exam, I looked up from my paper to see Jack enter the room.

Better late than never, but unbelievable. Astonishing. You had to admire his persistence. He had a bandage wrapped around his head, slightly stained with blood, stitches in his nose, which was swollen and purplish, and a swollen upper lip. He seemed subdued, but he was there to take the exam. To no one's surprise, Jack failed the exam and the course, but he had gone down trying. The year ended. We were rising sophomores. Jack returned to his home in New Jersey. No one heard from him over the summer. No one expected him back in the fall. He had made it through that brutal freshman year. What more could he do? Not much, but he tried.

Jack, to everyone's amazement and delight, returned for the sophomore year. He lasted about three weeks. On a Sunday morning march to the Summerall Chapel, after a Saturday night of serious drinking, Jack fell out of the ranks with another seizure. The parade ground was a lot softer than the quadrangle and he was probably still drunk from the night before, so this time he wasn't physically injured. He was distraught, though. Turned out he and the Citadel had struck a deal. He was allowed to return, but he had to keep his epilepsy under control. One more episode and he was out. Jack told us this as we helped him pack. "There are other colleges," someone said. "Colleges that don't frown on epilepsy, nor drinking neither."

"If the Citadel frowned on drinking a little more," Jack replied, "maybe I'd still be here. Maybe someday I'd have worn the ring."

None of us ever heard from him again. For a number of years a small group of us at class reunions, mostly the group Jack taught to drink, gathered for drinks at the Francis Marion Hotel in honor of Jack. We no longer do that. We wear the ring. We've always wished Jack did, too. Admirable courage.

My best friend from knob year and I planned to room together sophomore year. His grades were poor, so he went to summer school trying to pull them up. It didn't help. He flunked out. He badly wanted to wear the ring, so he went to community college for a semester, did pretty well, and was readmitted to the Citadel. We roomed together second semester sophomore year. He flunked out again. He was never the drinker Jack Zwiller was. One evening, though, he came in from general leave very drunk. Plastered. Bombed. He lay down on his bunk and came close to dying. Jack Zwiller all through his epileptic seizures at the Citadel never swallowed his tongue. My best friend and roommate came in so drunk this one night he swallowed his tongue. Fortunately for him several of us were in the room with him. We looked over at him and he was turning blue. Quick thinking saved his life. When his tongue was pulled back into place there was a loud sucking noise as air flowed back into him and filled his lungs. Frightening, yet gratifying. I wear the ring. He doesn't. It makes no difference. Friends still. We share the common bond of the Citadel. He was and is one of us. We share the common bond of one near tragic night. I never mention it to him. He doesn't remember. He was too drunk.

Phil Kimble was another member of our class remembered well. He was in another company and wasn't at the Citadel long enough for us to get to know each other well. We got to know each other later. He dropped out of the Citadel and joined the army. Served with distinction in Vietnam. Came back to the Citadel under the GI bill and graduated as a veteran student. He wore the ring, but not the ring of his class. He attended a few of our class reunions, fully accepted as a member of the class. I saw him a few weeks after his last reunion. We shared memories of our class and the reunion. He seemed well and in good spirits. Late one cold winter night a few months later, suffering from post-traumatic stress disorder and separated from his wife, he shot himself to death.

The Citadel's knob year experience supposedly prepares you to handle whatever life throws at you. Who's to say it takes more courage to stick it out at a place like the Citadel than to quit and leave, to pull the trigger or refrain from pulling it? Not me. *I wear the ring.*

CAPTAIN SCHIERICK

Tac officers. Short for tactical officers. Regular U.S. Army or Air Force officers stationed at the Citadel and assigned to the companies by the commandant's department to oversee the companies' military training. One tac officer to each company. Their primary duty was to teach military science or aerospace studies and their duties within the companies was an add on. Military science and aerospace studies at the Citadel were academic subjects. A cadet's major, his other academic load, or whether he planned a military career mattered not. Every cadet was required to take one of these courses each semester.

The commandant's department and the departments of military science and aerospace studies, as well as office space for the tacs and arms and supply storage were located in Jenkins Hall, which was situated on the northeast corner of the parade ground. Named for Confederate Brigadier General Micah Jenkins, Citadel Class of 1854, Jenkins Hall was better known as the Tool Shed, for most of the tacs and all the administrators at the commandant's department, the Boo being the sole exception, were first class tools.

Captain Wiggins, an air force officer, was F Company's tac during the Class of 1968's knob year. He was not a tool. Legend had it that he once flew an air force plane underneath the Cooper River Bridge for the sheer fun of doing it. The roadway of the bridge was a mere one hundred and ninety feet above the surface of the water at its highest point. This low flying daredevil feat elevated him to hero stature.

Major Gillespie, an army officer who was F Company's tac during the Class of 1968's sophomore and junior years, by comparison to Captain

Wiggins, was undistinguished. He was a typical tool. F Company was glad
to see him go. To a man the company hoped for another Captain Wiggins.
What they got was Captain Schierick.

The Class of 1968's senior year. The two top ranking members of the
class in F Company were no longer in the company. They had been promoted to second battalion staff. Squeaker Dorfner was battalion commander, with the rank of cadet lieutenant colonel. Don Palassis, whose
nickname was the golden Greek, was battalion supply officer, with the
rank of cadet first lieutenant. Except for the company commander and
maybe one or two others, the mentality of the rest of the F Company senior class, including most of the company's officers, was that of a senior
private. Nothing could have prepared them for Captain Schierick.

Schierick was a West Pointer, fresh from the battlefields of Vietnam,
having served one tour of duty there and volunteered for a second. Instead, he was assigned to the Citadel. He was sorely disappointed and considered service at the Citadel a bit of a letdown. He decided to try to make
the best of a bad situation. He saw his duty clearly: it was to train and
inspire fighting men; to fill them with hatred for America's enemies, the
Viet Cong; to instill them with a desire to go to war, to kill the enemy, and
win medals.

The year did not start off too badly. Just a few years older than the seniors, Schierick decided to build camaraderie by inviting the F Company
seniors to a party at his Charleston apartment. An unprecedented event.
All the seniors felt obligated to attend. The invitation was viewed as a
command, attendance mandatory. Schierick was recently married, a cute
little blond with a page boy haircut. It was difficult to see what she saw in
Schierick. He still wore a knob style haircut. Maybe she loved short hair.
The Schiericks put on quite a spread. Plenty of food, most of it prepared
by Mrs. Schierick. Plenty to drink. Beer and liquor. All the seniors were
at least twenty-one, so no laws were being broken by serving alcohol to
minors. The beer and liquor flowed freely.

Schierick was dressed casually in civilian clothes, but his demeanor
was still stiff, his voice formal and his manner military. As the evening
wore on he drank little and remained in complete control of himself. He

definitely was not one of the boys. Mrs. Schierick was a different story. She was dressed somewhat alluringly in a short skirt and low cut blouse, just enough to be appreciated. She drank and laughed along with the troops. If the evening had a savior, it was her. All was going well enough until Dave Medlin, one of the senior privates, suddenly bolted through the front door. The sound of barfing permeated the apartment. At least it was coming from the outside. Things got worse. Someone else laughingly, drunkenly, lacking good sense, drew back the curtains and blinds from the front windows and switched on the front porch light. There, on the front porch, clearly exposed for all to see, was poor Dave, bending over, sick, and retching into the potted plants. Everyone laughed, except for Captain and Mrs. Schierick, both of whom failed to see the humor.

Later, Dave claimed a bad oyster, not the liquor, had made him sick. Someone else was in the bathroom and all he could do was run outside. It was better than spoiling the carpet. "It would have been fine," Dave said, "if another drunk hadn't opened the blinds." The other drunk pointed out to Dave that "oysters weren't on the menu."

The party became known as the party that "grossed out Mrs. Schierick." To their credit neither Captain nor Mrs. Schierick ever mentioned the party, nor did they ever hold another one for a large assemblage of cadets. As a builder of camaraderie between authority and those under authority it was a failure. Otherwise, it was a success, of sorts.

Squeaker Dorfner, of course, had attended the party. He admired Captain Schierick for making the effort, but if Squeaker ever entertained any doubt as to whether or not Schierick was a tool, all doubt was removed on the morning Schierick requested Squeaker accompany him on an impromptu room inspection of the F Company area. Schierick found fault with every room and wrote up every member of F Company for demerits. The tour took place in the morning, so few of the rooms were occupied. In a knob room that was occupied, Schierick pulled a field cap from a press and addressed the knob: "This field cap is dirty," Schierick told the knob. "Didn't I tell you before to get rid of this cap?" The cap looked fine to Squeaker.

"Yes, sir," replied the knob.

"Then what's it doing in your press?"

"I haven't been wearing it, sir. Just haven't gotten around to throwing it away."

Schierick confiscated the cap and told Squeaker to write the knob up for DDVO. Had Squeaker not once been written up himself for the same offense, he wouldn't have known what it was. Direct disobedience to a verbal order. The knob had no idea. Probably wouldn't know when it came up on the DL. Schierick was a tool. Without a doubt.

Schierick sported a chest full of military decorations, medals, awards, and ribbons, several rows of them, which he proudly wore on his uniform. Quite an array for so young an officer. He was bent on getting back to the war and winning more. He felt his time at the Citadel would be well spent if he could inspire as many cadets as possible to follow in his footsteps: to love America, to hate the VC, to love war, and to love winning medals. Squeaker and a number of other F Troopers, from the seniors all the way down to the knobs, were in Schierick's military science classes. In class it was easy to distract Schierick from the lesson at hand. Just ask him a question about his time in Vietnam or about one of his decorations and he would be off and running, the lesson forgotten.

Most veterans were reluctant to talk about their experiences in war. Not Schierick. He described combat, from full pitched battles to smaller actions while on recon patrols in the jungle. His word pictures were vivid enough, but he wasn't satisfied with that. He had a large collection of slides made by himself and others, and he brought them to class. Many of them were innocuous: scenes of lush, green, peaceful landscapes, posed shots of soldiers in combat gear; others were horrifying: row upon row of dead VC, scattered about, and splattered with mud and blood.

Not surprisingly, the impact of Schierick's slide shows on most of the cadets who viewed them was the opposite of what Schierick intended. Only the most severely gung ho types could possibly be inspired by Schierick's war stories or his slides. As for the rest, Canadian citizenship was looking like a much better option.

Second semester senior year Sammy Graham, best known as the company barber and for his hand to hand combat with an upperclassman in the showers knob year, was lucky enough to have Captain Schierick for military science. Charles Hutcherson, another F Troop senior, was in the same class. They had been forewarned about the slide shows and had already heard most of the war stories from their classmates. Academically, Charles stood out head and shoulders above the rest of the F Troop seniors. A business major, Charles had been awarded gold stars, the Citadel's highest honor for academic achievement, every semester. As that semester began, Charles was in the process of applying to the Harvard Business School for graduate studies.

What Sammy and Charles had been told about the slides and war stories didn't do them justice. You had to be there, to see and hear it firsthand. They were appalled and repelled by Schierick, but at the same time fascinated by him. They had to admit he seemed a soldier's soldier. No need to worry about him ever being afflicted with post-traumatic stress.

Captain and Mrs. Schierick held no more parties for the cadets. Instead, they took to inviting F Troopers to their home for dinner, only two or three at a time, mostly the senior officers and the ranking junior sergeants. Cocktails were served, but with a strictly observed two drink limit. Gradually Schierick seemed to open up a bit and reveal a nonmilitary side which had been kept hidden. Though still considered a tool, the ranking F Troop seniors and juniors, if no one else, began to think somewhat better of him. As the second semester began neither Sammy nor Charles, both senior privates, had been invited to any of these dinners. A few weeks into the semester Sammy unexpectedly was promoted to the rank of cadet second lieutenant. A few weeks later both Sammy and Charles were invited to dinner with the Schiericks on the same evening. They assumed it was because Schierick had gotten to know them, since they both had a class with him, Sammy was now an officer, and Charles had a special status from wearing gold stars.

Both Sammy and Charles enjoyed their evening with the Schiericks immensely. Charles talked of his hopes of going to Harvard Business School and Sammy divulged his plans of going to law school. To their surprise, and perhaps to Mrs. Schierick's too, Captain Schierick announced that Mrs. Schierick was going to have a baby. "We just found out," he said. "You two are the first ones in the company to know. You can help us spread the word."

"Consider it spread," beamed Charles, raising his glass in a toast of congratulations.

Sammy offered congratulations, too, and added, "The baby will be born in Charleston. That's great. Being Charleston born is something of note. Ask any Charlestonian."

"Well," said Schierick, "That'll depend on my new orders."

"He's hoping to be reassigned to Vietnam," Mrs. Schierick said. She looked none too happy about it.

"There's a war on," Schierick said. "Can't win glory, medals, and promotion sitting around in the states." It was the only down moment of the evening. Tool Schierick had reappeared.

Tool Schierick was still around the following Thursday at company drill. Recently promoted from cadet private to cadet second lieutenant, Sammy had now exchanged his rifle for a sword. Captain Schierick asked Sammy to perform the sword manual for him. He wasn't impressed. He pulled Sammy from the ranks and walked with him over to an isolated corner of the parade ground. He required Sammy to stand there by himself and practice sword manual. Sammy spent the next half hour practicing his sword drill. Squads, platoons, and entire companies purposefully marched near him to hoot, laugh, and ridicule. Sammy was embarrassed and humiliated. His newly found regard for Captain Schierick evaporated. Finally, Schierick came over to Sammy, observed a minute, and said, "you're doing better. Keep practicing in your room." Evidently Schierick also took note of Sammy's personal appearance, and didn't like what he saw. "Your shoes and brass don't look too good, Mr. Graham," Schierick told Sammy. "You're no longer a senior private. You're an officer now. You have to set an example for the knobs. I'll expect improvement."

"Yes, sir." Surely he's kidding, Sammy thought. I'm only a few months from graduating. At least he didn't burn me. Sammy informed his knobs they'd have to spend more time on his shoes and brass, since he was an officer now and Captain Schierick expected him to be more shined up. Sammy drew the line at practicing sword manual. Schierick wasn't just a tool, he was a super tool.

The few months remaining until graduation passed all too quickly. Sammy was accepted into law school at the University of South Carolina; Charles not only was admitted into Harvard Business School, he was offered a full scholarship. Both were granted deferments of their military service until completion of their graduate studies. Everyone who knew Charles, including Captain Schierick, was astonished when a week before commencement Charles announced he had decided not to go to Harvard. "I'm just tired of school right now," Charles said. "I need a break. I'll go ahead and get the army out of the way and go to grad school later."

As unbelievable as the thought was, Sammy couldn't help wonder if maybe Captain Schierick's rah rah patriotism nonsense maybe influenced the decision, and so he asked Charles about it. "No way," came the reply. "I really am burned out with studying right now. Schierick's full of shit. If I go to 'Nam, the VC have nothing to fear from me. I intend to keep my head down and stay alive. There'll be no medals for Hutcherson. I'm no hero." Though he didn't understand and disagreed with Charles's decision, Sammy believed what Charles told him.

August of 1969. Having successfully completed his first year in law school, Sammy was back in Charleston working as a law clerk for a Broad Street law firm, a dream summer job. He received word that Charles Hutcherson had been killed in a helicopter crash in Vietnam. So much for keeping your head down, he thought. What a waste! A few weeks later, just before returning to Columbia for his second year of law school, out of the blue Sammy received a surprising phone call. It was from Captain Schierick. Sammy had no idea how he had tracked him down. He had just heard about Charles and was upset. He was concerned he may have influenced Charles not to go to Harvard. Sammy assured him that wasn't the case. He told him he had wondered the same thing, and told him of his conversation with Charles. Schierick was relieved to hear it. "All the same," he said, "I wish I hadn't carried on so much about winning medals and all the rest. War is a brutal, dirty business."

Sammy asked about the baby. "A little girl," Schierick replied. "I have to confess, she's changed my whole outlook on life."

"Born in Charleston?"

"Yeah. Against my wishes the army made me spend another year as F Troop tac, so I was here when she was born."

"That's great. Always a Charlestonian. Congratulations to you and Mrs. Schierick. You still want to go back to Nam?"

"Truthfully, not so much anymore. Changed world view and all that, but, being in the army, I'm sure I'll be going back. Next time, though, I'm not looking to win any medals. I plan to keep my head down."

"Be a good idea to stay out of helicopters, too." Captain Schierick did go back to Vietnam. He didn't keep his head down. He flew in helicopters. He won more medals. He came back without a scratch. Never won the Purple Heart. Go figure.

ENCOUNTERS
WITH THE BOO

O f the many good and great men who served the Citadel in the twentieth century none held the hearts of the corps of cadets as did Lt. Colonel Thomas Nugent Courvoisie. Affectionately known to the cadets of the 1960s as the Boo, he roamed the campus in his green Comet or afoot, stealthily uncovering unacceptable cadet behavior, meting out punishment with his Boo touch, and deftly handling every situation.

Born in Savannah, the Boo entered the Citadel as a knob in 1934, left after three years, but later returned as a veteran student and graduated with the class of 1952. He came to the Citadel as an army officer in 1959, serving as a tac and professor of military science. He retired from the army in 1961 and accepted the position of assistant commandant of cadets, a position he held through 1968. The Boo's primary responsibilities were in the area of discipline, a task which brought him into constant contact, often conflict, with the cadets. Boo grew to love the cadets. He called all of them his lambs. Once asked why he called cadets lambs, he replied, "because I am the good shepherd." Boo had two other names for cadets. Whenever Boo was aggravated or annoyed with a cadet, at the moment of aggravation or annoyance, he called the cadet a bum. More often than not, though, the Boo referred to cadets as "bubba."

The class of 1964 dedicated the *Sphinx,* the Citadel yearbook, to the Boo. Pat Conroy's first published work, *The Boo,* is the story of the Boo's years as assistant commandant of cadets, in charge of discipline at the Citadel. Conroy further immortalized the Boo as the character the Bear in his novel *The Lords of Discipline*. Sadly, the Boo's career at the Citadel ended with him in charge of supply and property rather than discipline, relegated to an office in the warehouse, where there was little contact with the cadets, an undeserved, unimagined fate. Equally hard to imagine is even a single cadet who attended the Citadel between the years 1961 and 1968 bereft of his own, very special, personal encounters with the Boo.

Sammy Graham's first direct, upfront and personal, encounter with the Boo occurred a scant six weeks into his knob year. Prior to that, at different times Sammy had heard, seen, and smelled the Boo's fierce presence on campus. Boo's distinctive gravelly voice, when shouted, was loud enough to be heard from one end of the parade ground to the other, and was known as the Boo roar; observing his craggy, sometimes scowling, face, even from a distance, was a truly frightening experience; the Boo's approach was always known before his appearance from the stink of his ever present thick brown cigar, forever dangling from the corner of his mouth.

Sammy's beloved grandmother, his father's mother, passed away on October 17, 1964, at age seventy-eight. She had entered the hospital a week before her death. Sammy's mom and dad, not wishing to add to Sammy's stress, had not told him she was sick and in the hospital. Sammy learned of her death at a noon meal in the mess hall. Mr. Freeman, F company commander, came up to Sammy's mess and whispered something to Chris Lauton, the mess carver. With Mr. Freeman's approach, all three of the knobs on the mess pulled their chins in hard in the brace position. Mr. Freeman did not speak to Sammy, but touched him lightly on the shoulder and looked at him as he walked away. Mr. Lauton, in an unusual, surprisingly normal, voice cleared his throat and said, "at ease, Graham." Sammy didn't know what was coming, but he obeyed the order and relaxed his chin into its normal position. Lauton continued in the most unmenacing manner Sammy had ever seen him use. "Graham," he said, "you've had a death in the family. Your grandmother. Your mother's on the way here now to get you. I'm to take you over to the assistant commandant's office to fill out the paperwork for a special pass for you to attend the funeral." Perhaps it was the numbing trauma of the past six weeks, perhaps it was the unexpected surprise coming in such an unexpected setting. Whatever it was, the expected emotional response did not come. Sammy did not react. He said nothing. Later, he would remember thinking *which grandmother?* Then he remembered. He knew which grandmother. His other grandmother, his mother's mother, had died when he was still in high school. But Lauton hadn't known that. He'd only said your grandmother. The jerk.

The meal over, Lauton and Sammy walked out of the mess hall together. Sammy was still unable to show any reaction, even though he had just learned of the loss of the person he loved most in the world outside his parents and brothers and sisters. He walked beside Lauton in silence. They left the mess hall area and walked through Number Two and Number One barracks, crossing the red and gray tiled quadrangles of each, where freshmen weren't allowed, except during required formations. Lauton didn't speak until they were crossing the quadrangle of Number One barracks. He lapsed back into the role of an F Company sergeant. He began in a quiet, but venomous voice: "Graham, this'll be the only time you'll ever walk across one of my quadrangles. You're the most screwed up knob I've ever seen. Don't come back from this leave. Don't even think about it. If you come back, I'm gonna make it my personal goal to make your life a hundred times more miserable than it's already been. You'll never last. This is your chance. Quit now. Just don't come back. You're a waste. A disgrace to the school. Hell, you're a disgrace to yourself." Sammy didn't reply to this harangue. By the time they reached Jenkins Hall Sammy's passive dislike of Lauton had turned to active hatred.

Sammy feared all upperclassmen, especially those of F Company, but he was petrified at the thought of being in the Boo's legendary presence. Sammy had never before seen Mrs. Petit, the Boo's secretary, but he had heard of her. If a cadet needed something from the Boo, it was prudent to go to her first and she could smooth the way. Sammy hoped the Boo would be out and the business could be handled by Mrs. Petit.

Lauton and Sammy climbed the Jenkins Hall stairway to the second floor, walked a short distance down a long corridor and entered an open doorway into an outer office. Lauton seemed familiar with the office, as

126

though he'd been there before. Mrs. Petit was a tall, thin, attractive, gray haired woman with glasses. She had been expecting them. As they came into her office, she picked up some papers from her desk and walked into an inner office, saying, "I'll let the colonel know you're here."

Mrs. Petit returned in a moment and ushered them into the presence of the Boo. Lauton stood at attention and saluted. Prepped by Lauton ahead of time, Sammy saluted too, and they both stood at attention in front of the Boo's desk. The Boo, a tall, stocky, imposing figure wearing fatigues and combat boots, stood up behind his desk and returned the salutes, his cigar all the while dangling from the corner of his mouth, and sat back down. "What can I do for you, gentlemen?" the Boo asked.

Lauton, adopting the proper somberness and military bearing the circumstances demanded, replied, "sir, cadet Sergeant Lauton, F Company, reporting as ordered, sir, with cadet Private Graham, who is in need of special leave to attend his grandmother's funeral, sir."

"I know, Bubba," the Boo said quietly, a little sadly. Turning to Sammy, the Boo asked, "Bubba, are you requesting leave?"

Sammy's throat was dry and it was an effort to keep his knees from trembling, but he managed a weak, "sir, yes, sir," the first words he'd spoken since leaving the mess hall.

The Boo signed the two pieces of paper Mrs. Petit had brought him. Handing one to Mrs. Petit to be filed and the other to Sammy, he said, "Bubba, this grants you one week special hardship leave to attend the funeral, beginning now. You do plan to attend?"

"Sir, yes, sir." Sammy's voice was stronger, but his throat still dry and his voice cracked a little.

"You should be back sooner, if possible, but by no means should you be late. If you're late, you'll be AWOL, and you'll be walking tours. Neither you, your dearly departed grandmother, who no doubt loved you dearly, nor the Citadel, nor you want that, do we, lamb?"

"Sir, no, sir."

"You do intend to come back, Mr. Graham?"

"Sir, yes, sir."

"I'm counting on it," said the Boo. "Mr. Lauton, you boys in F Company have been mighty rough on the new lambs. If you lambs want to repeat as honor company, you may want to watch your step a bit."

With a half-smile, half smirk, Lauton, to Sammy's surprise, replied, "well, colonel, you know how it is. Some of 'em, despite everything we do to make 'em happy, decide they'd rather be at Clemson."

"I know, Bubba," laughed the Boo, "but watch it. Dismissed."

Sammy didn't need the full week for the funeral, but he took it. He needed the time to rest up, nurse his wounds, and steel himself for his return to the Citadel. Grandma Graham had been proud of him and had looked forward to seeing him in his Citadel uniform. He felt her loss and he wasn't about to let her down by not returning to the Citadel. He thought the Boo's way of extending sympathy and support was letting him know he was one of his lambs; making him aware he knew F Company was tough, but he had his eye on the situation; and telling him he was counting on him returning. Lauton and the rest of the F Company upperclassmen, after Sammy's first encounter with the Boo, couldn't have blasted Sammy out of the Citadel with dynamite.

Pete Creger's first close encounter with the Boo didn't take place until near the end of his sophomore year. It wasn't that he'd been deliberately avoiding the Boo. Until then he just hadn't had a pressing need that only the Boo could fill. Pete's steady girlfriend was very special. She was two years younger than Pete, pretty, smart, warm, and tender. She came close to being Pete's first love. Pete and Joyce had been dating for about six months. He had taken her to the Corps Day hop that March. Joyce was still in high school and it didn't surprise him when she invited him to her prom in early April. "I want to show you off in your Citadel uniform," she told him. Pete, of course, accepted immediately. Then she told him there was another, smaller, event afterward, a party chaperoned by her parents at their home on the front beach on Isle of Palms for Joyce and her closest friends and their dates. It would go on for most of the night. That presented a problem.

Pete had already used up his allotted weekend leaves for the year. He had taken the last one over Corps Day weekend. Pete didn't have the heart to tell Joyce. He didn't want her to have to worry about it, didn't want anything to dampen her big weekend. He thought of the Boo. The Boo handed out special passes all the time. Pete had a good record at the Citadel. He had kept his nose clean. He had never before asked the Boo for a favor. The Boo loved all his lambs, and as lambs went, Pete was one of the better ones. This was a very special circumstance and Pete felt the Boo would grant him his wish of another long weekend leave. He decided to consult Mrs. Petit first.

Pete went over to Jenkins Hall to see Mrs. Petit. He chose a time when he thought the Boo wouldn't be in his office. He didn't want to run into the Boo. This was a small matter and he didn't want to bother the Boo with it more than was necessary. He figured Mrs. Petit could probably talk to the Boo for him and all would be well. Mrs. Petit was full of sympathy, understood how important it was, and acted like it was no big deal. "I'll talk to the colonel," she said. "Come back in two days."

Two days later Pete trekked back across the campus to Jenkins Hall, full of happy expectations.

"This is proving a little harder than I thought," Mrs. Petit said. "Don't know what's going on with the colonel. So far, he's only agreed to extend your general leave for Saturday night till three A.M. He's in now. Come on. Let's go see him together. We'll beg." Pete followed Mrs. Petit into the Boo's office.

The Boo was seated at his desk. Papers were strewn across the desk and the Boo seemed a little distracted by the paperwork. A half smoked cigar rested on a clear glass ash tray in a corner of the desk, no longer smoldering. It was the first time Pete had seen the Boo without a cigar protruding from his mouth. Pete noted the cigar and the Boo weren't far apart. Cigars were the Boo's friends. Mrs. Petit was magnificent in her pleas. "Colonel," she said in a pleading voice. "You simply must allow Mr. Creger this weekend leave. His girlfriend Joyce will be so disappointed if you don't."

The Boo picked up the dead cigar, popped it into his mouth, relit it, took a few short puffs, then a long one, leaned back in his chair, smiled, and asked Pete a question. "Mr. Creger, do you think you're smarter than the Citadel?"

Pete had no idea where that question came from nor where it was going. He hesitated, then gave the only answer possible. "Sir, no sir."

"Bubba, you don't need a weekend leave for this. I'll allow you an extra three hours. That's it. You used up your last weekend leave the month before over Corps Day. You shoulda planned better. You shoulda known you'd need a weekend for this prom thing and not taken one Corps Day. You did take Miss Miller to Corps Day, didn't you?"

"Yes, sir, but Colonel, this is really important."

"How old do you think Miss Miller's parents are, Bubba?"

"I don't know, Colonel. Pretty old, I guess. Maybe around your age."

"I'm not that old, you bum." The Boo sneered and raised his voice a little. Pete knew his chances for the leave were slipping away. How was he going to tell Joyce? "Tell me, lamb, did you know Miss Miller has three older brothers, all Citadel graduates?"

"Yes, sir, I did know that, Colonel."

"What you probably don't know is that they were all bums, just like you, lambs who needed a lot of looking after. I got to know Mr. Miller rather well while they were here. I called Mr. Miller up and asked him how he felt about me giving you this extra weekend leave. What do you think he told me, bubba?"

Pete thought he had a chance. Joyce was her daddy's darling little girl. He seldom denied her anything. "Oh, I'm sure he approved, sir."

The Boo laughed out loud. "Wrong!" he shouted. "He told me not to give you the leave. He said he and Mrs. Miller are too old to stay up all night and all the boys are to be out of his house no later than two thirty A.M. The girls are staying all night, but not the boys. "

Pete left the Boo's office feeling lucky he still had the three A.M. leave. Lucky but disappointed. Did Joyce know the Boo had talked to her dad? It turned out she didn't. The two of them talked and decided it was best not to talk to him about it unless he brought it up. He never mentioned it to either of them. It occurred to Pete that the Boo might have made the whole thing up, but he dismissed the thought as improbable. Prom night went well. The prom was fantastic, the party at the beach even better, shortened though it was. The problems began at the end of the evening.

All the other girls' dates left on time by two thirty in the morning, but Pete had trouble tearing himself away from Joyce.

He came close to panicking when he realized it was two forty and he had only twenty minutes to make it all the way from the Isle of Palms to the Citadel in downtown Charleston. It couldn't be done, but Pete tried.

He gave Joyce one final, hurried kiss and ran from the house to his car as fast as his legs would carry him. He was doing ninety as he crossed the Breach Inlet Bridge from the Isle of Palms onto Sullivan's Island. He kept up that speed all along Coleman Boulevard as he passed through Mt. Pleasant. There was no traffic, which helped, and he kept a wary eye out for the fuzz. He was making good time, but not good enough. It was five till three as he began the ascent on the Mt. Pleasant side of the Cooper River Bridge and he knew he wouldn't make it. Cresting the top of the span he saw flashing lights in the distance, whether at the far end of the bridge or on a Charleston street he wasn't sure, but it was a cause for concern. He slowed his pace. Miraculously, when he reached the end of the bridge, the flashing lights were gone. That helped, but it was past three A.M. and he was late.

The sergeant of Lesesne Gate was an F Company junior whom Pete knew well. "Been expecting you," he said, as he waved Pete through onto the campus. "You're late, but not too late. I'll call the OG of Number Two, let him know you're on the way. I won't report you. Maybe he won't either, but hurry."

"Thanks," said Pete. Maybe I'll get by all right, he thought. But he drove slowly through campus. He didn't want to attract the attention of the JOD, who patrolled at night in a jeep. The sophomore parking lot was at the back of the campus near the marshes of the Ashley River and on the other side of the tracks of the Southern Coastline Railroad, which crossed the river and the marshes before winding its way through the Citadel campus. As Pete crossed the tracks he looked to his left and saw the headlights of a northbound freight train hurdling through the marsh. Alarmed, he drove as fast as he could along the line of parked cars, frantically looking for an empty parking space. Pete was aware there was a train that passed through the campus each night around midnight. Many a night he and other cadets had barely made it across those tracks in front of that train in time not to be late returning from general leave. He had never known there was another train at three in the morning. He parked as quickly as he could and ran faster than he thought possible, trying to beat that train.

He didn't make it. The train was faster than he was. He pulled up at the crossing, panting from his exertions, taking in big gulps of air, heart racing, fought back his frustration, and watched the speeding freight go by, car after car, wondering if his luck was out. As he stood there, fearing a punishment order, his thoughts turned to the Boo. Looking toward the marsh, he imagined he saw the Boo out there.

Years ago a cadet returning late from leave and seeking to elude the colonel had run into the marsh. The Boo followed after him. Looking back at the colonel chasing him, the cadet thought he looked like a stranded caribou. Shortened to Boo, the nickname had stuck with him. It was a perfect fit. It was a long train. Nearly ten minutes. When the caboose finally rumbled past, Pete prepared to resume his race to the barracks. He was still in a trot, not nearly to full speed, when he thought he saw a figure approaching. Pete slowed to a walk. He couldn't believe his eyes. It couldn't be. It was. The Boo. Complete with fatigues, field cap, boots, and glowing cigar. Pete was so startled he scarcely knew how to react. Fortunately it took a few minutes before they stood next to each other, time for Pete to reflect. "Good morning, Colonel," Pete said. "Thanks for waiting up."

"I have to make sure all the lambs are in, Bubba, even the ones who are bums at heart," the Boo said.

"Colonel," Pete begged, "I can explain."

"Save it for now, Bubba. You owe me an ERW." The Boo walked with Pete all the way to Number Two barracks. "Don't worry about writing this man up for being late," the Boo told the OG. "I'll do it."

"Good night, lamb. Sleep tight," the Boo told Pete. Pete thought he heard the Boo laughing as he got into his green Comet which was parked in front of the barracks.

Knowing an ERW was going to be required of him, Pete gave the matter some thought and was ready when the next D/L made its way to the company bulletin board. The item read from left to right on the D/L: "Cre-ger, PW, 4/22/66, Late returning from extended general leave, EXPLANA-TION REQUIRED WRITTEN." Pete's ERW, dated 23 April, 1966, dripped with gratitude and plead for mercy:

> "SUBJECT: Explanation of report: "Late returning from extended general leave."
>
> TO: The commandant of cadets
>
> 1. The report is correct.
>
> 2. I am most grateful for the assistant commandant's kindness and generosity, which led him not only to grant me an additional three hours general leave but to lose his own sleep and rest awaiting my safe return to the warmth and security of the barracks. Alas and alack, I have sinned. My amorous attention to my paramour caused me to lose track of the time. Leaving her home on the Isle of Palms, I failed to allow sufficient travel time for my return to duty. I repent and beg for mercy.
>
> 3. The offense was unintentional."

In due course of time, Pete received the Boo's response, a copy of his original ERW, embossed across its front with the Boo's famous red DROP DEAD stamp, which generally meant a punishment order was to follow. The Boo, however, had scribbled something, partly illegible, across the bottom of the page. Pete wasn't sure, but he thought it read *limited mercy granted.* The part that Pete could read said *you're still a bum.* It was signed *The Boo.* Whatever it said, Pete held out hope he might retain his corporal stripes. On the next DL Pete was handed out eight demerits. It could have been a lot worse. Pete ran over to Jenkins Hall and thanked the Boo pro-fusely. The Boo laughed and said, "you're welcome, Bubba. Make sure the repentance holds. Next time you'll be walking."

Sammy Graham's final encounter with the Boo as a cadet occurred near the end of his senior year. He was recently promoted to second lieutenant, but was no more shined up than when he was a senior private. Maybe less so, given that graduation was a few months away. Every cadet has one pair of shoes that are less well cared for than his others. He wears them to class and drill. They're called his shitkickers. They're seldom shined, and in the case of senior privates, they seldom see any polish at all.

One morning between classes Sammy was at the checkout desk in the library, checking out a book he sorely needed as a source for completion of his senior essay, a graduation requirement. He was wearing his shitkickers. They were turning gray from lack of polish. Sammy first smelled the cigar, then he felt the heat from its tip, close to his face, then he saw the red glow, so close had Sammy not been wearing glasses and had he not instinctively turned his head away, he would have lost his right eye. Sammy had never before seen the Boo in the library.

The Boo didn't speak. He smiled crookedly. He looked down at Sammy's shoes. He pointed down toward them with his right index finger. Sammy followed the Boo's downward glance. When Sammy looked up again, the Boo was holding both his hands out, palms upward. Somehow, without a spoken word, Sammy knew the Boo meant for him to give up his shitkickers. Sammy reached down, took off his shoes and handed them over to the Boo. He never saw his beloved shitkickers again. He hurried across the parade ground to the barracks in his socks, put on his second best shoes, and somehow made it to his next class on time. The next month's DL reported: Graham, SR, "no polish on shoes," five demerits.

After graduation from the Citadel Sammy and a number of other members of the Class of 1968 attended law school at the University of South Carolina in Columbia. Several, including Sammy, returned to Charleston to practice law. Hearing of the Boo's banishment to the warehouse, the former lambs paid frequent visits to the Boo at his office in the warehouse, where they usually found him in good spirits, taking care of business and chomping on his trademark cigar. He missed not being able to take care of the new lambs, but he was good at making the best of a bad situation.

For a number of years Kyle Gallagher and Bobby Hankins, former lambs from F Troop, hosted a Saturday morning breakfast on homecoming weekends during the Class of 1968's five year reunions. A special invitation was extended to the Boo and he attended when he could, long since retired, wearing civilian clothes, but still with the ever present cigar.

The Boo's passed away now, gone to glory. He lives in one of those mansions in heaven, a very big one, by a river with marsh lined banks. Across the river is a fortress with high gray walls, reminiscent of the Citadel. The Boo never goes there. He doesn't want to. He's retired. It's only there for his viewing pleasure. He receives frequent visits from many of his former lambs, like him, gone to glory. They remember his goodness, his kindness, his mercy, and his love showered upon them. They were his lambs once, when they were very young, and he was their good shepherd.

A MUTUAL FRIEND

Patti Lazicki was a heartbreaker. A real heartbreaker. Even as a child. As she grew up, she became a Greek goddess. She and Sammy Graham knew each other as children. They were playmates and classmates in school. Patti's family lived on Sumter Street on the Charleston peninsula in a large, white, two story, frame house, with wide piazzas. Sammy's family lived around the corner on South Tracy Street in a much smaller Charleston single house. Patti and Sammy were the same age and they were in the same grade at Mitchell Elementary School. From first grade on, with other neighborhood kids, they walked to school together in the mornings and back home together in the afternoons. With other kids, they played together in the neighborhood and on the Mitchell playground.

Patti's family was Greek. After regular school ended, along with other Greek kids, Patti was required to attend Greek school at the Greek Orthodox Church, a few blocks away on Race Street, several afternoons a week. The Greek school kids were allowed a recess period and sometimes Sammy and other non-Greek kids from the neighborhood would play with them during their recess. As Patti grew older, the prettier and prettier she became. She didn't notice, but Sammy was rather taken with her. By the time she reached high school she was a real beauty. Tall, slim, and curvaceous. Long, raven black hair. Dark, creamy skin. Big brown eyes. A lovely face. Lovelier ways. Sammy, a bit of a nerd, worshiped her from afar. Sammy never told Patti and if Patti ever noticed, she never said anything to Sammy. Patti was very popular, but she always found time for Sammy. They remained the best of friends. Following their freshman year in high school, Sammy's family moved from the city of Charleston to the suburbs of West Ashley, and Patti and Sammy lost touch.

Sammy began his knob year at the Citadel in the fall of 1964. Unknown to Sammy, Patti enrolled at the College of Charleston that same fall. Knob year Sammy's squad leader was cadet sergeant Elliott Johnson, a junior, and the assistant squad leader was cadet corporal Dana Weller, a sophomore. Weller happened to be the roommate of F Company guidon corporal John Osterhout. The squad leader and assistant squad leader were the two upperclassmen most directly involved in administering the plebe system to the knobs. Some upperclassmen were downright mean and went way overboard, inflicting serious physical abuse to the knobs. Neither Johnson nor Weller misused their authority. They were both hardnosed and tough, but fair. As hard as the system was, Sammy felt fortunate to be in their squad.

That fall, shortly after Thanksgiving and several weeks before the Christmas break as Sammy stood bracing at his assigned place in the squad during a Sunday evening formation, he was approached by Weller. There was nothing unusual in this. Weller inspected the knobs in the squad at almost every formation. Weller had just finished looking at Sammy's brass, turning his brass belt buckle over to look at the back as well as the front, when he stepped back, smiled broadly, and said, "Mr. Graham, I've just met a most interesting young lady. We spent an enjoyable time together this weekend. Old friend of yours, I believe. She asked me to ask you if you remembered her. Do you remember Patti Lazicki?"

A name Sammy had not spoken nor heard spoken in quite a while. There could not be more than one Patti Lazicki. It had to be her. Sammy was pleased Patti remembered him. He couldn't think of any possible reason for his being a topic of conversation between Patti Lazicki and Dana Weller. He couldn't help smiling.

"I take it you remember her," Weller said.

"Yes, sir," said Sammy, still smiling.

"Wipe that smile off your face, mister," Weller said. "She's Miss Lazicki to you now, knoblet. Suppose you drop down and do fifteen pushups in honor of Miss Lazicki." Sammy hit the quad for fifteen. When he was done he popped back up and resumed bracing.

"At ease, Graham. So, anything you can tell me about Miss Lazicki? Anything I should know? Anything you can tell me that might be of benefit in my courtship of Miss Lazicki?"

"Sir, I haven't seen her in over three years, sir. Not since ninth grade, sir." Suddenly Sammy felt a twinge of something, of what, he wasn't sure. If not jealousy, envy.

"I think I sort of like Miss Lazicki, even if she is a former friend of yours. Anything you'd like me to tell her?"

Sammy could think of a lot of things he might like to tell Patti Lazicki, but not through Dana Weller. He decided to try to play it safe, although he wasn't sure how to do that. "Tell her I said hello, sir," he said.

Weller looked at Sammy for a minute without saying anything, as if he was trying to decide whether to tell him something. Finally, he said, "Miss Lazicki says to tell you hello. I've done that." He took another minute, and then said, "she also said I should be nice to you." Weller laughed. He took his place in the squad and the company marched off.

After that, Patti Lazicki became a regular topic of conversation between Dana Weller and Sammy Graham, usually, like the first time, at the Sunday evening formations following a weekend. Weller would tell Sammy about their dates. Sometimes Sammy felt he was talking to Patti through Weller.

Over time, though Sammy had no clue how Patti felt about Weller, it was crystal clear to Sammy that Weller was pretty well smitten with Patti. If she still looked as good as she did in ninth grade, that was not a surprise. It was a subtle change, but Sammy could sense a change taking place between himself and Weller. He was still a knob and Weller was still an upperclassman, and not just any upperclassman, but Sammy's squad corporal, but a bond of sorts was forming between them. Weller seemed to enjoy talking to Sammy about Patti. For his part, Sammy no longer felt that twinge of envy or jealousy or whatever it was. Sammy realized he had come to like and respect Dana Weller. He was, like Patti, dark complexioned, dark haired, smart, and well rounded. He and Patti no doubt were suited for each other.

Dana Weller was a member of the Citadel cadet choir. The choir sang hymns in the Sunday morning services at the Summerall Chapel, and presented an annual program of Christmas carols. Several performances were held each year, all in the Summerall Chapel, and the public was invited. The final performance of the year, attended by the corps of cadets, was held on the Sunday evening before the corps left on Christmas furlough. A formation was required and the corps was to march across the parade ground to the chapel. As F Company was forming up on the quadrangle of Number Two barracks, Elliott Johnson came up to Sammy and said, "Mr. Graham, Mr. Weller asked me to tell you that Miss Lazicki is coming to hear the choir tonight. She wants to hear him sing. She'd also like to see you. As you leave the chapel after the performance, she'll be standing on the sidewalk off to the right, near the steps." Sammy was amazed and elated. He couldn't believe it! Once inside the chapel, Sammy tried to spot Patti, but quickly gave up. He was surrounded by cadets and there was a capacity crowd. He wondered why Weller hadn't delivered the news about Patti himself. Weller, of course, had to go over earlier with the choir and wasn't at the formation. He was astounded Patti wanted to see him. What had he ever been to her? Certainly not a boyfriend. Just her little geeky pal from the old neighborhood. She couldn't possibly be as excited about seeing him as he was about seeing her. On the other hand, she had set this up through Weller. Weller must have told her their best chance of meeting was after the performance. No formation was required then. Each cadet made his own way back to the barracks. The knobs had to walk around the parade ground. He hoped he found her right away. He'd only have a brief few minutes.

Sammy was distracted, his thoughts on Patti, not the music. He was certain the music was inspiring, even though he heard very little of it. As soon as it was over, he pushed his way through the overflow crowd of cadets and civilians. It took longer than he would have liked. Would Patti be waiting for him? She was! He saw her as soon as he made it through the doorway onto the Chapel steps. Right where she'd said she'd be. He had no trouble recognizing her. He doubted she'd recognize him. At least his garrison hat covered his shaved head. Sammy walked up to Patti and said, "Hi, Patti."

Patti Lazicki looked at Sammy Graham, no sign of recognition on her face. An instant later her brown eyes widened in disbelief. She reached up and removed his garrison hat from his head and said, incredulity in her voice, "my goodness, it is you. You've gotten so tall. You used to be short. I was looking for someone much shorter. I used to be taller than you."

Sammy laughed. "Not anymore," he said. "I was a late bloomer. I've grown a lot since ninth grade."

"It's so good to see you again, Sammy!" Patti exclaimed. She pulled him to her and held him tight.

For a moment Sammy thought he might be in heaven. "It's great to see you again, too, Patti," Sammy said when their embrace ended.

"I'm so glad Dana told me the best way to get to see you."

"So our meeting was Dana's idea?"

"No, mine. As soon as Dana invited me to come and said the corps would be here tonight, I thought of it. Dana just told me the best way to do it. I think he was a little reluctant, but I assured him we were just old friends."

At that moment Dana walked up. He was all smiles. "Sorry it took me so long to get here," he said. "Glad to see two old friends become reacquainted." The two of them exchanged hugs and Dana pecked Patti lightly on the cheek. Sammy thought they both acted happy with each other. All the while another girl had been standing close by and Patti now introduced her to Sammy.

"Sammy, this is Gloria. Gloria's one of my roommates."

"Glad to meet you, Gloria," Sammy said. Sammy thought she was very nice looking, but he only had eyes for Patti. He hoped Weller didn't notice. Gloria, Patti, and Sammy all told Dana how much they enjoyed the choir.

"The choir was great, Mr. Weller," Sammy said, remembering as he said it that he'd hardly listened. "And thanks for arranging for Patti and me to meet. That's been great, too."

"You'd better be heading back to the barracks, Mr. Graham," Weller said. Sammy said his goodbyes and moved to the gutter on the edge of the street to begin his walk around the perimeter of the parade ground back to the barracks. As he did so, Patti slipped a piece of paper into his hand. "It's my phone number," she said. "Dana's leaving this week on Christmas vacation. He'll be gone two weeks. Call me. Let's get together and catch up." Sammy wasn't sure, but he thought Weller frowned. He thought it best not to reply. He walked off in the gutter, feeling very much like a knob, but a happy one.

Sammy and Dana Weller only had one other conversation about Patti Lazicki before Christmas break. As usual, it was at a formation. Weller asked, "well, Graham, did you enjoy your meeting with Miss Lazicki?"

"Very much, sir."

"Was she as you remembered?"

"Even prettier, sir. You're very lucky, sir," Sammy added, thinking he was probably saying too much, but Weller seemed pleased. "Thanks again for letting me see her, sir" Sammy continued, surprised at his own boldness.

Weller was smiling all over himself. "She insisted," he said. Sammy had a feeling Weller wanted to say something more, but was restraining himself. If he had been Weller, he would have ordered his knob not to call her over Christmas. He would have confiscated the phone number. Weller need not worry. Sammy had no intention of calling her. Too dangerous. His position as a knob was too tenuous.

Sammy's Christmas break was a busy one. He spent a good bit of the time cutting hair in his dad's barber shop. Beginning at age thirteen, his dad had taught him the trade. All through high school it was his weekend and summer job. The money was good, but sometimes he felt like an indentured servant. In the evenings, when he wasn't fretting about his return to the Citadel in the New Year, a return which he dreaded, he studied. Exams loomed in January. Sammy's fantasies focused on quitting, but knob year was half over. Leaving the Citadel wasn't in the cards for him, and it would never do to survive the year with failing grades. All of that barely left time for Christmas shopping or old friends. Sammy had some thoughts of Patti Lazicki, but not of calling her. Two evenings before Christmas Eve he was at home hitting the books when the phone rang. His mother answered it, spoke for a few minutes, and then called to Sammy. "You won't believe this," she said. "The most amazing, unexpected, and wonderful thing. It's for you. Patti Lazicki."

Sammy felt a little guilty about not calling her. It was unbelievable she'd called him, but he was thrilled. "Merry Christmas," said Patti.

"Merry Christmas," Sammy returned.

"I'd been hoping you'd call."

Feeling like a skunk, Sammy said, "Patti, you wouldn't believe how busy I've been."

"I would. Me too," she said. Then, "I've a favor I'd like to ask of you. I really couldn't think of anyone else to ask." Sammy had trouble believing this. "You remember meeting my roommate Gloria?"

"Yeah." Sammy wondered if Patti was trying to be a matchmaker.

"Well, she's Catholic. She wants to go to midnight Christmas mass at the cathedral on Broad Street. She wants me to go with her. She's finished school and is working as a nurse at Roper hospital. She gets off work at eleven thirty. She wants me to pick her up at the hospital and then we'll go to church together. I feel funny about it. I've never been to a Catholic service before. I don't want to be the only non-Catholic there. Would you be sweet enough to come by the apartment, pick me up, and go with me?"

Sammy was a little stunned. "What about your family?" he asked. "Aren't you spending Christmas Eve with them?"

"Of course," Patti replied. "But that'll start and end early. My parents are usually in bed by ten. Won't you come?"

Sammy was reluctant. "I guess I could probably do it," he said. "Our family celebration on Christmas Eve likely will end early too."

Patti took that as a yes. "Great!" she exclaimed. "I'll meet you at my apartment at eleven fifteen." She gave Sammy directions. It would be easy to find. Downtown on Ashley Avenue, two doors from Baker hospital and across from Colonial Lake, on the top floor of one of dozens of stately antebellum homes surrounding the lake, standing like elderly dowagers lining the walls of a wedding reception.

Sammy's reluctance centered around Dana Weller and his own status as a knob at the Citadel. He mastered his concerns quicker than he thought possible and by Christmas Eve morning he was looking forward to his midnight tryst with Patti and Gloria more eagerly than that evening's celebration with his family.

Sammy was nervous and excited as he parked on Ashley Avenue by Colonial Lake promptly at eleven fifteen. The center of the lake was adorned with a tall Christmas tree decorated with sparkling colored lights which reflected off the shimmering water. The upper part of the house's thick, oaken front door framed a beveled glass almost, but not quite, as thick as the door itself. In response to his ringing of the doorbell, through the glass Sammy saw Patti come bounding saucily down the steep stairs just inside the doorway. Patti was ravishingly beautiful. *A Greek goddess* thought Sammy. "Merry Christmas," she said again as she came through the door. Her face beamed. She continued on breathlessly, "thank you for doing this. Gloria thanks you too." She pecked Sammy on the check.

"The pleasure's all mine," Sammy said. In the car on the way to Roper, Sammy said, "I've never been to a Catholic church either. Should be different."

"I'm sure it will be. Dana's Catholic too, you know."

"I didn't know that. Mr. Weller and I don't talk much."

"Does he ever talk about me?"

"The little he ever talks to me is all about you."

"Really?"

"Really." It suddenly dawned on Sammy that Patti was interested in seeing him not to catch up with each other, but to find out what Weller said about her. He decided he wasn't going to tell her anything. "Does he know we're going to Catholic mass together on Christmas Eve?"

"No, and you're not to tell him either."

"Your secret's safe with me."

Sammy drove to the emergency entrance to Roper where Gloria was waiting for them. The whole way there Patti had chattered away, much of it about Dana, but Sammy held to his resolve. Gloria saw them through the glass doorway. She was wearing her nurse's uniform, a long cloth coat over it. The night was cool. As soon as Gloria got in the car Patti stopped talking about Dana. The three of them sat together on the car's front bench seat, Patti in the middle, close to Sammy. It was a short drive to the cathedral, an imposing structure fronting on Broad Street, a small parking lot adjacent. Sammy knew trying for a spot in the parking lot would be hopeless. Luckily, he found a space on the street only four or five blocks away. It was one of the largest churches in Charleston, a city filled with large churches, aptly called the Holy City. Inside the church was packed, but they were able to squeeze into an already crowded pew near the back. Glowing chandeliers hung from the high ceilings. Christmas greenery mixed with the red petals of poinsettias was everywhere.

Outside lighting, cleverly placed, illuminated stained glass windows depicting scenes from the life of Christ. At the front, to the left of the altar, stood a crèche, the figures almost life-sized. Promptly at midnight, Christmas bells announced the hour, the coming of Christmas Day. When the last bell chimed, all was still, silence prevailed. A procession proceeded down the center aisle to the altar: a dozen or more acolytes carrying scepters topped with crosses and candles, banners and ribbons, and censers filled with burning incense, its acrid smoke wafting about; dozens of bareheaded priests wearing long, flowing robes; and the bishop wearing his miter and priestly vestments, and sprinkling holy water along the way.

Sammy's seat was at the end of the pew by the center aisle, giving him an unobstructed view of the proceedings. As the bishop went by, holy water splashed onto his head and shoulders. It may have been holy, but it was cold; one drop found its way into his right eye, causing him to flinch. Gloria, seated next to him, whispered "a person sprinkled with holy water at Christmas receives a special blessing."

This was both Sammy's and Patti's first exposure to the pageantry and ritual of the Catholic service. It was far different from the more informal style of Protestant worship to which Sammy was accustomed. It made a definite impression, but, special blessing notwithstanding, Sammy did not think he would convert any time soon.

Christmas Day was well into its second hour by the time the service ended. Both Patti and Gloria tried to insist Sammy join them for a short nightcap of Christmas cheer in their apartment, but Sammy begged off. Gloria was yawning, tired from her long day at the hospital, and Sammy didn't want to give Patti further opportunity to press him about Mr.

Weller. He drove Gloria to the Roper parking lot to pick up her car and dropped Patti off at the apartment. Sammy didn't know it at the time, but it would be nearly another three years before he would see Patti Lazicki again.

Christmas vacation 1964 ended. The South Carolina corps of cadets returned to the Citadel. Sammy Graham and Dana Weller each resumed their roles as knob and corporal. Dana and Patti dated all through the rest of that year. Dana kept Sammy informed about Patti. Sometimes Sammy wished Dana would let it go. Sometimes Sammy felt the bishop's holy water was a curse, not a blessing: he was destined to listen to Mr. Weller's accounts of his romance with Patti Lazicki. A romance Sammy wished was his, not Mr. Weller's. Sammy's knob year, thankfully, came to an end.

Sammy spent that summer working in his dad's barber shop. He dallied with the idea of calling up Patti and asking her out. He was no longer a knob. School year romances, like summer ones, end with the change of the school year. Dana and Patti's relationship had survived a two week separation at Christmas; it wasn't likely to last over the three months of summer. Sammy wasn't sure why he didn't call Patti. He just didn't. Maybe it was because he was waiting for her to call him. She'd called him over Christmas. More likely it was because she had turned into a Greek goddess. He wasn't in her league. She was his fantasy. It had nothing to do with Dana Weller.

That summer ended and the South Carolina corps of cadets returned to the Citadel for another school year, Dana Weller as a junior sergeant and Sammy Graham as a private, but a sophomore, an upperclassman. Dana and Patti's relationship did last over the summer, and they took up where they had left off. Being in the same company, Sammy and Dana saw each other, but not as often as the year before when Dana had been knob Sammy Graham's corporal. Dana would occasionally mention Patti to Sammy. She was now Patti, not Miss Lazicki, just as Sammy was Sammy, not Mr. Graham, and Dana was Dana, not Mr. Weller. Sammy didn't mind much. Patti wasn't much in his thoughts. He went out with other girls, but he had no steady girlfriend. Patti and Dana only went out with each other. By the end of that year Dana Weller and Patti Lazicki had been a couple going on two years. Dana began thinking seriously of Patti in terms of a much longer relationship. The next year he would be a senior at the Citadel, Patti a junior at the College of Charleston. Half the cadets of each senior class were engaged by the beginning of senior year and married within weeks, if not days, of graduation. Dana determined to be among them that next year. He decided he would propose to Patti at the Ring Hop, held over parent's day weekend in early October of each year. He would have just received his Citadel ring, his parents would be in town, and he would present Patti with a ring as the two of them stood in the giant Citadel ring, which all senior cadets passed through with their dates. Patti would enter the ring as his date and emerge from it and pass with him under the umbrella of crossed swords of the junior sword drill as his fiancé, his future wife. What could be more romantic? Dana made these plans with absolute certainty of Patti's answer.

Dana Weller aspired to become a member of the Summerall Guards. Comprised only of members of the senior class and named after former Citadel president, General Charles P. Summerall, the silent drill platoon performed at various events throughout the year, and exemplified the exactness with which Citadel cadets were trained. Selection as a Summerall Guard was a high honor and a singular achievement. Before becoming a Summerall Guard his senior year, a cadet first had to become a Bond Volunteer near the end of his junior year. Named for Colonel O. J. Bond, another former Citadel president, the Bond Volunteers were the training platoon for the next year's guards. Administered by the current year's guards, the training was demanding physically and mentally. Essentially a mini plebe system, the volunteers were harassed, abused, and hazed by the guards as if they were knobs. It was a rigorous ritual, submitted to and survived only by the most determined and committed. Among the required rituals was obtaining a shaved head, the same as a knob.

Dana Weller was justifiably fond of his wavy, coal black head of hair, the exact shade of darkness of his beloved's, Patti Lazicki's. Patti did not think of membership in the guards as a big deal the way Dana did. She didn't consider the whole ordeal worth the loss, even temporarily, of his lustrous hair. They even had words over it, their first argument of any kind.

In an effort to make himself somewhat more presentable to Patti, Dana asked Sammy, the former F Company barber, to do the honor, thinking a properly shaved head would look better than one butchered by one of the barbers at the Citadel barber shop. To his dismay, Sammy turned him down. He said the barracks barber shop was closed and he had retired as company barber. He also said a shaved head was a shaved head and he couldn't perform a tonsorial miracle and make it what it wasn't. Dana told Patti Sammy wouldn't shave his head, but he was going to be a Bond Volunteer anyway. Patti transferred her peevishness to Sammy. Dana was glad, Sammy indifferent. He was well into not letting Patti Lazicki matter to him one way or the other.

Not everyone who became a Bond Volunteer made it through to become a Summerall Guard. Some quit along the way. There were just so many positions available in the platoon. Cuts were a cruel necessity. Dana Weller, though, was strong, athletic, well drilled, loved the military and, like his roommate John Osterhout, also a Bond Volunteer, was considered a shoo in. No one was surprised when both of them survived all the cuts and became Summerall Guards.

Rankings for the next year were also decided at the end of the year. Osterhout was a strong contender for regimental commander, cadet colonel, the highest ranking cadet on campus. Weller, too, was highly ranked within F Company. Osterhout was not well liked. His selection as regimental commander was met, not with surprise, but with some sense of dismay by many. Weller was very popular. His selection as a mere second lieutenant, assistant platoon leader in F Company, was surprising to everyone, and a big letdown for Weller. Still, he was a Summerall Guard and he would wear stripes his senior year. And, early in the year, he would become engaged to the love of his life, his Greek goddess, the most beautiful, loveliest girl in the world, Patti Lazicki. He was very happy.

That summer Dana, like all the rising Citadel seniors who had accepted commissions to become army officers upon graduation, was required to attend army summer camp, which took up half the summer. After summer camp Dana made a quick trip to Charleston to see Patti. Overall, the time with Patti, as almost always, was fabulous. At times, however, Patti exhibited a slight petulance. Though Ring Hop was a ways away, Dana asked Patti to attend with him and she said yes, as Dana had known she would. She was very excited about it and Dana was tempted to go ahead and ask her to marry him.

He hadn't bought the ring yet, though, and he didn't want to ruin the surprise he had planned when they went through the ring together. Dana returned to his home in upstate New York not giving any thought to the small, uncharacteristic irritations Patti had shown. Everyone, even the world's most perfect person, was entitled to be out of sorts once in a while. While at home Dana, with a loan from his dad, bought the world's most perfect person one of the world's most perfect diamond rings. He knew Patti would love it. He couldn't wait to return to Charleston and begin his senior year at the Citadel.

Patti was annoyed with herself, not Dana. She was in love with Dana. At least, she had thought she was. Until now. Now she wasn't sure. It was her own uncertainty which annoyed her and made her irritable. Dana was sweet. He was handsome. She was sure he cared about her. She knew she cared about him, but how deep did that caring go? She was beginning to think not too deep. Otherwise, how could she be drawn to someone else? Someone she didn't even know. Someone she'd only just met and might or might not ever see again. That summer, thinking she might lighten her load her junior year at the College of Charleston, Patti decided to take a few courses in summer school. Between classes she and her friend Arlene went to lunch at a sandwich shop on George Street near the College. There they ran into professor Grant Hale. Was there such a thing as love at first sight? Even if there wasn't, the lunch with Professor Hale, brief as it was, was causing Patti to question her feelings for Dana. She couldn't stop thinking about the professor. Even when she was with Dana that summer, she thought of the professor. Even when Dana asked her to the Ring Hop, and she, naturally, said yes, she was thinking of the professor. What was she going to do?

Grant Hale had recently completed his doctorate in history and the College of Charleston was his first teaching position. He had agreed to teach summer school because he needed the extra money. He was single and had just moved to Charleston. He was thirty years old, unattached, and had vowed to himself to never, not under any circumstances, become involved with a co-ed. The sandwich shop that day was very crowded and he was seated alone at a table for four. He recognized Arlene as one of his summer school students. He couldn't remember her last name. There was another girl with her. They were looking for a place to sit. The other girl was stunningly attractive, in a dark, Mediterranean sort of way. He told himself that was not the reason he offered to share his table, but by the time they were seated, his vow was a distant memory.

Patti had paid no particular attention to Grant Hale until she and Arlene were seated. Arlene made the introductions. Patti was smitten immediately. She couldn't help it. Patti had always felt Dana was good looking, handsome. Grant Hale was beyond good looking. She had never before in her mind applied the term gorgeous to any male, but, to Patti, Grant Hale was gorgeous. Stunning blue eyes, sparkling white teeth, lustrous blonde hair. Perfect features. Unconsciously, she looked at his left hand to see if he was wearing a ring. He wasn't and her heart leapt. Then her mind told her many men didn't wear wedding rings and she felt deflated. She looked into his eyes and fell in love. Later, she couldn't remember any of the conversation, but she was certain he had talked brilliantly on a number of subjects. Arlene was pretty sure he wasn't married, but, of course, knew nothing of his personal life. Arlene also said his lectures were engrossing, one of the best professors she'd had at the College.

Later still, afraid she'd never meet him again, and trying to remember everything, the only other thing she could remember was that the summer's hit song, *Ode to Billie Joe,* had been playing on the sandwich shop's jukebox. Patti found out what courses Professor Hale was teaching in the fall, dropped one of her electives, and signed up for his course on the French Revolution. It might be a futile effort, but she had to try. She doubted he would even remember her.

That doubt was removed on the first day of class. After introducing himself to the class, Grant Hale looked straight at Patti and said, "let's see, Miss Lazicki, before we begin, can you tell the class exactly what the hell it was that Billie Joe McAllister threw off the Tallahatchie Bridge?"

He remembered. He remembered her. He knew her name. Like her, he remembered *Ode to Billie Joe* was playing on the jukebox that day in the sandwich shop. The whole class laughed. For them, it was nothing more than an ice breaker to begin the semester. For Patti, it was much more. Strange as it was, at that moment Patti was certain she was in love with Grant Hale. He must love her, too. He simply must. She must do something to make an impression. She tried to think fast, but she was nervous, addled. She tried to give a serious answer. She said, "no one knows what Billie Joe threw off the bridge. Whatever it was, he didn't throw it alone. The preacherman claimed a girl was with him. What is known is that later he threw himself off the bridge, and the girl, the singer, lost her appetite over it."

"Were they lovers, you think?" Professor Hale asked.

"Maybe," Patty replied. There were titters, but no outright laughter, from the class. Patti felt her face growing warm, the beginnings of a blush.

Speaking to the class, not looking at Patti, Professor Hale said, "Interesting. Let's get on to the goings on in France in the late eighteenth century." Patti was delighted with the exchange. It was a beginning.

Patti wished she had broken up with Dana when she'd seen him back in the summer. She'd known then it had to be done, but she couldn't bring herself to do it. She wanted to let him down gently, but she didn't know how. It wasn't as if she and Grant Hale were already seeing each other. They weren't, but Patti was sure it would happen. He was the one. Dana really was a great guy and she really did want to go to the Ring Hop. Briefly, she considered not breaking up with him until after the big dance, but that would be too cruel. Better to get it out of the way, sooner rather than later. That way, he'd have time to find another date. She didn't want him to miss it because of her. They had gone out every weekend since the new school year had begun and she hadn't been her old self. Surely, Dana had to have noticed, but if he had, he hadn't said anything. Somehow, she had to find the right time. She couldn't just spring it on him all at once. What she needed was a good argument, even if it started over a triviality.

The weeks passed and no opportunity to break with Dana presented itself. Why did he have to be so nice? She studied harder in Grant Hale's

French Revolution class than she'd ever studied before, striving to impress him. So far, he was being very professional, he the professor and she the student, but Patti knew in her heart she was more than a student to him. She could tell by the way he looked at her. She adored being in his class. He was the greatest of lecturers. She adored him. Patti knew a breakthrough was coming soon and their lives would be forever changed, forever entwined. She decided to tell Dana the truth: they had to stop seeing each other because she was in love with someone else. A quick, clean break was best. Ring Hop was two weeks away. Plenty of time for Dana to find another date. She hoped he would take it well, as well as Billie Joe McAllister's death had been taken, if it had been taken well, because she was dead to him. It was over.

Dana was stunned. He hadn't seen it coming. It hurt too bad to cry. "How can you be in love with someone else?" he asked. "You're supposed to be in love with me."

The two of them were in the front seat of Dana's car, parked on the Battery, a romantic place frequented by lovers, not a setting for a breakup. Patti touched Dana's arm and said gently, "I'm sorry, Dana, I don't love you."

"I love you," Dana said. "I thought you loved me. I was sure of it. You did love me, didn't you?"

"I thought I did, but now I know what love is. Please understand. Someday you'll find someone else, and you'll know what true love is."

"I know it now, and it's killing me. There'll never be anyone else."

"Don't say that, Dana."

"It's true. I have to say it. Who is this guy? When did you meet him? When do you see him? You've been going out with me."

"It doesn't matter who he is. I met him this summer. I wanted to tell you then. Should have told you then. I didn't mean to hurt you, Dana. Please believe me. Please forgive me." Patti began to cry. Softly. Quietly. She reached in her purse, took out a tissue, and began wiping her cheeks and eyes. "I think you should take me home now." Dana sat in silence. "Please take me home."

Dana turned the ignition key. The car's engine hummed to life. Dana pulled away from the curb. They rode in silence to Patti's house with the wide piazzas on Sumter Street. Dana felt numb. He pulled to the curb in front of the house. They sat in the car, neither speaking, neither knowing what to say. Patti made no move to exit the car. Finally, Dana said, "it's hard to believe you're serious."

Patti looked squarely at Dana. "I am," she said. She leaned across the seat and pecked him lightly on the cheek. "Goodbye, Dana," she said as she got out of the car. "I'll always remember you." She ran toward the house without looking back. Dana wanted to say something, anything, but words stuck in his throat. He couldn't get them to come out. He wanted to scream *Patti, don't do this! It doesn't have to be this way. You can't mean it!* But somehow he knew she did. He waited until she was inside the house, and then he drove off, thinking *I'm not going to beg. She'll call me. Before Ring Hop, she'll call me.*

As much as Sammy Graham tried to think and act indifferently about and toward Patti Lazicki, deep down he knew he had always carried a little spark for her. That's all it was, nowhere near a flame. He was amazed two years had gone by and he hadn't run into her, especially since she and Dana had dated all that time. There wasn't a lot of socializing between the classes, which explained it some. Sammy seldom had a steady girlfriend. He liked to play the field. He attended all the hops, never with the same girl, and was surprised he'd never run into Dana and Patti at one. He knew they'd been there. Hops were crowded, which was the only explanation he could think of. He had a date for the upcoming Ring Hop and knew he'd see her this time because all the seniors went through the ring with their dates.

The seniors went through the ring alphabetically. Their names, along with the names of their dates, were announced over the PA system as each couple entered the Ring. Sammy stationed himself and his date so they'd have the best possible view. Sammy told Kay, his date, he particularly wanted to see his friend Dana Weller walk through the ring, not mentioning it was really his date Patti Lazicki he was interested in seeing. The announcements of the seniors going through the ring went from Wakefield to Wilson. No Weller. Strange. Sammy and Kay stood where they were, waiting, watching. Somehow out of order. They waited and watched all the way through to Zinsky. The end. No Dana. No Patti. Kay asked Sammy, "what happened? Where are they?"

"I don't know. I can't imagine them not being here." Sammy was worried. Sammy knew barring death or serious injury Dana and Patti would not have missed the Ring Hop. Maybe there had been a terrible accident. He and Kay went around the dance floor asking other F Troopers if they knew anything about where Dana Weller was. No one knew anything. They were as puzzled as Sammy.

Finally, Sammy ran into John Osterhout, Dana's roommate. Surely he would know something.

Osterhout was sad for Dana. "They broke up," he said in response to Sammy's question. "She dumped him."

"When?"

"Two weeks ago."

"Wow! I hadn't heard."

"Dana wanted to keep it quiet. He kept hoping she'd change her mind and they'd be here."

"How's he doing?"

"Not good. She broke his heart. Otherwise, he'd be here with another date."

"So it's over."

"Looks that way. Best not to say anything to Dana."

"I won't."

If Dana's heart was broken, he didn't let it show. Outwardly, his life at the Citadel went on as before. He never again mentioned Patti to Sammy. In February the Summerall Guards made their annual trip to New Orleans to march in the Mardi Gras parade. Dana and the other guards returned full of tales of riotous revelry and high living and drinking on Bourbon Street. Seemingly, Dana had moved on. Sammy wondered. In early June Dana graduated from the Citadel and entered the army.

That summer found Sammy again working in his dad's barber shop. Dana was gone, but Patti, like Sammy, was still in Charleston. He still had the scrap of paper with Patti's phone number on it, which she had handed him outside Summerall Chapel before Christmas his knob year. He hadn't actually seen Patti since that Christmas Eve, but from time to time she crossed his mind. He wondered if she was still in the apartment by Colonial Lake. He was a rising Citadel senior. Patti should be a rising senior at the College of Charleston. She and Dana were history. He decided to call her up and ask her out. What did he have to lose? He thought he had an unbreakable heart.

They went to LaBrasca's Pizzeria on upper King Street. LaBrasca's had the best pizza in Charleston, maybe in the world, followed by dancing and drinking at the Merchant Seaman's Club on East Bay Street. They were carded, but they both had just turned twenty-one, rising seniors, and they were legal. Sammy couldn't believe he was actually, at long last, out on a date with Patti, who was more of a Greek goddess than ever. They did the fast dances and the slow ones. During the slow ones, holding Patti close, Sammy thought he might be falling in love. Between dances they sat alone at a table, drank, red wine for Patti, and gin and tonic for Sammy, and talked. It was like they were kids again on the Mitchell playground, they were that comfortable with each other. Neither mentioned Dana Weller, but Sammy thought of him and wondered if Patti did, too. He would have liked to have known the details of their breakup, but didn't want to hear them from Patti. The evening would have been perfect, except Patti mentioned she'd just broken up with someone. She even said his name, Grant Hale. She gave no other details, except that he had broken off with her. He couldn't imagine anyone breaking off with Patti.

Maybe it serves her right, though, he reflected, remembering Dana. Sammy had the impression that, for Patti, it was a pretty big deal, but that she was done with the guy. *All the better for me,* he thought. Sammy and Patti dated all through that summer and into the fall. Sammy discovered that Patti only dated one guy at a time. Patti became his first steady girlfriend. He thought she might become his one and only. Sammy grew to love the apartment on the top floor of the house by Colonial Lake. Patti agreed to be his date to the Ring Hop on parents weekend. Patti said she'd always wanted to go to the Ring Hop. Sammy was quite sure she'd at one time dreamed of going with Dana Weller and couldn't help puzzling over what had changed her mind. Dana was never mentioned by either of them. Their Ring Hop evening was a dazzling success. Patti was in her top Greek goddess-like form: beautiful, vivacious and fun. Sammy was certain no other cadet who walked through the ring that night did so with a girl the equal of Patti. They both had a wonderful time. It wasn't until days later that Sammy gave a thought to the previous year's hop and Dana's disappointment. He was pretty sure Patti hadn't given it a thought either. Sammy was very happy with Patti.

The only troubling aspect of their relationship was that, from time to time, Patti continued to bring up Grant Hale. Nothing too specific was ever said, but enough was said to make Sammy think that Patti, if she did not love him, thought she did, and probably was not over him. He hoped he wasn't merely Patti's transition boyfriend, merely someone who happened to be there when Patti needed someone. He hoped he was more than that, although, unlike Dana and many other Citadel grads, he had no intention of walking down the aisle with anyone, not even Patti, immediately following graduation. He had plans for law school and beyond.

Patti and Sammy were still a couple the following spring. Patti celebrated with Sammy when he learned of his acceptance to law school. They capped the evening with champagne in the apartment, an apartment which, by then, Sammy considered, if not his own, a part of him. "You know," Sammy said, "my dad's just a barber. If I make it through law school, which I will, that'll be pretty good for a barber's son."

Patti looked at Sammy, batted her eyes, and replied mischievously, "I'm just a grocer's daughter and I'm going to be a teacher." Patti's dad ran a corner grocery, a very successful one in downtown Charleston that had been in the family for several generations.

"Your students will love you," Sammy replied. "They'll have a Greek goddess for a teacher." In his mind Sammy often had thought of Patti in that way, she was that alluring, but this was the first time he'd ever told Patti he thought of her as a Greek goddess.

Patti laughed. "Thanks," she said, "but I'm not sure what that means."

"It means you're beautiful and very special."

"You're special, too," Patti replied. "You're one of my best friends."

The conversation was turning serious. Feeling like he might be about to walk off a cliff, Sammy asked, "could I ever be more than a friend?"

Patti was slow to answer. As always, they had been talking together easily, talking like two old friends, but Patti laughed nervously. She measured her words. "We've known each other since forever," she said. "I'll always want you in my life."

Sammy wasn't sure what that meant. His old insecurities about himself and Patti floated to the front of his mind. His instincts told him this was the time to take her in his arms, kiss her passionately, and declare himself, but something held him back. "I'm glad," he said. The moment passed. Later, much later, thinking back, the moment would remind Sammy of the Shakespearian line from *Julius Caesar*: "there is a tide in the affairs of men, which, taken at the flood, leads on to fortune." This was a floodtide moment, and he hadn't set sail. Fortunately for Sammy, there would be other tides.

Sammy and Patti both graduated from college. Sammy went on to law school and Patti began her teaching career in the Charleston public schools. They saw each other from time to time after that, but the chance for real romance between them faded. Sammy graduated from law school and landed a job with a small, but prestigious, law firm on Charleston's Broad Street. On his return to Charleston, not having seen or heard from Patti in a while, Sammy decided to give her a call. They were both still single, but in placing the call Sammy harbored no romantic illusions. He was merely calling an old friend. Over the phone, Patti was ebullient.

"I'd been thinking of calling you," she said. "I wanted you to know. I'm engaged! I'm getting married!"

Sammy felt a momentary twinge. Disappointment? Uncertainty? He didn't know.

"Congratulations are in order," he said. "I hope you'll be very happy."

"I can tell you're brokenhearted," Patti said. Sammy thought she sounded serious.

"Patti," Sammy said, "you've broken many hearts, but not mine. I wiggled off the hook." He thought of Dana Weller.

"Not that many," Patti protested.

"Plenty," Sammy countered. "Who's the guy who finally won your heart?"

"Grant Hale. He's wonderful."

The name sounded vaguely familiar to Sammy. "Do I know him?" he asked.

"No. You should know the name. I used to talk to you about him all the time."

Sammy thought back. "He's not the one you'd broken up with just before you and I started going out?"

"Yes! He's the one. I loved him from the moment I first saw him. We managed to get back together. Now, it'll be forever. You will come to the wedding, won't you, Sammy?"

"Of course I will."

The invitation came a few months later. Sammy intended on going right up until the last minute, but when it came right down to it, he couldn't bring himself to go. For some weird reason he kept thinking of Dana Weller. He supposed he was thinking a bit of himself, too. He read about the wedding in the newspaper. Grant Hale was a professor at the College of Charleston. Patti must have been one of his students. That was a bit of a shock. He hoped she knew what she was doing. How much older than Patti must he be?

The law firm Sammy had joined was a general practice one, but each of the members practiced in a different area. He stayed there and eventually became a partner, with his name on the shingle. His area of practice was family court work. He married and he and his wife Myra became the parents of three children. Their marriage was solid. Given his career work, Sammy knew how horrible it was for a married couple to end up in divorce court.

As the years passed Sammy and Myra accumulated many friends, but Patti and her professor husband weren't among them. The two couples moved in different circles. Patti and Sammy were no longer a part of each other's lives. Sammy had never met Grant Hale. One afternoon Sammy received a telephone call from a Mrs. Grant Hale. He knew it was Patti before he picked up the receiver. He knew it was an unlikely social call. He hoped Patti was a volunteer and the call was a fundraiser or something of that nature. It wasn't. After exchanging the required pleasantries of a lapsed friendship, Patti Hale stated she needed Sammy's professional advice, needed it badly. An appointment was scheduled.

Patti had aged, but she was in as good a looks as ever, one of those women who became even more beautiful with the passage of time. Hoping to put her more at ease, Sammy began with, "how's my Greek goddess?"

She broke into tears. Sammy led her to a chair beside his desk and handed her a full box of tissues, an unfortunate necessity of his chosen trade. He waited for the tears to subside. Still red faced and teary eyed, Patti finally looked up and said, "I feel like I've wasted my life."

It was not a pleasant divorce. Grant Hale had turned out to be an incorrigible womanizer. Multiple affairs. Arrogant in the extreme. Verbally abusive. Patti had loved him, but finally she had had enough. Sammy listened patiently to the sad tale of woe, a tale he'd heard many times. His heart went out to Patti and the two children, but not to Grant Hale. Sammy made him pay. Sammy never mentioned it to Patti, but throughout the prolonged proceedings, he kept thinking Patti should have married Dana Weller. Sammy didn't know the full story of their breakup. He didn't know Dana had planned to propose to Patti at that Ring Hop so long ago. Sammy had to stop and think how long it had been. Twenty-five years. Hard to believe. He and Patti were the same age. Forty-six.

Her divorce was final. Sammy wondered if Patti would marry again. It would be sad for her to spend the rest of her life alone. That might be a waste. Once again, Sammy thought of Dana Weller. He hadn't seen him in all those years. He wondered what had become of him. Through the years Sammy, Myra, and their children had been frequent visitors to the Citadel campus, usually on football weekends. They had attended all of Sammy's five year class reunions but one. Citadel homecoming was coming up within a few weeks. The children were teenagers now, with their own active social lives, but Sammy had no trouble talking Myra into going with him. Sammy realized this would be Dana Weller's twenty-fifth class reunion. A big one. He hoped he might finally run into Dana. He had an eerie feeling, a premonition, that he would. He didn't mention it to Myra. Sammy and Myra arrived on the campus early on Saturday morning. That afternoon there was a football game. That morning there was a parade and a performance of the Summerall Guards on the parade ground. Sammy scanned the crowd, hoping to spot Dana, though he wasn't sure he'd recognize him. Dana found Sammy. They were standing on the edge of the parade ground near the bleachers, watching the Summerall Guards. The performance had just ended. An army officer, wearing the insignia of a bird colonel, approached them, held out his hand to Sammy, and said, "how's it going, Sammy?" Sammy recognized the voice, but he had to look closely before he was sure it was Dana.

Sammy shook Dana's hand. "I can't believe it," he said. "My old corporal, now a full colonel in the real army." Sammy introduced Myra.

"You might not believe this," said Myra, "but I've heard lots and lots about you."

"I wasn't as mean to him as he's told you," Dana said. "Back then, we had a mutual friend who insisted I be nice to him."

"Her efforts at intervention weren't effective," Sammy said.

"They worked better than you ever knew," Dana said.

"I've heard of the mutual friend, too," Myra put in.

"Oh? I might like to hear about that sometime," Dana said.

They talked for a long while, standing there on the parade ground. Dana had been assigned to the Citadel as a tac officer, an assignment he had requested. It was a three year assignment and it would be his last. He planned on retiring and staying in Charleston when it was completed. They quickly capsuled their lives since their Citadel days. Dana's wife of seventeen years had passed away of breast cancer three years ago.

"This year would have been our twentieth anniversary," Dana said.

"We're so sorry," Myra said. Women were much better at expressing sympathy than men.

"It's been hard," Dana said, "but it's getting better."

Before parting company, Sammy and Dana exchanged telephone numbers, both saying they'd have to get together and stay in touch. The usual stuff. Stuff which seldom happened, but Sammy knew this time would be different. Before going more than a few steps, Myra said, "are you thinking what I'm thinking?"

"You know I am."

Women are much better at social arrangements than men, too. Sammy was glad to leave everything to Myra. It was a little more difficult and took longer than Myra had expected. Both were reluctant: Patti because she was still reeling from the reality of divorce; Dana because he was still grieving; both of them because of the end of their long ago relationship. Myra persisted and eventually succeeded in bringing Dana and Patti together.

Myra and Sammy hosted an annual Christmas drop-in. She invited both of them, letting them know the other would be there. Myra wasn't one for surprises. They both came, honoring their promises to Myra. Sammy and Myra kept their fingers crossed. No need to worry. If it wasn't love at first sight the first time, it was the second time around. The new romance between Dana and Patti progressed much more quickly than either Sammy or Myra ever would have imagined. By Easter they were engaged. They waited a few more months, to give their children, all teenagers, time to adjust, and were married the first Saturday of the following July at the Summerall Chapel in a small, informal wedding attended by family and a few friends.

At the reception held at the alumni house John Osterhout, Dana's Citadel roommate, told Sammy that Patti's engagement ring was the same one Dana had bought for her when he was a cadet and that he had planned to give it to her at the Ring Hop that year. Details Sammy had never known. "Hard to imagine that he kept that ring all these years," John said.

"Oh, I don't know," Sammy replied. "I've still got a scrap of paper with Patti's phone number on it she gave me back then. Dana's keeping that ring makes a lot more sense than me keeping a piece of paper."

John didn't say anything to that. "I don't think Dana ever told his first wife anything about Patti," he said.

"Why would he?" Sammy asked. "There are things about Patti I've never told my wife."

John looked across the room at Patti. "She's still very attractive," he said.

"She's a Greek goddess," Sammy said.

"That's one I wouldn't tell my wife," said John.

Patti and Dana walked up. "Be careful of your new wife. She's a heartbreaker, you know," Sammy teased.

"Not anymore, she isn't," laughed Dana.

Sammy had a certain feeling, a premonition, that Dana and Patti, finally, would live together happily ever after.

SCUM

Most teachers generally are thought of as occasionally being a bit ditzy, arguably an undeserved reputation. College professors in particular are often thought of as absent-minded professor types. There's the Disney movie *The Nutty Professor*. Overall, the Citadel faculty of the 1960s deserved its well-earned standing of excellence. To a man, for there were no women faculty members then, they were outstanding in most respects, including in their eccentricities. Strangely, those with the highest scholarship and best oratory were the quirkiest.

One oddity they all shared was that none of them was called "professor." Even those holding the coveted Ph.D. degree were never addressed as "doctor." The Citadel, being a military college, required all its professors to wear a military uniform and to join the South Carolina Unorganized Militia. SCUM.

SCUM was an exclusive club, membership limited to the Citadel's teaching faculty and a few key academic administrative positions. There were no enlisted personnel. Only officers. Those faculty members who at one time or another had actually served in the military were allowed to wear the uniform of the branch in which they had served. The others wore army uniforms. The rank within SCUM was determined by academic rank within each academic department. There were a few lowly lieutenants. Most were captains or majors. Some were lieutenant colonels. All the department heads were full bird colonels. There was only one general: the academic dean, and he was a mere brigadier with only one star. SCUM did not want to be perceived as thinking too much of itself militarily. In truth,

162

it was not a military organization, though all of its members wore military uniforms and were addressed by their military rank.

Pete Creger entered the Citadel as a premed major. For two and a half years, through the end of the first semester of his junior year, he survived with passing but less than stellar grades. Entry into medical school was a fading, forlorn hope. The course that ultimately made Pete see the handwriting on the wall was organic chemistry. More accurately, it was Major Hemmings, who taught organic. More accurately still, it was the major's sloppy lab procedures, the F Pete received in the course, and a conversation between the two of them that led directly to Pete's giving up on medical school.

Pete wasn't in the lab on the afternoon of the explosion. He heard about it secondhand. The cadet involved blamed Major Hemmings. Major Hemmings blamed the cadet. Pete wasn't real clear, but someone had poured hydrochloric acid into a beaker of other chemicals in too close proximity to a lit Bunsen burner, which caused rising gases resulting from the mixture to ignite, leading to the explosion. Fortunately, only Major Hemmings and the cadet conducting the experiment under Major Hemmings' supervision were injured. They both had cuts from flying glass, superficial burns, and sore throats and lungs from inhaling ghastly gaseous fumes, but they recovered nicely over time. It could have been worse, a lot worse.

To Pete's way of thinking, at the very least Major Hemmings was guilty of improper management of the lab. Major Hemmings, Pete thought, had a bad tendency to give hurried instructions, quickly throw a few chemicals together in test tubes or beakers, and walk away, expecting the poor, befuddled student to instantly grasp what was to be done. There had been a few other small mishaps before the big explosion, which had rapidly become the talk of the campus. A fire in a chemical lab full of all sorts of solutions, mixtures, and volatile substances was dangerous. The fire department was called. Luckily, the fire somehow was contained to the single lab. The lab was completely destroyed, but the rest of Bond Hall survived the explosion and fire unscathed and intact. It took months to restore the lab, which seriously impacted the whole chemistry department's completion of required laboratory work. The serious students stewed, but the marginal ones, the ones like Pete, didn't mind so much.

Even before the explosion Pete had begun to question the soundness of conducting continuing chemical procedures under the auspices of the never-watchful Major Hemmings. After the explosion Pete was convinced that when Major Hemmings was in charge of the lab, the lab was an unsafe, perilous place. It was a distraction Pete didn't need. His interest in all things chemical, all things organic, all things scientific, and all things medical waned. Before the explosion Pete's grades in organic were poor, but he believed he was passing; after the explosion his grades plummeted. The F at the end of the semester was a shock. Pete had never before received an F. He went to talk to Major Hemmings. He hoped he could talk him into changing the F to a D. That was the only reason he had requested the conference. He had already decided to change his major.

Major Hemmings ignored Pete's pleas for a D. Strangely, he seemed to think Pete was there to discuss his chances of getting into medical school. He was also Pete's academic advisor. He was unkind. He was blunt. He said, "Mr. Creger, even before this F, you had no chance of medical school. Changing it to a D would be of no help."

Pete said, "that's not the reason I'm asking you to change the grade. I'm no longer interested in medical school. I'm changing my major. I just don't want an F on my record. I've never had an F before. Not in anything."

"You do now," said Major Hemmings. "Does your family maybe own some sort of business? Maybe your father could take you into that."

Pete felt a flash of anger. The major's words were unnecessary. Were they purposefully cruel? Pete remembered Major Hemmings was reputed to have once, cruelly, absentmindedly, inflicted a near fatal injury to his pet Chihuahua. Major Hemmings lived on campus in faculty housing. Allegedly, he had been walking the dog on campus before class and lost track of time. If he took the dog home he would be late for class, so he took the dog to class. He didn't have time to go by his office. He placed his hat and coat on one of the wall hooks in the hall outside the classroom. The dog was on a leash, so he put the looped end of the leash over one of the hooks, too. That might have been fine had the leash been longer, or the dog larger and well trained. The near fatal combination of small dog, short leash, and wacky professor left the poor animal dangling precariously, his short legs inches above the floor, neck stretched through his collar, yelping and struggling against the wall, fighting for life and freedom from restraint, choking and gagging, as the inattentive, oblivious Major Hemmings walked into his classroom and closed the door.

Minutes passed. The hallway was empty. Luckily for poor Fido another professor happened by, recognized the canine's peril, and released him from his deathtrap seconds before he would have lapsed into unconsciousness. Pete had not personally witnessed this episode either, but he had heard of it and did not doubt its veracity.

Pete had seen the sandwich salute first hand. It was proper military custom for cadets to salute uniformed officers, including SCUM, when walking past them on the campus grounds. One morning Pete had left Capers Hall and was walking toward Mark Clark Hall and he saluted Major Hemmings as the two of them passed each other. The major was carrying a number of books, held against his left side with his left arm and hand. In his right hand he carried a brown sandwich bag, apparently containing a sandwich, probably his lunch. The major returned Pete's salute, still holding the sandwich bag in his right hand. Intrigued, Pete turned around and watched as the Major continued past dozens of other cadets, rendering the unorthodox sandwich salute.

Reflecting on Major Hemmings' idiosyncrasies saved Pete from lashing out verbally. The major wasn't deliberately cruel. He didn't mean to burn down the lab. He didn't intend to harm his dog. He didn't disrespect military convention. He didn't realize his words were insulting. He was just distracted and often thoughtless. He was peculiar. He was SCUM.

Pete let the family business remark pass without comment. He made himself an appointment with Colonel Chappell, head of the English department. Pete told Colonel Chappell he wanted to transfer to the English department. He realized he was unsuited for premed and would never get into medical school. He loved English literature. The English department was where he belonged. He also wanted to graduate on time with his class, in four years. He couldn't bear the thought of hanging around the Citadel longer than that, becoming a five year man. To Pete's amazement, relief, and delight Colonel Chappell said it could be done. There was a lot of leeway in the English department. All the required courses Pete had taken in premed, from chemistry to biology to physics to calculus, could be counted as electives. He would have to go to summer school, but it could be done. He was three semesters and summer school away from graduation. No more musty chemistry labs.

Pete and the English department were a perfect fit. The professors were eccentric, but they were eccentricities Pete loved. His newly assigned faculty advisor in the English department was Colonel Strawhorn. Not a full colonel, since he wasn't the department head. A mere lieutenant colonel. A strange specimen, a terrific teacher. He was aptly named, for he was tall, well over six feet, lean and lanky, resembling a straw with a horn attached to one end: the horn being his large, long, thin, beaked nose, placed squarely in the middle of his craggy, formidable face. His age was hard to guess. He may have been older or younger than he appeared. He had large, bushy, gray eyebrows, and a mop of unruly, gray hair, which made him seem old. It was his energy which made him seem young. His limbs, arms and legs, were exceedingly long, and he marched back and forth across the front of the classroom in quick, lengthening strides, arms flailing, in constant motion, motion which would have exhausted an older man. His lectures, delivered in a rich, baritone voice, exuded an intense energy and enthusiasm.

Pete was enthralled. It was a rare occasion when Colonel Strawhorn stood still in front of the class. When he did he sometimes pulled the wooden chair from behind his desk, placed one of his size twelve feet on the seat of the chair, left the other on the floor, and leaned forward with his right hand holding his chin, his bent elbow resting on his foreleg near his bent knee. He resembled Rodin's statue of *The Thinker*, but the pose was short lived, only a moment of rest before returning to restless activity.

Once Colonel Strawhorn went too far with his chair trick. He pulled the chair away from the desk as usual, but instead of placing his size twelve on the chair, he stretched his leg all the way to the top of the desk. The class was astonished. Everyone had known Colonel Strawhorn's legs were incredible extensions, wonders of flexibility, but this feat was truly amazing, worthy of the rubber man from India.

The show got better. Sitting on the floor beside the desk was a round, olive drab, metal waste basket, about eighteen inches high, probably military issue. Colonel Strawhorn's age showed. His legs weren't as supple, his vision not as sharp, as he supposed. As he brought the leg down from the desk, meaning to return his foot to the floor, he stepped into the basket. The step was with such force that his size twelve foot became stuck, wedged in the bottom of the basket. He took a few stumbling steps forward, but fortunately managed to maintain his balance. The class was too stunned, the colonel too close to taking a dangerous fall, for immediate laughter.

The expression on the colonel's face never altered. He continued his lecture as if unaware of and unhampered by the protrusion. He took a couple of steps, not his normal long strides, toward the classroom door, all the while lecturing. He stopped. It was as though he was considering going into the hallway, possibly to remove the basket, but had thought better of it. He turned around, clomped back to the chair, sat down, and after several minutes of trying finally succeeded in getting his foot unstuck.

Only then did he pause in his lecture. He looked at the class and smiled. Laughter, brief but fun-filled, erupted, followed by hearty applause. He acknowledged with a wave of the hand and another smile and went on with his lecture.

As class ended that day Jim Blake, a member of the baseball team, said to Colonel Strawhorn, "Colonel, my baseball coaches have always warned me against stepping in the bucket. Until today, I'd never thought that warning also applied to the classroom."

The colonel took it good naturedly. "Today's performance wasn't poetry, was it, Mr. Blake," the colonel said. "At least it was comedy, not drama." No one else mentioned the episode to the colonel, then or later, but for a while it was all the talk among Colonel Strawhorn's students, adding to his reputation as a bit of an odd duck, a flake, but an unparalleled teacher.

One of Colonel Strawhorn's favorite literary works was *Chaucer's Canterbury Tales*, particularly the raunchy ones about cuckolded husbands and farts. Another of his favorite authors was Lewis Carroll. His fondness for *Alice's Adventures in Wonderland* knew no bounds. Pete Creger was no particular fan of Chaucer, whom he considered too profane, but he loved Lewis Carroll and, thanks to Colonel Strawhorn, he came to consider Carroll's *Alice* and *Through the Looking Glass* the world's foremost masterpieces of children's literature. His head rang with passages, such as "'The time has come,' the walrus said, 'to talk of many things: of shoes and ships and sealing wax, of cabbages and kings.'"

Pete thought of Strawhorn as an enigma. How could his taste in literature range from the fleeing farts of *The Miller's Tale* to sweet *Alice*? Nonetheless, when Pete decided to write his senior essay on Lewis Carroll, he was delighted when Strawhorn agreed to become his faculty advisor on the project. Colonel Strawhorn had a tendency toward long-windedness. That trait and Strawhorn's role as Pete's advisor on his senior essay got Pete into trouble with another of the Citadel's offbeat professors.

Colonel Madden was the strangest of the strange when it came to assessing the Citadel's faculty. Among the Citadel's many outstanding professors, Colonel Madden had the reputation of being the best, the greatest of them all. Pete had to find out for himself if it was true. He simply couldn't finish his Citadel career without experiencing Colonel Madden. Madden wasn't even an English professor. He was a history professor. His specialty was a course entitled "the history of England." The full course covered two semesters. Pete signed up.

Even with the occasional weird behaviors, Colonel Madden's class was the zenith, the highlight of Pete Creger's academic experience at the Citadel. Colonel Madden, due to his academic prowess, was the only faculty member to hold the rank of full colonel without being the department head. The chairmanship of the history department had been offered to him and he had declined, rather rudely, so the legend went. He couldn't let "administrative details which could be handled or mishandled by any nincompoop interfere with his more important teaching duties" was his reputed stance on refusing the "dubious honor of the department chairmanship."

Colonel Madden was a big, strong, powerful man of enormous girth. At a full six feet and one inch tall, he stood regally, with broad shoulders thrown back, and an erect, perfect posture exuding confidence bordering on arrogance. He was a handsome man with dark, well-groomed hair graying around the temples, but he was morbidly obese. Part of the legend surrounding him held that he had been a superb athlete in his youth, a boxer and weight lifter, and that it was his youthful obsession with weight training, coupled with an enormous appetite for fine dining in middle age, which created his vast bulk. Colonel Madden possessed an irascible temperament, a mind filled with an unending storehouse of knowledge and learning, teeming intelligence, and a quick wit. Yet, paradoxically, he was among the most obstinate, prejudiced of men. He loved England, the English people, English royalty, and all things English. He loathed Irishmen, Scotchmen, and Welshmen. After a few months in his class, Pete came to suspect his hatreds were not as tremendous as he claimed. As to the non-English residents of the British Isles, if he did not love them, he at least loved hating them. It was his strong personality more than his great size which gave rise to the name by which he was known amongst all his students. He was called "the Beast."

Students of the Beast thoroughly enjoyed his classes. He was a gifted lecturer who also taught by allowing stimulating, challenging discussion. He carried his lecture notes to class in a small, but thick, black, loose-leafed notebook. His turning of the pages as he spoke was so delicate, his downward glances at his notes so muted, that few in the class were aware he consulted them at all. He would march into the classroom promptly at the appointed hour, expecting his students to be there before him, stand behind the speaking podium, place his notebook, opened to the predetermined page, and begin. Woe to the foolish student who entered his classroom once the lecture had begun. Tardiness was one of his many pet peeves.

Prior to that fateful day when Colonel Strawhorn's verbosity caused Pete to incur the wrath of the Beast, Pete had heard of many of the Beast's untoward outbursts, but he had never witnessed any of them, much less himself been victimized by the Beast's antics. Quite to the contrary, until that day he had been basking, he thought, in the glow of being one of the Beast's favored students. There had been one small, semihumiliating incident. The Beast had been remarking upon the exquisiteness of the facial features of the pure Anglo-Saxon blood line and lamenting upon the fact that the strain had been so decimated by comingling with other, less desirable blood, that it scarcely existed in the modern world.

Another student asked the Beast if he could describe those exquisite features precisely. Instead of giving a verbal description, the Beast looked around the classroom. "Let me see," he muttered, "is there anyone in here who might come close? No, I don't think so." Then his gaze fastened upon Pete. Their eyes locked. "Mr., Creger!" the Beast exclaimed emphatically. "Remove your glasses!"

Pete took off his glasses. "Turn your head. Let me see a side view. Yes! That's it! That's pretty close. Gentlemen, behold the pure Anglos-Saxon bloodline." The entire class stared at Pete. At first Pete was embarrassed. He felt his face about to flush pink. Then he thought, this is actually pretty cool. "I'll bet your ancestry is English," the Beast said. "Am I right, Mr. Creger?"

So far as Pete knew, his paternal ancestry was indeed English, with a smattering of Cherokee Indian thrown in. Pete thought it best not to mention that. He also kept quiet about his mother's family's reputed German and Scotch-Irish background. "Yes, sir, that's correct," he said. The class applauded. Pete didn't join in the applause, even though he assumed it was for the Beast, not him. He was okay with being considered a pure blood, of sorts. Aren't we all Americans by now, he thought.

Pete's proudest moment in the Beast's class came one day when the Beast was telling the class that in the centuries preceding the nineteenth, research had shown that the peoples of Europe, including England, were considerably smaller in stature than in the nineteenth and twentieth centuries.

Pete raised his hand and asked what he thought was a simple question: "Were the animals smaller, too?"

The Beast's normal serious countenance took on an even sterner look. He sighed. "Regretfully, Mr. Creger," he replied, "I don't know. There hasn't been much research. What little there has been is inconclusive. The answer is unknown." Pete had stumped the Beast! He was thrilled. Then the Beast said, "let us continue considering facts of more historical moment." He proceeded with his lecture.

Pete coveted an A in the Beast's class. Try as he might, he couldn't achieve it. Every test, every written research paper, was returned with a grade of B. Pete was assigned a paper on the Venerable Bede, an English monk who lived from 672 to 735, mostly at a place called Jarrow. Pete worked as hard on that paper as he did on his senior essay. He didn't see how the Beast could fail to give him an A. The paper came back with one comment, written in red ink, "vicissitudes of Jarrow?" Graded B. Vicissitudes indeed! Why, that paper was filled with vicissitudes. Pete began to suspect that the reason the Beast gave him B's instead of A's had nothing to do with his work. It was because his major was English, not history. As an English major, he came to realize that the phrase "vicissitudes of Jarrow" had a certain ring to it. He liked it. It was his only consolation. Pete blamed Colonel Strawhorn for his trouble with the Beast. Second semester senior year Pete had a free period right before the Beast's class. As he neared the completion of his senior essay on Lewis Carroll, a conference with Colonel Strawhorn was scheduled for that hour. Pete felt a certain, but indefinable, uneasiness as the conference began. Both Pete and Colonel Strawhorn were enthusiastic fans of Lewis Carroll, they both enjoyed discussing him, and before Pete knew it the hour was nearly over and he could tell their talk was incomplete, nowhere near its end. He told Colonel Strawhorn he had to go, he had to make it to Colonel Madden's class on time. Colonel Strawhorn ignored him and kept on talking. He tried to leave several more times without success. Short of walking out, there was nothing he could do.

By the time Pete extricated himself from Colonel Strawhorn, he was a full ten minutes late to the Beast's class. He briefly considered not going, but quickly dismissed that option. His conference with Colonel Strawhorn running over its allotted time might be an excuse for tardiness, but certainly not for missing an entire class. He hoped the Beast was in a good mood, but he feared the worst. He opened the classroom door slowly, carefully, and closed it as quietly as possible after entering the room. The Beast was well into his lecture. He tiptoed to his seat, which happened to be near the dead center of the room. The Beast took no notice. He went on declaiming, in full lecture mode. Fifteen minutes went by. Pete was breathing easy, thinking he was sitting pretty.

Suddenly, without warning, the Beast stopped in midsentence. He glared at Pete. He closed his notebook, picked it up and slammed it flat onto the podium, picked it up again and slammed it to the floor. "God damn it, Mr. Creger!" he cried aloud. "Have you no decency? How rude and inconsiderate can you be? To interrupt the class in the middle of my lecture!"

The entire class sat in stunned silence. Pete was horrified. He attempted an apology. He got out a stammered, "sir."

The Beast stopped him with another glare and a raised hand. "Stop, swine," he said. "Not now. Wait a few days. Come see me at my office during office hours."

"Yes, sir."

The Beast picked up his notebook from the floor and resumed his lecture, perfectly composed, as though nothing had transpired.

Pete was flabbergasted. He found it impossible to listen to the rest of the lecture. He left the class that day without looking at the Beast. He imagined he may have seen his last B from the Beast. He was glad he'd been instructed to wait a few days. He needed time to mull over the Beast's outburst. He thought of telling Colonel Strawhorn what had happened, but decided against it. This was between himself and the Beast. Involving Colonel Strawhorn might not help and it might make matters worse.

A few days later Pete approached the Beast's office door anxious, but determined to stay calm. He was prepared to expect the unexpected. He knocked on the door. "Enter," came the growled voice of the Beast from within. The Beast was seated behind his desk. "Oh, it's you, Mr. Creger," he said as Pete came into the room and shut the door. "What have you to say for yourself?"

Pete stood before the Beast, his field cap in his hand. He began with an apology. "I'm sorry for disrupting your class," he said. He then explained. He couched it in terms of a dilemma. He mentioned Colonel Strawhorn, his senior essay advisor, by name, but did not give the topic of the essay.

"And what, or who, may I ask," said the Beast, "is the subject of this essay which outweighs by far the history of the world's most glorious country?"

"Lewis Carroll, sir."

"You can't mean it. A most unworthy subject. You do know he was a pedophile, don't you?"

Pete surprised himself with his own audacity, but his ire was peaked. "Sir, you are impugning the name of an Englishman. There is no more proof of that scurrilous charge than there is to prove the actual size of animals on the European continent prior to the nineteenth century."

"Careful, young man, the evidence may be wholly circumstantial, but many scholars believe it to be so."

Pete was inflamed. "Sir," he said," you teach at an all-male college and I am a student at that college. Would you be so reckless with your scholarship as to assert those facts as a circumstance that would support the accusation that you or any of the other professors here or myself or any of the other students here are homosexuals?"

The Beast glared at Pete, a glare that by now Pete knew all too well. Pete had a fleeting thought the Beast might suggest he should withdraw from his course. Instead, a broad smile spread across the Beast's face. He burst out laughing. He kept on laughing. He laughed and laughed. Pete didn't laugh.

He had been standing all this time. Now, without first having been asked, Pete sat down in a chair across from the Beast. Moments later, when the Beast had finally managed to control himself and stop laughing, he said, "Mr. Creger, you have saved yourself. My apologies to Mr. Carroll. Now, mind you, if he had been a Welshman, I'd never apologize." Still chuckling, the Beast made it known he'd planned to punish Pete severely, but he couldn't do it now. "This is too good," he said. "It deserves a reward. The reward is that you receive a reprieve. See that nothing like this happens again."

"It won't, sir. Never again, sir."

From that time on, Pete ceased thinking of the Beast as a beast. From then on, to Pete he was Colonel Madden. Peculiar, yes, but by no means a beast.

Compared to Colonel Madden of the history department, and for that matter just about all of the other professors in the English department, Lt. Colonel Weiss of the English department was completely normal. He was unusual in one respect only: he was a lover of poetry, a love he attempted to share with all his students, most of whom weren't that appreciative, poetry by and large being the misunderstood stepchild of the world of literature. He did succeed in making a few disciples, among them Pete Creger. Until Colonel Weiss, Pete had considered men who admitted to liking poems unmanly. Colonel Weiss was anything but. A decorated combat veteran of the Korean War, he was more like a Citadel tac officer than a member of SCUM. He wore his army uniform, including medals, with faultless pride and military bearing. He stood ramrod straight and was quick of step, with closely cropped gray hair. He believed poetry should be read out loud, not merely silently; and he would stand before his classes and read or recite from memory with perfect pitch and timing in his masculine, gravelly voice. After Colonel Weiss, Pete no longer minded admitting he liked poetry. He considered it the ultimate artistic expression of language. Colonel Weiss became one of his heroes.

With Colonel Weiss's reading before the class of the long pastoral poem "Michael" by William Wordsworth, Pete knew he was hooked for life. He had never heard anything so wonderful. Later, he read the poem to himself over and over again. Michael was a shepherd who, late in life, was severely disappointed by the behavior of his only son Luke. Pete came to love the entire poem, but his favorite lines were these: "There is a comfort in the strength of love; / 'Twill make a thing endurable, which else / Would overset the brain, or break the heart."

Under the tutelage of the English department, Pete came to admire a wide range of poets, among them, Donne, Keats, Eliot, Yeats, and many others. He thought it sad that Colonel Madden probably did not approve of Yeats, since he was Irish.

His last three semesters at the Citadel, thanks to the English department, Pete made the dean's list. He had gold stars second semester his junior year. But for the B's in Colonel Madden's history of England class, he would have made gold stars both semesters his senior year, too.

Pete didn't mind too much. The phrase "vicissitudes of Jarrow" was some consolation. When Pete first applied to graduate school, it was mostly to avoid Vietnam; he had no desire to duplicate Colonel Weiss's exploits in Korea. Pete loved graduate school. Eight years later, after expanding his senior essay on Lewis Carroll into enough originality to satisfy his dissertation committee, he emerged with a Ph.D. in English literature.

Pete put in several stints at colleges where the students called their teachers professor or doctor. Eventually he landed his dream job: a position in the English department at the Citadel. At first he was a mere captain, but he worked his way all the way up to the rank of lieutenant colonel. He tried hard to emulate his hero, Colonel Weiss, including the reading and recitation of poetry. The day he read the poem "Michael," he knew he had arrived. He had become SCUM.

MESS

T he French word *mes* is roughly translated food, or a portion of food. That word, in turn, comes from the Latin word *mittere*, which means, among other things, to send for. The word "mess" means to send for food. Sometime around the fifteenth century the English military began using the term mess to describe soldiers eating together. In the military, as well as in the civilian world, mealtime is an important part of the day. The Citadel world of the 1960s revolved around mess. The Citadel mess hall churned out three square meals a day, seven days a week. On Mondays through Thursdays there were three mess formations per day, one at six-fifteen A.M. for breakfast, one at noon for lunch, and one at six P.M. for dinner, which all cadets were required to meet. On Fridays, due to general leave, the six P.M. mess formation for dinner was optional; on Saturdays both the noon and evening mess formations were optional, general leave still being in effect; and on Sundays the noon mess formation was optional, since attendance at religious services was required in the morning and general leave ended at six P.M. The cadets met these formations in the barracks and marched off to the mess hall, a sprawling building located behind the barracks, large enough to accommodate the entire corps of cadets, some two thousand strong, at one seating.

Each company was assigned its own area of the mess hall. The meals were served on long tables covered with white tablecloths, fourteen cadets to a table, one mess at each end of the table, each mess consisting of seven cadets. There were two, sometimes three, knobs at each mess, and either four or five upperclassmen. As each company reached and entered the mess hall on the march, the individual cadets dispersed to their assigned company areas and to their assigned tables. Except for the knobs, everyone stood quietly behind their metal chairs awaiting the saying of grace over the meal. The knobs were busy: hurriedly preparing to serve the upperclassmen, filling their glasses with juice, their cups with coffee, if it was morning; their glasses with ice and pouring the beverages, usually water or tea, if it was noon or evening.

The table settings, knives, forks, spoons, plates, and napkins, had been placed ahead of time by the waitresses, called *waities,* by the corps. The communal blessing completed, the corps sat down, the knobs careful to sit on the front three inches of their chairs. The waities brought the food to each table, balanced in large serving bowls on even larger serving trays and placed it on the tables or handed it directly to the knobs, who passed it on to the upperclassmen. Only when all the upperclassmen were served, their plates and glasses full, were the knobs allowed to serve their own plates. Even then, before eating each knob in turn was required to hold his plate in front of his face, the edges of the plate grasped between the fingers of each hand, and ask permission of the mess carver, who sat at the head of the table, to commence eating. Gaining consent to eat was not easy. Sometimes perfect recitation of an obscure bit of plebe knowledge, such as the number of bricks in the smokestack attached to the laundry, or the direction in which the eagle on top of Bond Hall was facing, was a prerequisite. Often permission to eat was denied throughout the meal. Knobs were accustomed to little or no food passing through their gullets into their stomachs during the typical mess hall dining experience. Knobs had to keep a close eye on the food and hand off as quickly as possible to a passing waitie any empty or near empty serving bowl for refilling. No matter how unpalatable a dish might be, an upperclassman kept waiting for a second helping spelled trouble for all the knobs on the mess. Teamwork among the knobs was essential for the running of a happy mess and directly related to whether the knobs on that mess did or did not manage to eat.

All knobs, even those who entered the Citadel as string beans, skinny as rails, lost weight at the beginning of the year. It was the inevitable result of an unprecedented regimen of exercise and physical activity and little food. Once classes began, many knobs resorted to gorging themselves on chips, candy, and snack crackers from the vending machines at the knob canteen next to Mark Clark Hall, which thankfully, mercifully, was off limits to upperclassmen. It was their only hope of warding off starvation.

The mess hall was equipped with a PA system. Each meal began with the blessing, usually given by the regimental commander over the PA microphone. The blessings were normally very short and mostly similar, something like "bless this food we're about to receive, Amen" or "Lord, thank you for the blessings of your bounty, Amen." They waxed longer only if the chaplain or some other clergyman was visiting and was asked to do the honor. Each meal ended after about twenty minutes with announcements, again given over the PA microphone, sometimes short, sometimes long, usually by the regimental commander. Following announcements all were free to leave on their own, except that a knob could not leave without permission so long as there was an upperclassman still at the mess.

The knobs were glad to leave the mess last. It was their only chance to eat a complete meal. One rainy morning early in the knob year jelly doughnuts were served at breakfast. Sammy Graham's mess carver, as he was leaving the mess hall, wrapped one of the doughnuts in a paper napkin and placed it on the table next to Sammy's plate, saying, "see if you can smuggle this into the barracks without getting caught." No other instructions were given. Generally, cadets weren't allowed to take food from the mess hall. Hence, the need for smuggling. Sammy assumed it was probably a trick. The members of the mess would be waiting on him inside the barracks and would give him a racking if they found him with the doughnut. He thought of just leaving it on the table. He hadn't been told the doughnut was for anyone or for any particular purpose. Luckily, because of the rain, raincoats were being worn, which made it easy to conceal the doughnut as he left the mess hall. On the way to the barracks Sammy considered what to do. He decided on a trick of his own. As always, he was ravenously hungry. He ate the doughnut, stuffing the whole doughnut into his mouth and chewing as fast as he could. He wiped his hands with the napkin and discarded it, his first act of littering on the Citadel campus.

His thinking was that he was going to get racked no matter what. This way, he was following instructions. The doughnut would be inside the barracks and he wouldn't get caught with it. Besides, none of the knobs had been allowed a doughnut at mess, and it tasted damn good.

They were waiting for him just inside the sallyport, as Sammy had known they would be. All five of them. "Hit it for fifteen, screwhead." When he was done with the fifteen pushups, "Now get up and hand over that doughnut."

"Sir, I can't sir."

"Why not? Where the hell is it? You were told to bring it into the barracks, weren't you?"

"Yes, sir. Sir, it's inside the barracks, sir."

"Then give it to me, dumbhead."

"Sir, it's taken on a new form, sir. It's all chewed up. It's inside my stomach, sir."

"What? You ate it?"

"Sir, yes, sir."

"Hit it again, shitbrain. Keep going until you're told to stop, turdface. You're the dumbest knob ever. Get up, asshole." Sammy was pulled roughly to his feet and made to bend over at the waist, his face in a metal garbage can on the gallery. "Puke it up. Show me the doughnut." Sammy made gagging sounds, but nothing came up.

"You're going to stand here until that doughnut comes up."

Sammy stood bent over, his face in the can. He didn't know how long he had been standing there, probably not as long as it seemed, when he realized he was there by himself. He raised his head up, looked around, and, not seeing his tormentors, took off for his room. That wasn't as bad as it could have been, thought Sammy. Sort of a little victory, even. Upperclassmen 1,000. Knobs 1.

Mess was never a pleasant thing for any of the knobs, but as the year wore on it did get better. The sitting on the edge of your chair thing was relaxed. All the knobs got better at their roles of table servants. More and more food made its way to their stomachs. Once, at the noon mess, Sammy mistakenly announced that a bowl of soup was vegetable soup when in fact it was bean soup. He was made to eat the entire serving bowl. That, too, could have been worse. It was his biggest meal at any mess up to that time. Bean soup wasn't Sammy's favorite, but it wasn't gag city either. He did pass gas for days afterward. All knobs learned to be careful least the upperclassmen discovered their most disliked foods: once the secret was out, they were assured generous portions. The reverse of that was making them think you disliked something you really loved, but it could be tricky, even dangerous.

Sammy detested broccoli, especially the way it was served in the mess hall: overcooked, limp, and soggy. Sammy could barely tolerate it raw or gently, but crisply steamed; nonetheless, he always was attentive to putting small portions on his plate and putting some of it in his mouth.

As a rule, most knobs avoided the optional meals. Open mess. No assigned seating. Upperclassmen grabbed the few knobs present and pressed them into service, often only one at a mess. A knob nightmare. Sammy only attended one the whole knob year. Afterward, he vowed never to do it again. Knobs were allowed seventeen demerits per month. Any above that meant one confinement per each excessive demerit. A confinement was served only on the weekends, lasted two hours, and was spent in your room in the barracks wearing a white waistband with brass waist plate and a pair of white, cotton gloves, meeting an hourly formation on the quadrangle to assure the confinee's presence. Only six confinements were allowed to be served per weekend: one Friday evening, three on Saturday, and two on Sunday, effectively amounting to restriction to campus. On the first monthly DL knob year Sammy had twenty-nine demerits, which meant twelve confinements. Two weekends. All the knobs had excessive demerits and Sammy's were by no means the record number. On late Friday afternoon of that first weekend, after parade but before the first confinement period, along with several classmates Sammy managed to grab a quick bite at the sandwich shop in Mark Clark Hall. On Saturday funds were running low, so he decided to meet the noon formation and dine in the mess hall. Big mistake.

On entering the mess hall Sammy was immediately grabbed by an unknown upperclassman from another company and pressed into service at a full table where he was the only knob. Seated at the head of the table was an extremely tall, well-built senior wearing two diamonds on his collar, whom Sammy had seen before, but not up close. The regimental staff was housed adjacent to the F Company area in Number Two barracks. What in God's name was the regimental executive officer doing eating in the mess hall on a Saturday? He couldn't possibly have confinements. Maybe he was from a poor family and couldn't afford to eat out. Sammy was kept so busy he scarcely was able to eat himself. He kept thinking he would have a chance after all the upperclassmen left.

There was a short blessing, but no announcements. Everyone just left when they were finished eating. The regimental exec was the first to leave. Sammy had no idea exactly how tall he was, but when he stood up, he stood out like Saul among the Israelites. The meal had consisted of soup, salad, and sandwiches. Cold cuts, made at the table from platters of meat, with tomato, lettuce and condiments provided. To Sammy's ultimate horror, before leaving the cadet lieutenant colonel walked over to him and told him to make him two sandwiches before he left and to bring them by his room when he left. "Stay and eat as much as you want," he was told, "but don't fail to bring me my sandwiches." Sammy was given the room number.

Sammy figured there would be no trouble over the order, since, after all, it was given by the second highest ranking cadet on campus. Wrong. Sammy made the sandwiches as soon as he could, while the fixings were still available. He had just started to wrap them in paper napkins when Mr. Bennett, an F Company junior private seated at the table, took them from him. "So good of you to make these sandwiches for us, Mr. Graham," Bennett said. He handed one to another junior at the table and bit into the other.

Sammy tried to protest. "They're for Mr.—" That's as far as he got.

"Not today, they're not," said Bennett. "Your meal is over. Get out of here."

Sammy hesitated. "I've got to take—" He was cut off again.

"I said get the hell out of here. "Now move!"

The sound of laughter reverberated in Sammy's ears as he scampered from the mess hall. What was he to do? What could he do? He thought of going by the exec's room and telling him what had happened, but, no, that wouldn't do. He'd want to know the name of the cadet who'd made him leave the mess without the sandwiches. That would probably cause trouble for Mr. Bennett, which in turn would mean trouble for Sammy within F Company. There was nothing he could do. Maybe the exec would forget about the sandwiches. Maybe he wouldn't remember which knob was supposed to make the sandwiches and wouldn't be able to find him. That, thought Sammy, was his best hope. It was his only hope.

Back in his room Sammy told his roommate, Tim Hagan, all about his mess hall difficulties. Tim was serving confinements, too. "Tell ya what," Sammy said, "I'm never going to another optional mess."

"You're in deep shit. I wouldn't want to be in your shoes," said Tim, who was a straightforward, practical sort of guy, not prone to negativity, but in tune with the realities of knob life at the Citadel. Sammy knew Tim was right. They hadn't been back in the room ten minutes from their next confinement formation, both sitting at their desks studying, at least Tim was studying, Sammy was worrying, when the door to their room flew open and the tall, imposing regimental exec stalked in. He was a fearful figure. Both Sammy and Tim stood and popped to in the brace position. Tim stood there wide eyed and quaking while Sammy received a terrible racking. Sammy braced harder than he ever had before. He was put against the wall and made to do deep knee bends, then pushups, then sit-ups. It went on and on. Sweat poured from Sammy. Great beads of it formed on his forehead and dripped into his eyes. His face turned beet red. His arms, knees, back, and stomach ached. All the while Tim stood there, bracing and watching the agony, growing more and more concerned. The whole time Sammy was hollered at and cursed for being a stupid, worthless piece of shit. Incredibly, the sandwiches were never mentioned. Sammy knew if they had been, he'd have broken and named Mr. Bennett as the one responsible for the sandwiches not being delivered. The whole racking, the whole episode, was beyond bizarre. It was as though the exec was in the room fine tuning his racking skills and Sammy had been a randomly picked victim.

Suddenly, right in the middle of a sentence telling Sammy what a waste product he was, the exec stopped, gave Sammy one more menacing look, turned on his heels, and stalked from the room. Could it really be over? Sammy collapsed on his bunk. Tim sat in his desk chair. He hadn't been put through the racking Sammy had endured, but he was bracing the whole time, and was thoroughly traumatized. Tim looked at his watch and said, "we've only got about five minutes until the hourly confinement formation on the quad." He went over to the sink, returned to Sammy with a wet wash cloth, and began wiping the sweat from his face.

"I thought we'd probably missed the formation," said Sammy.

"No, the racking only lasted about forty minutes," said Tim.

Talking it over with Tim and the rest of his F Company classmates later, Sammy was halfway convinced the whole thing was a set up. The exec didn't want the sandwiches and Bennett was in on it.

None of it made any sense. The Citadel didn't make sense.

Between the jelly doughnut incident and the sandwich incident Sammy was gaining a reputation. One rumor had it Sammy had eaten the sandwiches between the mess hall and the barracks, just as he had the doughnut. Whatever, it took balls to mess with the regimental exec, and in the eyes of his classmates Sammy Graham had balls. No one was surprised when he went to the showers to fight an F Company junior who had been giving him a hard time at mess.

For knobs, there were good messes, and bad messes, hard one and easy ones. The mess Sammy was on when he fought in the showers became much easier after the fight. New mess assignments were made about every four to six weeks. Sammy Graham and Pete Creger once had the misfortune to be on a mess together that they both later described as the mess from hell. The mess carver was a junior sergeant named Ned Marone, a dark haired, dark skinned, small, wiry character, who was a stickler for mess facts and miscellaneous information. Sammy and Pete were the only two knobs on the mess. Serving the mess wasn't hard. There were no mean spirited, hard asses on the mess, and that included Marone. It was Marone's infernal, incessant, obsessive need to be entertained with limitless minutiae which made the mess increasingly intolerable.

When Marone wasn't requiring them to recite endless plebe knowledge from the *Guidon,* he was peppering them with questions, questions which usually required research to find the answers. There was class-work, homework, and messwork. It was like adding on another academic course. The mess course covered historical events as well as current ones. He would ask questions about literature and authors, scientists, and medical breakthroughs, newspapers and magazines, musicians and concerts, movies and radio shows, awards and rewards, cities and states, countries and continents, planets and galaxies. No subject was too small, none too broad. Even politics and religion weren't out of bounds.

It wouldn't have been so bad if he at least would have allowed sufficient time for the research, but he did not. Worse, when answers weren't forthcoming quickly enough, he would assign pushups as punishment. At breakfast he once asked Pete to name the two currently serving U.S. Senators from North Dakota. When Pete didn't know, he asked Sammy, who didn't know either. They were meted out fifty pushups each for ignorance. "You should know stuff like that," he said. "Find out and give me the answer at lunch." Both had a full morning of classes. Neither had any idea off the top of his head how to go about finding the answer, and not enough time to find out anyway. At lunch they were meted out another fifty pushups each for stupidity, and another question was asked: "Who is the current governor of North Dakota?" Fifty more pushups each for not knowing the answer. "I'll expect you to know that and the entire North Dakota congressional delegation by dinner this evening." Eventually, the correct answer was rendered, and another insufferable topic was entertained. Meanwhile, the pushups mounted.

Sometimes, Marone would just throw out a question. He once wanted to know the author of the Uncle Remus and Brer Rabbit stories. Pete knew that one, one of the few not requiring looking up or finding out. "Sir, it's Joel Chandler Harris, sir," Pete answered.

A rare smile formed on Marone's face. "Very good, Mr. Creger," he said. "At ease. You've earned at ease for the rest of the meal. Hell, I'm in a good mood. I'll even reduce the number of pushups you owe me. How many do you owe now?" Pete and Sammy were required to keep track of the accumulating pushups. They had been working them off by driving by

Marone's room after every meal and performing pushups on the gallery outside his room, usually a minimum of fifty at a time.

"Six hundred and fifty, sir," Pete replied.

"Okay, I'll knock off fifty."

That's the way it went. Marone would add pushups when he was displeased, which was most of the time, and graciously subtract them when he was pleased, which was rarely. Sometimes, instead of asking questions, Marone required Sammy and Pete to bring mess facts to the meals. It could be a fact of their own choosing, but it had better be something Marone didn't already know, and something that he liked, something that entertained him. More often than not, Marone's reaction to the mess facts was something like, "you dumb shit, you think I don't already know that. That's fifty more pushups."

Once, after a string of four consecutive days of unacceptable mess facts, Marone shamed Sammy and Pete by making them cover their faces with their hands. "You two are so dumb, I can't stand looking at either of you," he said. Naturally, they were expected to continue serving the mess with their faces hidden. Marone drank the last of the tea in his glass and held it out to be refilled. Luckily, Sammy, peeking through his slightly spread fingers, noticed at the exact moment Marone chose to throw the glass. Sammy held out his right hand and amazingly caught the glass in midair as it was passing him on its flight down the table. If he hadn't caught it, it probably would have hit the mess carver at the other end of the table. Sammy refilled the glass and placed it by Marone's plate. Marone was the happiest either Sammy or Pete had seen him the entire mess. He broke out laughing. He led the mess in applauding Sammy's remarkable, lucky catch. "At ease, both of you!" he proclaimed. "Mr. Graham, your pushup debt is reduced by a hundred."

Mercifully, with the periodic mess changes, the mess from hell finally came to an end for Sammy and Pete. Ned Marone was not named a mess carver for the next cycle. Sammy and Pete were glad for the sake of their classmates in F Company. No further descent into mess hell for them. Sammy and Pete each owed Marone over a thousand pushups when the mess ended. It took weeks and weeks of daily driving by Marone's room to work them off.

Some of the dishes served up in the mess hall weren't that bad, even tasty, but most were pretty unappetizing. Among the worst was an awful concoction consisting of chipped beef swimming in what was thought to be (no one was really sure) lumpy, brown gravy, served over toast in the mornings and claiming to be breakfast. The cadets called it SOS, or shit on shingles. Unbelievably, a few lapped it up. Most passed, preferring their toast dry, maybe with butter and jam. There were several varieties of some kind of unknown meat, collectively called mystery meat. Even though the burgers themselves were a little rubbery, mess hall hamburgers weren't that bad, and were a favorite meal.

The down side of hamburgers for the knobs were the condiments: mayonnaise, mustard, and ketchup, placed on the tables in plastic squeeze bottles on hamburger days. The favorite mess hall sport, other than not allowing knobs a sporting chance to eat, was sending a knob under the tables to mayonnaise the shoes of an unsuspecting mess carver, usually a high ranky, such as a member of regimental or battalion staff, or a company commander. Mustard or ketchup made a mess on shoes, too, but it had been discovered through trial and error that mayonnaise, being oilier, worked best. A target would be picked out and a knob chosen for the mission. For the mission to succeed, the cooperation of all the other upper-classmen at the target's table was essential. The chosen knob, armed with a mayonnaise bottle, would slip stealthily under the table and crawl on his hands and knees up to the target. Squezze. Squezze, squish. Squish, plop, plop. It was a tricky business, the trickiest part of all the escape: crawl-ing backwards to the point of entry and emerging unscathed, a hero. Few missions were a complete success. More often than not, even if the attack ended in a mayonnaising, the knob was caught during the retreat, and the formerly cooperative upperclassmen turned on him. The counter-attack. The knob emerged from under the table covered from head to toe in ketchup, mustard, and mayonnaise, a pitiful red, white, and yel-low creature. The targeted ranky was getting off easy. He only had an oily white blob on his shoes. Often the mission was a complete failure: the knob was caught before reaching the target. However it went, the upper-classmen thought it great fun. They laughed their asses off. No knob ever volunteered for the job, nor did any knob ever refuse when drafted into service. The knobs dreaded being drafted and would have much preferred to be allowed to eat their hamburgers in peace.

Once in a great while a senior private was made a mess carver. Bob Andrews was a senior private who never racked knobs. He was even benevolent toward knobs whenever an opportunity presented itself. The knobs called him Uncle Bob. It was Uncle Bob who cut the deal with one of the barbers at the Citadel barber shop and knob Sammy Graham that turned Sammy, himself a trained barber, into the official F Company barber. Second semester that knob year Sammy operated a barber shop on Friday afternoons in Uncle Bob's room and Uncle Bob often heard Sammy complain of the mess from hell. It was Uncle Bob who was responsible for Ned Marone not continuing on as a mess carver. He got himself named a mess carver in place of Marone. He insisted Sammy be on his mess. He asked Sammy to name two other knobs to be on the mess. Sammy suggested Pete Creger, his fellow sufferer on the mess from hell, who, like himself, needed a break, and Tim Hagan, his roommate. It may have been the first mess in school history made up exclusively of cadet privates. The other three members of the mess were, like Uncle Bob, senior privates who never messed with knobs. It was the mess from heaven.

Sammy, Pete, and Tim were still required to serve the mess, but all three were given perpetual at ease. Uncle Bob even called Sammy by his first name. He would say things like, "Sammy, would you pass the salt please?" The knobs were even included in the conversations. But for the clamor going on around them, it would almost have been like a normal dining experience. George Todd was the mess carver at the other end of their table. He was a first lieutenant and platoon leader who felt racking knobs was one of an upperclassman's essential duties. The plebe system may have been on break on Uncle Bob's mess, but it was alive and in full force on George Todd's, and it was a constant source of irritation and annoyance to Uncle Bob. He would say things to the knobs on his mess like, "I wish you guys didn't have to listen to all that. It can't be good for your digestion. When I formed this mess, I should have made certain there were more compatible diners at the other end of the table." He was close to being apologetic.

Scattered throughout the mess hall were a number of large potted plants, greenery which provided the building's only interior decoration. Some of the plants had grown quite large, the size of very small trees. After a particularly loud, vexing outburst from the other end of the table, Uncle Bob, with help from Sammy, Pete, and Tim, picked up two of the nearby plants and placed them in the center of the table, blocking the other mess from view. "That's better," he said. "Now we won't have to witness all the crap that's going on down there. Maybe it'll keep out some of the noise, too." He asked the waities to see that they remained there. They did stay in place several weeks, until a tac officer noticed them. Uncle Bob explained to the tac why they were there. The tac talked to Todd and came back and told Uncle Bob that Todd had agreed to tone it down and he would have to put the plants back on the floor. Uncle Bob wasn't happy. The other end of the table was more civil for a while, but little by little Todd reverted to his old ways.

Not always, but sometimes, music played over the mess hall's PA system. A futile effort by the administration to provide the cadets with a more pleasant dining experience. Futile because most of the time it could barely be heard over the other ongoing racket anyway. Most of the popular songs of the day were played at one time or another. One of the most popular singers of the day was Bobby Vinton. Most of his songs were played and received well enough. Two of his songs, however, grated on upperclassmen as well as knobs. These two songs seemed to be played over and over, more than any of the others. They were "Mr. Lonely" and "Mr. Blue."

The lyrics to "Mr. Lonely" went: "Lonely, I'm Mr. Lonely / I'm a soldier, a lonely soldier / Away from home through no wish of my own / That's why I'm lonely, I'm Mr. Lonely / I wish that I could go back home," and the lyrics to "Mr. Blue" went: "I'm Mr. Blue / When you say you love me / Then prove it by goin' out on the sly/ Provin' your love isn't true / Call me Mr. Blue / I'm Mr. Blue (wah-ooh-wah-ooh)." Given the mess hall setting, it was understandable why these lyrics weren't favorites. One day at Uncle

Bob's mess the conversation drifted to mess hall music, Bobby Vinton, and these two songs.

Someone wondered out loud "who picks these songs?" The unanimous consensus of the mess was that the mess hall would be a happier place without them. Despondency among the cadets would be less prevalent if they were off the list. "I'll see if I can find out who picks the songs and if these two can be taken off the list," declared Uncle Bob. Sure enough, Uncle Bob succeeded in getting them off the list.

For the rest of that year "Mr. Lonely" and "Mr. Blue" ceased being heard in the mess hall. They remained near the top of the music charts, however, and the next school year and for a number of years afterward their mournful refrains were once again heard in the Citadel mess hall. Bobby Vinton songs were still being played in the Citadel mess hall when the members of the Class of 1968 reached their senior year. Throughout his Citadel career Sammy Graham had tried his best to emulate Uncle Bob, whom he considered the existential senior private. Near the end of his senior year, when he was surprisingly, against all odds, promoted to the rank of cadet second lieutenant, Sammy, like Uncle Bob before him, had never racked a knob. It just wasn't his thing. He had more important matters to attend to. The plebe system and harassing knobs wasn't on his list.

Along with his duties of being an assistant platoon leader, Sammy's new rank carried with it the role of mess officer, which meant he was responsible for making out the rotating mess assignments. He thought the task would be a simple one. It proved anything but. Everyone wanted to tell him who to put on what mess. His classmates were the worst. It was impossible to keep everyone happy. After a while he gave up trying, made up the assignments however he wished, and told everyone to feel free to swap messes if they could find someone to swap with.

Sammy had never been a mess carver. At first, he gave no thought to making himself one. Then, because of the aggravation, he decided to do it. Why not? He remembered how wonderful being on Uncle Bob's mess his knob year had been. He was a mess carver the rest of the year. At each mess rotation he handpicked three knobs for his mess, knobs whom he felt most needed respite from the system, knobs whose mindset about the

Citadel likely matched his own, knobs destined to be senior privates. He was also careful about the other upperclassmen on the mess. He picked privates. The only other senior was his roommate Tim Hagan. Sammy never resorted to potted plants or eliminating Bobby Vinton songs, but he was good to the knobs on his mess. He remembered a quote from St. Augustine: "Since you cannot do good to all, you are to pay special attention to those who, by accidents of time, or place, or circumstance, are brought into closer connection with you."

ABOUT THE AUTHOR

Tom Worley, a 1968 graduate of the Citadel and former member of the F Company, practices law in Charleston, South Carolina. He and his wife, Nancy, have two children and four grandchildren. Worley is currently working on a new collection of short stories and a novel.